MAKING SWEET MUSIC

THE SHOPS AT SUNSHINE BAY

JEANINE LAUREN

ISBN 978-1-7388343-7-2

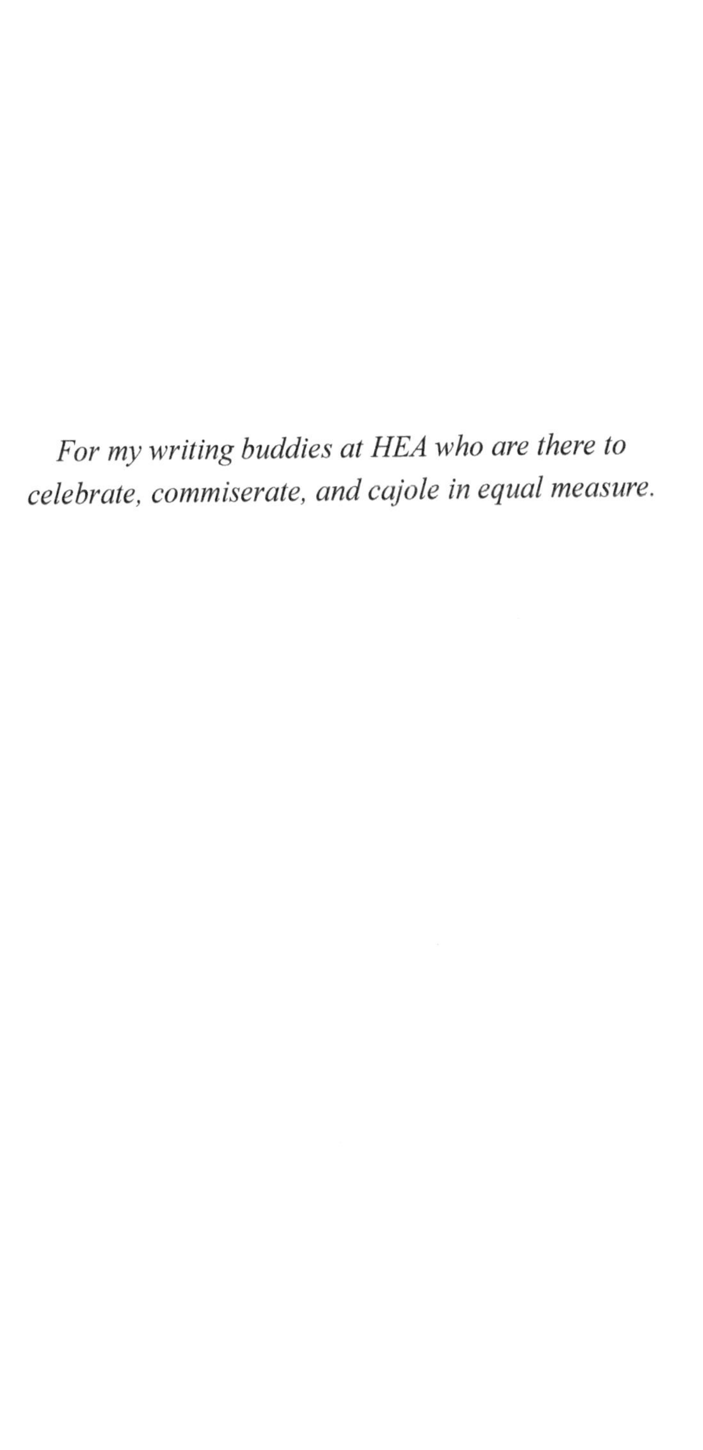

For my writing buddies at HEA who are there to celebrate, commiserate, and cajole in equal measure.

CHAPTER 1

The sun had just thrown off the petal-pink rays of sunrise when Doris Hudson stooped in front of her shop, Making Sweet Music, to pick up the local *Sunshine Bay News* from the brick-paved sidewalk. The window display advertised spring classes and the fundraiser Making Music for a Cause, which was only six weeks away. She would need to talk to Robert, her son and business partner, about changing the window soon. It was already May, and they needed to advertise the summer classes and band practice opportunities she had arranged. It paid to advertise early.

Doris walked around the building, let herself in the back door, and hastened down the little hallway, past two class-rooms and the large storage room, to the cozy office. The soft sage tones of the walls normally had a calming effect on her. But not today.

She listened for Robert and her grandson Zack and heard muffled voices coming from above. Good. They were still upstairs in their apartment. She shut the door before whipping the advertisement section from the newspaper and dropping it into a drawer with the five others she'd removed in the past week. Then she extracted the float for the cash register from the safe, picked up the rest of the paper, and went out to the front of the store to get ready to open.

Sunlight glinted off the three glossy pianos on the floor and the glass instrument cabinet, with its clarinets, saxophones, trombones, flutes, and trumpets—the instruments they most commonly rented to the local schools. The sight made her smile, but she frowned at the dust on the music books displayed against the far wall. She would have to get at that today or remember to assign someone else the task.

As she counted the money and put it into the cash register, footsteps landed on the stairs, and Robert yelled, "Get a wiggle on, Zack, or you'll be late!"

"Coming!" The toilet flushed, water ran, and a door slammed.

"Morning, Mom," Robert said, as he stepped into the room from behind the thick bottle-green curtain that separated the back of the store from the stairs to his apartment. He shook his head at the paper she held out for him. "No time this morning. I'm meeting Curtis for breakfast next door, but I'll be back in about two hours. We're going over the program for the fundraiser."

"Before you go, can you bring the box of books from the back room for me? I'm putting teaching packages together for the summer lessons."

"Sure." He fetched the box and placed it behind the counter, on the low table they used to unpack and price stock.

"Thanks," she said, picking up a knife to slice open the box. "What time are you going to Victoria tomorrow?"

"Early, I think. I'll know more after I talk to Curtis, and we make a list of what we need to pick up. The concert date is getting closer and we don't want to do too much last minute."

"After three years of running the fundraiser, everything's in hand. We've been over the checklist dozens of times."

"And yet there's already a new challenge: Curtis's sister-in-law is coming to town to play the harp."

"That will be an excellent addition to the program."

"Curtis is happy. He said it's taken her three years to face Maggie's loss. He thinks it will be good for her to do something positive. But now we'll have to find a van to transport the harp."

"I'm sure you'll sort it out. You've got a lot of help."

"Yes, but ticket sales are still down." He sighed. "There is still a lot that can go wrong."

"I think you worry too much. Making Music for a Cause is always a success. People like to help fight cancer. It touches so many. Besides, once Aria Winters does her radio spot tomorrow, the tickets will go. That woman could sell running shoes to a turtle."

Robert grinned at the mention of his old classmate, who hosted the local morning show. "She does have a gift," he said. "By the way, I put another book of tickets under the counter in case anyone comes in and wants to buy one."

Doris looked in the drawer under the till. "I'll see if I can move some today. And I'll put another poster beside the counter. Never hurts to advertise."

"Thanks, Mom. I'm glad you're here. The show is a lot bigger this year—more details—and we need all the help we can get." He glanced at his watch and frowned, then stepped back behind the curtain. "Zack," he yelled up the stairs. "Where are you?"

"Coming." Another door slammed, followed by a clatter of footfalls on the stairs. Soon the boy emerged, his red hair bright against the darker curtain. "I had to find my science book."

"I told you to put it beside the door last night," Robert grumbled, and the boy's face fell. "Say goodbye to your grandmother, and let's get a move on. Grab your coat." He pointed to the back door. "See you later, Mom."

"Bye, Grandma." Zack ran to Doris and gave her a quick hug around her waist. He was getting taller. Though he had only just turned ten, he was nearly five feet tall, and she was secretly pleased he would take after his grandfather in that regard. Neil was six-four—tall enough that, when they dressed up, she could wear heels without towering over him. She hugged the boy tightly. If her plan worked, she was going to miss him.

"Have a good day, Zack," she said. "I'll see you after school."

She watched until the pair disappeared down the hall to the back door, then finished unpacking the box and went to the back-room kitchenette to plug in the kettle for her morning tea. While she waited, she collapsed the box and put it out for recycling, set the flyer for the fundraiser in a standing frame, and added a label across the front that read *get your tickets here*.

Then, after the tea was made, she pulled her phone from her pocket and reread the text conversation she had had with her husband Neil six days earlier.

I'm not ready to come home. Those six words had kept her awake for two nights. First they'd reduced her to tears, and then they'd made her angry and she'd slammed doors around the empty house and beat up on furniture and pillows. The next day, she'd progressed to doing internet research about divorce, learned her options, cried again, and finally decided she needed a plan. There was no way that, after forty-one years, she was going to let her marriage go without a fight. She reread Neil's texts as though that might change what they said.

Neil: *I'm not ready to come home.*

Doris: *What do you mean?*

Neil: *We agreed. I said I needed time away to think about what I want next. You won't even notice I'm gone.*

Doris: *I don't remember agreeing to anything. Aren't you coming to help with the fundraiser?*

Neil: *That's Rob's thing. He's a grown man. He'll be fine.*

Doris: *He's not fine. He's still_heartbroken. He needs me to help with Zack and the store.*

Neil: *Does he? April's been gone nearly four years. He's had a lot of time to adjust. Have you considered it might be you who needs them? Zack is an easy kid, and the store practically runs itself.*

What did he think she did all day? But she responded as though she weren't gripped by rage. She tamped it down, as she had for years.

Doris: *That's not fair.*

She grimaced as her tepid response. When had she lost her voice?

Neil: *You never ran to help Nora, and she survived.*

Doris: *That's not fair either. I talked to her nearly every day when she and Crispin broke up. Besides, she didn't want me there. She had her friends and her work. I would have just been in the way. And I couldn't just leave the store.*

Neil: *Robert can run the store. He has friends who can help. You have staff.*

Neil was right, of course. Doris had planned to retire and leave the store to Robert to run—but what would she do then? Especially now, with Neil was always away—and maybe walking out of her life forever.

Doris: *What do you want? For me to stop working? Stop helping the kids?*

Neil: *There's more to life than running stores and looking after kids, Dory.*

Doris: *Alone?*

He hadn't answered for several moments, and she saw the years ahead like a long, empty tunnel.

Neil: *I need some time to think about what I want next.*

Doris: *We're supposed to be a team. Shouldn't we be figuring this out together?*

Neil: *We're a team but not a partnership. You are the quarterback. I just run interference.*

Interference? What was he talking about? They had agreed she would handle things while he was away so he could travel without worrying. That had been their deal, and now he was trying to change things.

Doris: *Why don't you come home so we can work through this together?*

Neil: *No. I need to do this on my own. Figure out what I want. Then we can talk. I'll let you know in a few weeks. Going to South America for the conference and then California.*

Doris: *What are you going to do in California?*

Neil: *I have a project there. And there's a model rail conference next month.*

Doris: *You haven't gone to one of those in a while. Why now?*

Neil: *Because I need to take a break. A sabbatical. I'll talk to you when I figure things out.*

Doris: *And then you'll come home?*

There had been no answer. She'd tried phoning him twice in the past four days, and her heart pounded hard every time he didn't answer.

She had all but given up, but she texted him one more time.

Doris: *Is there someone else?*

Neil: *I already told you I need a break. This isn't working anymore.*

That was the moment Doris has leapt into action. Neil might not want to come home, but she had a plan to change the situation.

She just hoped it would work.

CHAPTER 2

Robert pushed open the door of the Whisking Love Bakery and Bistro and walked into the din of breakfast conversations and laughter. The counter was busy. Two lines of customers stood nearby, one for pick-up and the other waiting to order. He scanned the room until he saw Curtis's checked flannel shirt and his salt-and-pepper hair.

Curtis was lost in thought as he watched the counter, and only seemed to notice Robert when he pulled out a chair and sat down.

"Morning," said Robert, hanging his messenger bag on the back of the chair and picking up the menu.

"I ordered for us already," said Curtis.

"How did you know what I'd want?"

"You always order the same thing, and it was getting busy."

"Well, Esther's breakfast always hits the spot, and I love her sourdough bread." And he could always rely on Esther giving him exactly what he ordered, Nothing else in his life seemed to be as reliable, except perhaps his mother. But even she seemed to be distracted recently, and he wished he knew what it was.

"It's all pretty lovable," said Curtis, gazing past Robert to the counter.

"You're drooling." Robert twisted to see Esther, the owner, serving a line of customers that didn't seem to be getting any shorter. "I'm sure the food will be ready soon."

"Hope so. I'm starved." Curtis said, still watching the counter.

"Why don't we go over the list while we wait?" Robert pulled his tablet from his messenger bag.

"Huh?" Curtis dragged his gaze to Robert. "Okay, but I've got to be at the Men's Shack by ten today to give some instruction on the saw. I'm trying to train a new guy."

"I thought you did that."

"I did, but there are more opportunities than when I was young. We have new guys cycling through faster than I can refresh a computer screen. I wish I could find a reliable employee who would stay for the long haul."

"What qualifications?"

"Somebody who is handy, can learn safety protocols, instruct on how to operate the equipment, has first-aid training, and, most importantly, is willing to listen to the guys and treat them with respect. It's a mental health support group as much as it is a workshop. Oh, and somebody who will work for a lot less than a tradesperson makes."

"Maybe you need an older guy, someone who wants a second career."

"Like me, you mean?" Curtis grinned. "I had Klaus, but the college recruited him to teach a course. I can't compete with those wages or their pension."

"There must be others. I'll keep my ear to the ground. Besides, this new guy may stick around longer than you think."

"What I really need is a few part-timers. At least I have Jack most weekends and a few extra days. He even volunteers some of his time. He's helping me today and filling in for me tomorrow, and the guys love him. He's been through some of what they've experienced."

"Jack's a good guy. Maybe he'll know someone."

"But in the meantime, I'll ask Esther to post an ad on the board before I leave." Curtis nodded toward the community bulletin board that gave people something to do while they waited for their orders. "But first, let's get the list done so we don't forget anything in Victoria tomorrow. I don't have time to go back for a few months. I need to do a lot more networking with donors this quarter."

"I'll take notes," Robert said, turning on his tablet. Curtis was clearly worried about funding for his non-profit again, and yet here he was, spending a lot of time raising money for cancer research instead. Robert didn't want to waste his time.

They discussed their plans between bites of breakfast and sips of fair-trade coffee until Robert finally turned off his tablet and stowed it away. "I think we've got it all. When I get back to the store, I'll confirm that my mother's taking care of the decorations and food."

"Sounds good." Curtis pulled a sign out of the folder he had on the table. "I'm going to catch Esther before she slips back into the kitchen. I'll see you tomorrow."

"Okay," Robert was about to rise when the server came around with the coffeepot and offered them a refill. He glanced up at the clock and nodded, then asked for the paper.

Relaxing in his seat, he flipped through the *Sunshine Bay News* and thought about Curtis's dilemma. Maybe he could advertise in the community section of the paper. Robert turned to the classified section and scanned it to see what it would cost, but halfway down the page, in bold type, an ad caught his eye that made him forget all about Curtis's problem.

What was his mother up to now?

~

*D*oris had finished organizing the teaching packages and was dusting shelves when the door opened, and an angry Robert stepped inside.

"What is this, Mom?" He was holding up the paper. She glanced over at the place she had left her copy. It was still there. *Damn.*

"What's what, dear?" She studied the well-dusted shelves and checked them for imaginary dirt.

"A nanny? You're hiring a nanny behind my back?"

"They prefer the term childcare worker now, dear." She concentrated on stepping down from the little ladder she was using, trying to buy time. She had been dreading this.

"You know how I feel about this after the last time."

"Not everyone is going to be like Christine."

"Well, I won't have it."

"You don't have a choice. I'm going to California to help my brother, and someone has to look after Zack while you're working."

"Nora's gone to help Uncle Jock, and he's got Sandy too. She's been working for him for years."

"I spoke to Sandy a couple of days ago. She sounds exhausted. And though the store is under control, Jock will need extra help when he gets out of the hospital."

"But isn't Eugene's there too? They'll be fine."

She held up her hand. "No, Robert. I need to help Jock, and it's a good opportunity for me to step away from this for a while." She waved her arm at the store. "The only way you'll be able to take over the business is if I leave you completely in charge."

"You sound like Dad."

"What do you mean?"

"He said I need to 'man up.' Take care of Zack. Get help."

"Your father may be right. And I agree that you should hire some help."

"But why did you go behind my back? I told you I would try to find a sitter for the summer."

"And that was when? A month ago? School's out in ten weeks, and I want to see my brother. It's been four years, and now with his accident…" She swallowed hard. How had she left such a long time between visits? She hadn't seen Jock since he had trekked up to Vancouver Island for April's funeral. "Well, now he needs me, and I have to go."

"But you aren't going before the fundraiser, are you?"

"Yes. Jock needs my help. And if I'm down there, maybe Nora can come and help you with the books."

"You think I need a bookkeeper? That I can't make a go of it without my sister to give me a hand?"

"No, no. Nothing like that." Where was this coming from?

"I know Nora is the one who always had the responsible, well-paid job. The career. And I've been a disappointment to you and Dad, but I'm not sixteen anymore."

"You aren't a disappointment. And I never said you weren't responsible. I simply want both my children to have what they need for their future."

"Nora won't want to come back to Canada to run a music store. She has clients and a business in Seattle."

"I doubt she has many. Most of the clients she had were connections she made through Crispin's family business. With the divorce, she has to start over. I want her to know she has the option of doing it here if she wants to."

"Mom, why would she want to come back?"

"Why would she want to stay? She's been living in a friend's basement suite in Seattle."

"I just don't want you to be disappointed."

"Why would I be disappointed?" She looked into his eyes. Sometimes her son made no sense.

"Because, with the way you're talking, it sounds like you're making plans for Nora without consulting her. Just like you do for me." He pointed to the paper.

"I'm only giving her options. There's nothing for her in Seattle. I wish she had listened to me before. I always thought there was something off about Crispin. He was too self-important. Too…"

"Smarmy?"

"Yes. Exactly."

"Mom, we have never once discussed Nora working in the business. I'm the one trained to take it over."

"You could do it together."

"She and I are very different. And not once in fifteen years has she ever mentioned coming back."

The words stabbed at Doris. Nora—her lovely, headstrong daughter who had made a life for herself despite the man she married—had never considered coming back, just as Doris had never once thought of returning to Cataluma where she had grown up. Once you left a place and grew in a different direction, it was hard to imagine going back.

But she and Nora were different. Doris had a business and was part of a community. Nora had nothing left, and though Doris knew Nora was a grown adult, a part of her still wanted to reach out, draw her home, and look after her.

"Maybe so, but she might want to now. She could help with the books while she sets up her own business. I could give her the cabin out by the lake until she finds her footing."

"I don't need help with the books. I've been doing them for two years."

Doris stood to her full height and glared at her son, just as she had when he was a little boy and been cruel to his sister. "Nora needs us, and you can help."

"It's always about Nora," he muttered.

"No. In case you've forgotten, the past few years have been about you and Zack and April."

And not, she reflected, about Neil.

"Fine." He turned toward the back of the store. "I didn't think you would abandon me too," he muttered.

"Pardon?" She had heard him but pretended she hadn't. The accusation was too close to how she felt. She didn't want Robert to feel abandoned; she knew all too well what that felt like.

He turned back. "Can't you wait until we have everything in place first? Nora has had a year to adapt, and Jock is still in hospital anyway. And what about the food and the decorations?"

"Honey, you have it under control. I booked the hall. Esther's doing the catering again, and I arranged for

Alexis Grant from the school to set up the craft room for the children. She's already getting volunteers lined up to do face painting and paper crafts."

"But we haven't sold nearly enough tickets. We'll end up owing money if we can't do that."

"I have Louise from the Belle Tones choir helping us. You know what a force she is. The choir is selling tickets and collecting donations for the silent auction. And they'll do the decorations. All you need to do is show up with the Pink Ribbon Band and play your heart out."

He looked doubtful, so she added, "And look at my sign." She motioned at the poster on the counter. "It's already helped me sell four tickets this morning. You'll be fine."

He seemed to relax, then looked at the paper he was carrying and rounded on her again. "When are we doing the interviews?"

"Tomorrow."

"When I'm not here."

"It's only the preliminary ones. You'll make the final decision."

"Well, at least that's something," he said.

"Sarcasm doesn't become you, Robert," she said. "Now, do you mind carrying that other box of books out here for me?"

"Fine," said Robert, stomping down the hall to the storage room.

Doris slumped against the counter. Well, that had gone better than expected. Now she hoped one of the three women who answered her ad would be suitable so she could go to California, see Jock and Nora, and find her husband.

She had to make Neil understand that even though he might not feel it, their marriage was her priority.

CHAPTER 3

*O*ut in the back room, Robert leaned against the closed door, took a few deep breaths, and worked on noticing the things around him. It was a grounding exercise he'd learned from Curtis, who attended the same grief support group. They'd both lost their wives to breast cancer.

Notice three things you can see, he told himself, and scanned the room, resting his gaze on the boxes on the floor that needed to be sorted, moved, and unpacked. Then he noticed the shelves that lined the room, and then a tiny cherry-red ball sitting on the floor near the bottom of the shelves.

The ball was a gift from April to Zack, who delighted in slamming it against the floor and seeing it ricochet around the room until it ran out of energy. Now it lay, abandoned in the dust, forgotten, like so many things Robert and Zack had shared with April. Tears welled up in his eyes and he swept them away with the back of his hand, turning his attention back to the exercise. *Notice three things you can hear.* His heartbeat, a clock ticking at the far end of the room, and the soft music now coming through the speaker. His mother must have turned on the classical radio station to bring calm to the store after their little blowout, as though she knew it helped him to settle down.

And it was helping. His breath came more evenly now.

Staying on task, he continued to notice things, this time smells: the musty odor from the books at the back of the room, and the scent of dust—he would need to get one of the staff to give it a thorough cleaning before he brought in more stock and collected the instruments from their school loan program. He walked to the little window high on the wall and slid it open, letting in the fresh scent of flowers from a planter on the patio above, where April's friend Yvonne lived. He couldn't place the sweet scent. April had been the one who knew flowers.

He closed his eyes and breathed in the scent again, willing his shoulders to relax, then worked to identify what he could notice with his sense of touch: the smooth surface of the window he'd just opened, the rough cardboard boxes as he moved two or three out of the way, the empty shelves as he searched for the books his mother wanted, and the rubber of the little ball he retrieved and placed in his pocket. He wondered if Zack would remember it too.

There was nothing to taste in here outside of dust, so he abandoned that part of the exercise. But he didn't need it. He was calmer now. His heart rate slowed. And if he continued to focus on what was in front of him instead of becoming anxious at the first sign of trouble, he could do this. He didn't need his mother, and he wasn't a child, no matter how much his mother sometimes made him feel like one. He had managed to live in Vancouver, work, teach music, and raise a child for five years before returning to the island.

But he hadn't done it on his own. April had been more patient and softer with Zack. She didn't get angry when their son took too long in the morning, or when his mind frequently drifted off into the clouds. As another anniversary of her death approached, Robert felt her loss as much as ever. He considered phoning Curtis to talk about this latest development, but Curtis had his own concerns today. Tomorrow, on their drive to Victoria, Robert could vent his anxieties about his mother leaving and all that entailed for him and for Making Music for a Cause. The fundraiser had been Curtis's idea—a way to make something positive from their collective loss—and his friend would step up if Rob needed it.

"I can do this," he mumbled to the empty room, as he looked for the box his mother needed. But he had his doubts about a nanny—no, childcare worker. The last experience had been a disaster.

He remembered the evening vividly. He had come home later than normal after asking Christine to stay while he and Curtis were playing a gig downtown with their new band. The crowd had enjoyed their music, and he had stayed afterward to share a drink with some friends and pretend for a few hours that his life was normal. He arrived home on a high of music making and camaraderie.

He'd thanked Christine for staying longer and held the door for her to return to her apartment across the hall. But she'd stopped in front of him and stood close. He held open the door and thanked her again, but she didn't leave. Instead, she reached up and kissed him in a way no child-care worker should kiss her employer. He hadn't returned the kiss, only stepped back, letting go of the door.

"No," he'd said, hands up in front of him.

"I thought maybe," she began, tears welling in her eyes, "you might be starting to move on."

He shook his head at her and stared in disbelief. Moving on? How could she think that?

"You seemed so happy just now. I haven't seen you like that in a long time."

"Happy?"

"I'm sorry. I misjudged things. It won't happen again."

"You need to leave." And the next day he had handed her severance in lieu of notice, while his mother stepped in to take care of Zack.

He could not go through that again.

He found the box his mother wanted and carried it out to the front.

"I'm not ready," said Robert, putting the box on the table then turning to face his mother. "But I'll suck it up. I know you've done more than your share of childcare the past few years."

"I know you don't feel ready, Robert, but you are more prepared than you realize. You've been doing the training and hiring for the store, and I believe in you. I'll be able to officially hand over the reins as soon as we get the paperwork from the lawyer."

"Paperwork from the lawyer?" What was she talking about now?

"I'm putting you on the store paperwork as a full partner," she said. "We talked about this."

"You said you were thinking about it. We haven't really talked about it. What's the rush?" Did he even want to run the store if Nora came back? The help would be nice, but if he was going to do this, he wanted to make it his own instead of depending on family to help him all the time.

"No rush. I was just thinking it might be time to retire. Your father has been talking about the possibility. I thought you wanted to run the store, so I started talking to the lawyer to move things along. You know me."

Robert laughed to cover the panic gripping his throat. "Yes, I do. Once you get an idea in your head, it becomes a thing in no time."

"Your ideas also find their legs, Rob. The ribbons, selling your house and moving in upstairs after April passed, learning how to do the books, the ordering, and managing people—you're a great manager—and all while raising Zack. Your little guy is a lovely chap. You've done well. I'm proud of you."

"I didn't do it alone," said Robert. "I had April, and then I had you to help after she died." How would he ever repay her for swooping in and taking charge of six-year-old Zack while they waded through the thick, sticky treacle of grief? Now that he was finally gaining ground, paying off debts, finding footing in his new world and learning to walk on his own again, she was leaving. And by the sounds of things, she was thinking of making it permanent. He was going to need help.

"What's the name of the first applicant? Do they have a resume?"

His mother beamed. "I'll forward them to you."

He had the suspicion he had just fallen into a Doris trap. His mother had a way of talking people into things they didn't even know they wanted. It was no wonder there were so many musicians in Sunshine Bay. She was one of the major forces behind the vibrant arts and music community in town. How would he do her legacy proud when he still awoke most nights from dreams of his happy family, only to find April's side of the bed empty?

He glanced again at the ad in the back of the paper and shook his head. He wouldn't be surprised if, by the end of the weekend, Zack had a new person in his life—and Robert had a new staff person to train. Hopefully whoever it was would be kind to Zack and keep him safe.

He had promised April. And, after failing her once, he couldn't let it happen again.

CHAPTER 4

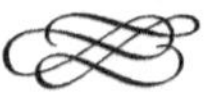

"I'll call you soon, Bhapa. Sunday. And don't worry, I'm fine." Kiran Misra clicked out of the call to her father and walked into the bathroom at the Whisking Love Bakery and Bistro, where she had just finished the most delicious roasted vegetable sandwich she had ever eaten.

She smiled at her reflection, not believing her luck. She'd been in town only one day, and already she had an interview for a childcare position. And she needed to get ready if she wanted to make a positive impression. Despite staying in hostels during her travels, she was running out of money, and with summer only a few weeks away, she wouldn't have a chance of getting a job as a substitute teacher, much less a full-time one, until September.

She pulled her brush from the oversized leather bag she'd toted across Canada and half of Europe and brushed it through her long dark hair. Then she took out her makeup case—a luxury she'd never given up despite nearly two years moving from place to place—and lined her dark brown eyes, applied mascara, and dusted on some bronzer to give her skin a sun-kissed appearance. She pulled her hair into a ponytail and straightened her blouse the best she could, grateful that she had put it on at the hostel this morning rather than wearing the same ratty T-shirt she had for the last week.

"Right," she said to the reflection. "You are ready to take on the world." Her reflection nodded in agreement, and she walked the few steps to the music store next door. Collecting her courage, she stepped inside, and a little bell rang to signal her entrance. She found an older woman speaking to a woman of about eighteen, who was chewing gum in a way that would have had Kiran sent to her room when she was that age.

Kiran didn't want to interrupt them, so she wandered over to a grand piano in the middle of the room and ran the tip of her finger over the glossy black finish. What she wouldn't give to play this instrument. When her relationship imploded three years earlier, she had sold her piano, and she'd played little since. She walked over to the music books and flipped through one to see what level it was.

The bell over the door sprang to life again, and another woman, about her age, walked right up to the counter and took the place of the younger woman, who was now leaving.

"You should have been paying attention," Kiran mumbled to herself, hoping that the woman behind the counter didn't admire people who marched up and started speaking without so much as a by-your-leave. She didn't relish going back to the café next door to continue her search for work.

The door opened again, but this time a boy stepped inside, about ten years of age, with bright orange hair and freckles. He glanced at the pair speaking at the counter and made a beeline to the piano. He opened the lid, stretched his hands, and then played an intermediate version of *Für Elise*. Kiran listened and then walked over to watch him play. The kid had talent.

When he finished, she clapped. "Bravo," she said. "That was fantastic."

He seemed startled to find someone watching him but soon found his voice. "Thank you," he said. "I'm practicing it for the MMFC."

"The MMFC?"

His face fell. "It's something my dad and I do every year. Well, Dad does most of it, but he said I could play this year if I practice really hard."

"Oh?" said Kiran. "Tell me more about that. I'm new here."

"It's a fundraiser," said the boy. "Its real name is Making Music for a Cause, but we call it the MMFC.

We raise money for cancer research. My mom died of cancer."

"Yeah?" said Kiran, realizing this must be the boy she was applying to look after. "So did my mom."

He peered into her eyes as though seeing her for the first time. "When?"

"Twelve years ago," she said. "I was away at university, learning to become a music teacher, when she got sick."

"You're a music teacher? Can you play the piano?"

"I haven't practiced in a long time. I've been traveling, and when you travel, it's not possible to take pianos with you. They don't fit in your pocket."

He laughed. "Do you want to play with me? I'm doing a duet with my dad, but he's always too busy to practice with me."

"Which song?"

He stood up, flipped open the lid of the bench, and grabbed a few sheets of music from the cavity in the seat. "This one." He pulled it out and handed it to her.

She read the sheet music, serious for a moment, then winked at him. "I'm pretty sure I can handle this. Which part do you play, the top or the bottom?"

"I'm playing top," he said, shifting his position and making room for her to join him on the bench. "You can take that part." He pointed at the sheet, and she sat beside him, stretching her hands as he had done and settling them onto the keys.

"Ready?" she said, reveling in the cool, familiar touch of the keys.

"One, two, three," he said. She stumbled a little in one section, but was otherwise proud when they got to the end of the song.

"You can still play well," he said.

"Thank you. What's your name? I'm Kiran."

"Zack," said the boy. "My dad and grandparents own this place."

"Nice to meet you, Zack." Kiran reached out to shake his hand as though he were a CEO in a boardroom. From her experience, it helped children connect with her when she treated them like equals.

"Should we practice this again? I missed some notes in a couple of places and threw you off."

"Okay." He grinned. "This time, can we play it faster? It's a boogie-woogie, and it's supposed to be played fast."

"You got it."

Zack counted down again then plunged into the piece. Kiran threw herself into the music too. Playing the piano was like visiting an old friend—a friend she hadn't realized she missed so much.

When they finished the piece, they stopped to talk about what was working. She pointed out a phrase where Zack could put more feeling into the piece and demonstrated what she meant.

He tried what she had shown him and laughed in delight when he got it right. And then they played it again. The bell over the door tinkled, and Kiran glanced over to discover that the second applicant was gone. The older woman, with a head of spiky gray hair, came toward them. Kiran missed a note. She quickly recovered, but she could tell by Zack's frown that he had noticed.

The woman waited beside the piano until they finished. "I'm sorry to keep you waiting. Is there something I can help you with? I notice you were looking at the music books."

"Oh, no. My name is Kiran. I'm here about the job."

"Really?" said the woman, brightening. That was a good sign, wasn't it?

"My name is Doris. Why don't you come with me over there so we can talk?" She pointed to the counter. "Zack, honey, you practice your other piece. When I'm finished with Kiran, I'll play your dad's part."

"Can't Kiran come back?" pleaded Zack.

"Perhaps later," said Kiran. "If I have time. But I would love to hear you play the other piece while we have our meeting."

"Okay." Zack's pout turned to a grin. "I'm really good with this one, and it has a crossover in it."

"He means he has to cross his right hand over his left to get the whole range of notes," said Doris.

"That's pretty advanced stuff," Kiran said to Zack. "You must practice a lot."

"Yep, two hours a day," said Zack.

"And he loves it," said Doris, patting Zack on the shoulder before walking with Kiran toward the end of the counter. "Let's have a little chat and see if this is a good fit."

They sat at the end of the counter in two tall chairs. They were the right size for Doris, but Kiran had to boost her five-foot-four frame into it while Doris asked her about her experience.

"I haven't been a nanny," said Kiran, wanting to be as truthful as possible. "But I have a teaching certificate, and I taught grades one through four for nine years—until two years ago, when I decided to travel."

"You've been traveling for two years?"

"Yes. I did the backpack-around-Europe-and-Asia thing, and then thought I would travel across Canada. I've never been to the west coast before this. I grew up in Toronto."

"And how long do you think you'll stay?"

"I would like to stay for at least a few months."

"I was looking for someone to stay the summer," said Doris, looking unsure.

"Oh, I'll be here until at least September," Kiran said quickly. "I'm applying for work as a teacher."

"That would get us through until Zack goes back to school in the fall," said Doris, brightening again. "I thought perhaps you would want to go home. Don't you miss your family?"

"I only have my father now, but he's remarried. I visit him once a year, and I see him every few months when he's traveling out this way." Those were the best times, from Kiran's point of view. It was like old times, before he married Rajani. Her stepmother always made her feel unwelcome.

"Do you live near here?" Doris asked, bringing Kiran back to the conversation.

"I'm staying in the hostel. Still looking for a place to stay."

"Well, we can't pay a great deal, but we do provide room and board," Doris said.

Kiran frowned. "I was hoping to find a place of my own." Though how she would afford it was another question.

"Actually, if you and Rob—that's my son—decide you're a good fit, there's a separate apartment upstairs," said Doris. "Across the hall from where Rob and Zack live."

"When can I meet him?" asked Kiran, hoping to wrap up the interview. She had a good feeling about this job, and she already liked Zack.

"Rob will be back soon. He went into Victoria to pick up some supplies and get a new soundboard for his band."

"Your son plays in a band?" Kiran knew band members. They weren't always terribly reliable. Maybe this wouldn't be such a great idea after all.

"He plays keyboard and sometimes guitar," said Doris, her voice rising with excitement. Kiran wondered if she was truly excited about her son's band—or if she simply overemphasizing the positives to gloss over something negative. She seemed almost *too* nice, like she was trying to rush things along for some reason. She glanced over at Zack, who was still playing the piano. Still, the boy seemed nice and well brought-up. It couldn't be all bad.

The band is practicing for a performance in a few weeks," said Doris. "They do it every year."

"For the MMFC that Zack mentioned?"

"That's the one." Doris's face lit up.

"He said it is in memory of his mother."

"April passed on a few years ago," explained Doris, growing serious. "Robert and his friends formed a grief group, started the Pink Ribbon Band, and they've been raising money for cancer research every year since, in the memory of their lost loved ones."

"That's a good cause. My mother died of breast cancer."

"I am sorry." Doris reached over to pat Kiran on the arm. "Was she very young?"

"She was forty-five," said Kiran. "Years ago. I'm used to living with her loss now. But it would be great to help raise money for research, even if this job doesn't work out."

"I'm sure we can find something for you to do for the big day. But Robert should be back soon. Why not come back in about an hour? I'll introduce you."

CHAPTER 5

Robert shifted the heavy box to one hip, unlocked the back door, and edged his way toward the storage room, past the strains of violins being played in one of the teaching rooms. It was a beginner's class by the sound of things.

"Robert, is that you?" His mother sounded anxious. He set the box down and rushed to the front of the store.

"What's wrong?" He glanced around the room and breathed out in relief when he found Zack working on his homework at the end of the counter.

"Nothing. Just wanted to make sure you were here. I have Kiran coming back in a few minutes."

"Kiran?"

"She's your new childcare worker," said his mother. "If you agree, that is."

"If I agree?" Did he have a choice?

"Please, Dad?" said Zack, hopping down from the stool to join the conversation. "I like her!"

"You've met her already?"

"She plays piano, Dad. She helped me play the middle part of *Für Elise* that I was having trouble with."

"Wow." Robert felt a tug of joy at Zack's smiling face. It had been a long time since his son had been so animated. If this Kiran woman had this effect on Zack, he might have to give her a chance.

He glanced from his mother to his son. "Well, I look forward to meeting her."

"She'll be here in a few minutes," said his mother, looking him up and down. "Perhaps you should clean yourself up?"

He glanced down at his pants. "I guess the boxes were dirtier than I thought." He made a mental note to ask one of their after-school student employees to help him clean the storage room of dust. How was he going to keep everything straight without help?

"You don't have time," said Zack, jumping up and down. "She's here!"

The bell on the door sounded, and they all turned to see a petite young woman glide through the doorway. She smiled at Zack when he came running up to her.

"I've been practicing, Kiran," said Zack. "Come listen."

She tilted her head as she listened to Zack, just as April used to do. Robert's heart squeezed. Zack needed someone to pay attention to him, and it seemed this woman would do that. She paused, put her hand on Zack's arm, and reassured him she would talk to him as soon as she spoke again to his grandmother. It was natural. Not as though she were putting on an act for an interview. She appeared to be genuine, trustworthy, comfortable around children. Not like Christine or the others they had tried.

Zack grabbed Kiran's hand and led her over. She turned in their direction, and Robert got a good look at her dark eyes, luminous with life and fun. Even in just tan pants, a worn brown leather jacket, and a yellow shirt, she looked elegant. Her clothes contrasted completely with the shades of green April had worn, and Kiran's dark hair was pulled up in a messy bun while April had always worn her long auburn hair down or in a quick ponytail.

He shook himself. Why was he comparing her to April? They were nothing alike, and she would be the nanny— no, childcare worker. He had to think of her not as a woman but as an employee. Though, when she thrust her hand out after his mother introduced them, he was aware that keeping her at a distance would take effort.

He stared down at her outstretched hand. Her fingers were long for a woman of such short stature: the slender fingers of a pianist. His mother elbowed him, and frowned as only a mother can, so he collected himself and focused on shaking her hand—and not giving in to the temptation to hold it longer than was proper.

Too late. He'd already crossed that line.

Zack bounced beside him, looking from one to the other, breaking into his thoughts, and Rob dropped Kiran's hand, but not before he saw the shock on her face. What must the woman think of him? Did she think he was one of those leches that hired vulnerable women under the guise of being his nanny?

He wondered if his mother had told her about all their failed attempts at getting reliable childcare. There was the young woman who thought it was okay to sing, even though April was dead and could no longer sing. There was the one who tried organizing Zack's every moment until the boy didn't have time to breathe. And then there was that last disastrous attempt with Christine. He couldn't deny that he was the common denominator in all those failed attempts.

"How about you take Kiran upstairs, show her your apartment where she'd work and the one where she'd stay? Then you can have a chat and ask her any questions you have. I've left her information on the counter in the kitchen, along with some muffins for you."

He nodded and motioned for Kiran to follow him. It was only when he was halfway to the back stairs that he realized he hadn't even said hello. No wonder the woman looked concerned.

He turned around to make sure she was following him and spied his mother's concerned frown and Zack's look of expectation. He'd best try to make a better impression.

"Come this way," he muttered, smiling in a way that he hoped didn't make him appear like a demented clown. He was a friendly employer. People liked working for him. If only he could untie his tongue long enough to prove it.

CHAPTER 6

I cannot work for this man, she thought as she passed his mother and son and followed him up the stairs. Though she was already quite smitten with his son, she could tell Zack's charm had not fallen from this tree.

Zack's mother must have been the charming one. This man hid his emotions, if he had any, behind penetrating eyes and a shock of wavy dark hair. He had examined her like she was an alien species and shaken her hand as though he found fault in it—all without saying a word.

No, she couldn't work for him. She would have look for another position, and soon, because there was no way she could ask her father for a loan. If she did, he would have to discuss things with Rajani, and she could not be in her stepmother's debt. Not even for a nickel. Thoughts of Rajani kept her rooted to the spot instead of turning to run out the door.

Robert turned suddenly when he got to the green curtain, and she nearly jumped back. "Come this way," he said, drawing the curtain aside to reveal a wide wood staircase lined with storage cupboards. She nearly looked back to ensure the boy and his grandmother were as real and friendly as she'd thought. This reminded her too much of a vampire movie. Then he tried to smile, and she revised her assessment. This was more like a movie about a serial killer who locked nannies in the attic. She nearly fled, expecting his awkward grin to crumple into maniacal laughter at any moment.

But Rajani's critical frown flitted into her mind, and she reminded herself that Zack seemed normal and appeared comfortable with his father. She was watching too many horror films.

Robert beckoned again for her to follow, and she stepped firmly over the threshold and walked up the stairs, careful to leave two steps between them. She owed it to Zack and her dwindling savings account to find out more about this post, even if her intuition told her to be wary.

At the top of the landing, he pushed open the door to a small room lined with hooks for coats and shelves.

"This is the back door to our apartment," he said, and she was relieved to find his voice sounded normal. Almost friendly. But hadn't Norman Bates seemed friendly to some?

They stepped into a hallway with a door at the other end. The walls were an off-white, and the crown molding was a glossy, brighter white, making the space feel clean and spacious. The pictures on the wall were of landscapes, local birds, flowers. They made the apartment seem like a home, not the Bates Motel. Kiran forced herself to relax and followed him into the comfortable, open kitchen and living area. It was tidy, though due to his efforts or his mother's, she couldn't say.

"Would you like something to drink?" He walked toward the kitchen area.

"Water is fine," she said, and he went to the fridge for a jug of filtered water, a small luxury she could appreciate.

"Let's sit at the table," he said, pointing toward a snug little nook.

The nook had a big window overlooking the street, with a peekaboo view of the ocean. She loved the ocean. The table beside the window would be a lovely place to give Zack his breakfast in the morning. And maybe on the weekends or during summer break, they could go to the waterfront. She had seen a playground there the day she had arrived in town.

She sat, and the wood table reminded her of her mother's. They had spent hours there. It was where she had done her homework and learned to cook; where she and her parents shared stories over meals she had helped prepare; and where, when she got older and her mother couldn't come to the table anymore, she would write letters to family, do the paperwork her father couldn't bear to do, and create lesson plans for her students.

The table was one of the first things Rajani had expelled from the house when she married Kiran's father. Kiran had come home one day to find a new square, lacquered table in its place, all hard edges and cold.

"We sent it to goodwill," Rajani said. "Some poor family can get use from it. We will use mine. It is newer. Much more in fashion."

Her father had been unconcerned about the change. "Your mother only kept it because, while you were growing up, there was no use getting a new one. But it was worn. Old."

"You didn't think I might like it?" she had asked, her voice breaking.

"Why would you want an old table?" tsked Rajani. "Really, Kiran, you need to get some style."

Her father didn't look her in the eye. Conflict was not his forte, and she knew it.

That evening, she had cried herself to sleep in her basement room. She had relinquished her old bedroom to Rajani's three-year-old daughter, Priti, and Sima, then two, had taken the other upstairs room so Rajani could have them both close.

Her father had allowed her to paint her room and make it hers, since her grandmother had occupied it before she died, and though she had loved her new space, she couldn't help but feel exiled by her father and his young wife, only a year after her own mother had passed.

"Everything okay?" Robert set a glass of water in front of her.

"Oh, yes. Fine," she said, shaking off the memories and forcing her frown into a smile.

"Are you hungry at all? I have some muffins Esther brought by yesterday. She often brings me day-olds."

She shook her head. "I can get something later."

"Well, do you mind if I have one?" He went to the cupboard, pulled out two plates, two knives, and a tin, and brought them all to the table.

"Humor me. You can tell me what you think of Esther's baking."

"Thank you," she said, giving in and taking a muffin from the tin. They smelled so good, and though she had eaten only an hour earlier, she was hungry.

"Now tell me. What is your real dream? Is being a nanny your dream job?"

She was caught off guard for a moment by the direct question.

"Those are two different questions."

"Well, let's start with the second one."

"No, being a nanny isn't my first choice."

His face fell, and she quickly added, "but I am available for at least the spring and summer. I was a teacher for nine years in Ontario, and I'm now looking for a teaching position or an opportunity to get on the on-call list. But that won't be until September. That is what your mother was most concerned about. The summer."

"That's true." He sat back and seemed to ponder this. "So that will give you about four months of work here, and a place to stay until then at least. And perhaps we can both re-evaluate in August?"

"Yes. Your mother seemed to feel that by then your uncle and your sister would not need much more help."

"I see." He reached for a second muffin and shook his head. "I should cook dinner instead of eating more of these. When can you start?"

"Could we go over the expectations first?" What was wrong with this guy? A few minutes ago, he couldn't be bothered to say hello, and now he seemed to be offering her a job.

"Okay, how about we agree to create a plan for this month and next that will give you some time to find an on-call teaching job during the day, as long as you are available to take Zack to school. He goes just down the road, so either my mother or I walk with him. I know it's close to the

store but could you pick him up? I worry about his safety.
"

"Yes, of course." She watched his face light up. He really was an odd one. "If I do get a day of teaching, could I arrange something different for those days? "

"That would be fine." Robert took a bite of muffin, and they sat in silence for a moment. Then he said, "Zack also needs someone to supervise his piano practice. I think you were already a great help there. And to make him meals and clean up after him. I have a cleaner come in once a week, but you could do the day-to-day clearing up. Do you cook?"

"I do. I enjoy cooking."

"Well, maybe we can go over a few foods Zack likes. If you can get him to try some new things, expand his palate, I would not be averse to it. Mom cooks plain fare, mostly because it's what my dad prefers after traveling and eating in restaurants all the time. And I'm afraid my attempts in the kitchen are more on the side of pasta and pasta. "

"Do you like spice? I make a rather good curry, and Thai food, and of course steak, seafood, fish."

"My mouth is watering already, "

So he was a bit of a foodie. She would file that bit of information away for future reference. A man who loved fine food couldn't be all bad. "Could you teach me how to make any of the dishes Zack learns to like? I need to be better. Mom gives him the basics, but, as I say, he needs to expand his horizons.”

“Happy to,” she said, and his genuine, ear-to-ear smile made her decide that, yes, she could work for this man after all.

“What do you think so far? Do you think this will suit for a few months?”

“Yes, I think so…”

“Before you make up your mind, let me show you around the apartment, and then I’ll take you over to the apartment that comes with the position. We are only able to pay minimum wage, but we do include accommodation and meals.”

She nodded and rose to follow, not sure what type of living quarters she could expect. But it had to be better than living like a sardine in a hostel, with people coming and going all the time. As long as she had privacy and could get a good night’s sleep, she would be happy for now. It would give her the summer to find something new.

He toured her around the small apartment, showed her Zack’s room and the bathroom. “It’s pretty small, but it suits us well enough, especially as we have space down-stairs. That’s where my office is and where we keep the pianos, of course.”

She marveled at the change in his demeanor and, as he chattered on, showing her where things were kept, she tried to remember any details she might need later.

He led her down the hallway to a door on the far side of his apartment and out to a larger hallway. "There are three other apartments here, and the main entrance to the building is down there" he pointed to a large set of double doors at the end of the corridor. "Esther, the baker lives there." He pointed at the door on the same side of the building as his own. "I rarely see her, though, unless it's at Whisking Love. She gets up early to bake and is generally quiet. By the time I get up here at night, I suspect she's asleep. She's usually at work by four or five."

He pointed to the other two doors. "This one, across the hall, is the one that comes with the job, and that one"—he pointed to the one across the hall from Esther's— "belongs to one of April's old friends, Yvonne. April was my wife." His expression changed as he said April's name, and Kiran's heart went out to him. Poor man, to have lost so young someone he so obviously cared about. Maybe he was just overwhelmed, and that was why he seemed so unapproachable.

"Does Yvonne run a store here, too?" she asked, to get his mind back to the present.

"No, she's a dentist. Her practice is down the street, in an old house that has been done over. She and April have known each other since they were children, and they sang in the same choir."

"There's a choir?"

"Yes," he said, as he pulled out his keys to unlock the door to the apartment. "The Belle Tones is an all-women's chorus. About twenty singers of all ages. They were a great support to my wife when she found out she was ill." His face was grave now, and he seemed to have drifted away on another memory.

He opened the door. "Come and look." Kiran was delighted. The clean, bright room held a couch and chairs at one end and a galley kitchen with a little kitchen table, complete with a vase of white daisies. She stepped forward to look out the window to the square below. "That's the library," he said, following her gaze. "There's a café down there, and the theatre across the street. Many people come here in the evenings, especially as the weather improves. Sometimes there's music in the park there." He pointed past the library to a green space edged with spring flowers and a bandstand in the middle.

"It's beautiful," said Kiran, and his smile was genuine this time. Maybe he was the type of guy who needed to warm up to a person. She considered something Doris had said during their interview—that Robert had been through a couple of nannies who didn't work out. *If I had a wonderful boy like Zack, I would be concerned, too.* She turned to him again. "It's so light and comfortable." But he was looking a little pained again, so she decided it was time to shut up.

"I'm glad you like it," he said. "Mom redecorated it a few months ago after the last tenant moved out."

"I like the painting." She pointed at a landscape on the wall in vivid acrylics.

"That's one of my wife April's paintings." They stood together, gazing at the bright blue skies, the bald eagles on the beach, and a starfish in the foreground. "It's from a picture she took when we were in Campbell River, when the eagles were plentiful. It was around this time of year," he mused.

"I love it," she said, wincing. He'd think she had a limited vocabulary if she kept telling him how much she loved everything. "I'd like to see the eagles there. Perhaps next spring break I'll get out that way. And I love the daisies." She pointed toward the kitchen table. Oh no, there she went again.

"Huh." He startled a bit, then turned to her. "Well, Mom is the one to thank for the flowers. She thinks they brighten everything up."

"I agree, especially spring flowers. They are a sign of new beginnings, better things to come."

"They are pretty to look at, anyway," he said, turning to gaze at his wife's painting again. Kiran took the opportunity to see what else the apartment offered. Behind one door she found a full bathroom complete with tub and shower. How long had it been since she'd had a soak in a tub? Years. She made a mental note to find some bubble bath. Then she investigated the bedroom and stifled a squeak. The bed was made up as though it were a high-end bed-and-breakfast complete with plush duvet, four fluffy pillows, and white wooden blinds—not the cheap ones people normally put into rental apartments. And the closet was large enough to walk in. She felt at home already.

Behind her, she heard a voice clearing, and she turned to find him in the doorway, watching her, a slight smile on his lips. "What do you think? Would this work for you?"

"Yes, this is perfect."

"There's a laundromat down the street," he said." But you could also use our washer and dryer if you like. One of the duties I would ask you to perform is laundry. Or at least help Zack with it. It's one of his chores to fold."

"It's good to teach a child responsibility early," she said. "His future partner will thank you for it."

He gave her a quizzical look. "Yes, I suppose that's true."

As she followed him out of the bright apartment, she turned around one last time to take it all in, her gaze settling on the daisies again. Those flowers were a sign of good things to come. Her mother had always thought so.

She decided that if they made the offer, she would take the job and ignore her intuition, which was still warning her to watch out.

Why did they need someone so quickly—and what had happened to the last person who was in the job?

CHAPTER 7

Zack and Doris watched the pair disappear up the stairs, and Zack turned to her. "Do you think he liked her?"

"I hope so. We'll know soon enough. Why don't you practice for a few minutes while we wait? I'll get the close-out done."

Zack sat at the piano and noodled around with his pieces, not paying full attention to the task, while Doris closed out the cash register and got the bank deposit ready. They waited a good forty minutes before finally they heard steps on the stairs.

Robert was grinning as he entered the room. "Mom, I'm going to drive Kiran over to the hostel to pick up her gear. We'll be back in about half an hour."

"Really?" said Zack, running up to Robert. "Kiran can stay?"

Kiran stepped out from behind the curtain. "Yes, Zack. Now we'll have more time to work on those pieces you're practicing."

"And you can help me with homework?"

"She absolutely can," said Robert, placing a hand on his son's shoulder. "I'll still have to keep my hand in, though. Otherwise, I might forget how."

"Okay," said Zack. "You can both help me."

"Sounds like a good plan to me," said Doris, feeling as though she had just won the lottery. "Now, off you two go." She shooed them away with both hands. "I'll meet you upstairs when you return and put some dinner on."

"Thanks, Mom," said Robert, kissing Doris on the cheek and patting Zack on the arm. "You can practice for another few minutes as well. We'll be back soon."

He opened the door for Kiran and followed her out to the sidewalk. When the door closed behind them, Zack turned to Doris. "He's going to let her stay!" he said, and raised his hand so they could high-five.

As Doris walked over to lock the door, Zack was already sitting and practicing the pieces in earnest. It was an excellent decision to hire Kiran, she thought. Both Zack and Robert agreed. Things were all going to be fine now.

~

While Zack practiced, Doris checked her messages on her phone and found one from Sandy, her old school friend who worked with Jock.

Sandy: *I need your help.*

Doris stepped into the back room and dialed Sandy's number; Sandy picked up after the first ring. "What's wrong?" Doris asked. "Is Jock okay?"

"I've just quit my job, and I need someone to stay with Jock at my place until he can go home. I'm leaving town for a while."

"What do you mean?" Sandy had worked for Jock ever since she'd been widowed more than fifteen years earlier.

"I can't do it anymore, Doris. I just can't."

"What happened? Are you unwell?"

"I'm fine. I've just had enough."

"Is it Nora? Or Eugene? What have they done?"

"It's not them. They've been a huge help. It's Jock."

"What did he do?"

"He's been seeing Virginia."

"Virginia?" Doris wracked her brain to remember where she'd heard the name. "Not Virginia from school." Sandy's old nemesis.

"Yes."

"And you don't want Jock to get hurt? Is that it?" Sandy was protective of Jock, which made sense. They had been friends a long time.

There was silence, and then a sob.

"He's a grown man, Sandy. I'm sure he can take care of himself."

The sobs got louder. "Just come," Sandy begged. "I can't have him living with me when he's going out with that… that… conniving, controlling witch!"

"When does he get out of the hospital?" asked Doris, calculating how quickly she could arrange to leave. Now that Kiran was starting, there wasn't much holding her back from going to California, and from there she could try to track down her wandering husband. Make him see that they needed to make their next plans together.

"They said three to seven days. He has a secondary infection that needs to be treated first."

"I'll make arrangements," said Doris. She hung up, finishing closing the store for the night, scooted Zack upstairs to start on his homework, and made a mental list of what she needed to prepare before she left: a passport, gas for the car, a ferry reservation, and her best clothes. She sorted through her closet in her mind, and settled on a few outfits, her favorite pair of high heels, and a commitment to buy a new dress. One that would remind Neil—and herself—that she still had some life left in her.

CHAPTER 8

On Monday morning, Kiran woke before the sun, propped herself up on her pillows, and dialed her father's number. She'd been avoiding him the past few days, but now she had good news to share.

"Beta." His face smiled at her from the screen. "I've been worried about you."

"I've been busy, Bhapa. But I'm doing well. I have a job for the summer and a place to live. Here, let me show you." She hopped out of bed and turned the phone screen toward the apartment to give him a virtual tour.

"What do you think?" she asked, turning the phone back so she could see his face." I'd show you the view, but the sun's not up here yet."

"It looks nice, Beta," he said. "Is it expensive?"

"That's the best part. It comes with the job. I'm a nanny for the summer, and I have my own apartment." She still couldn't quite believe her luck.

His face fell. "But what about your teaching?"

"I've applied for teaching jobs, but it's almost summer, so I needed something to do until September. It's a nice family, and the town is right on the ocean. You should come and visit me. I think you would like it."

"Yes, I've been to Vancouver Island, and it is beautiful. If I can come, I will. But if I can't, could you visit here? I miss you."

"I'll try to come in August, before the school year starts."

"I would like that," he said.

"Dad, you okay? You look tired."

"I am a little tired. There has been a lot to do. The girls have a lot of school functions."

"Well, get some rest," she said. "Sleep is important."

"I will, Beta. And I am glad you have a safe place to live."

They could hear Rajani calling him from the other room. "I must go. I promised I would drive the girls to school. I am glad you called. Call again soon, okay?"

"I will. Love you, Bhapa."

"I love you too."

Kiran stared at the screen where her father's face had been. She missed him. She'd have to make some time to go to Toronto in late August. Hopefully she'd have a teaching job by then.

She walked to the bathroom to start her shower when she heard a small thud and a rustle in the hallway.

"Darn it," said a woman's voice.

Kiran pulled a sweatshirt on over her tank top and peered out the door. A woman was bent over, picking up papers that had spilled from a box onto the hall floor. Kiran rushed to help.

"Oh," said the woman, whom Kiran recognized from the bakery. She sat back on her heels when Kiran handed her a pile of papers.

"Sorry to startle you," said Kiran.

"I'm sorry to have woken you up," said the woman. She glanced at Kiran's pajama bottoms and grinned at the cartoon kittens that covered them.

"It's okay," said Kiran. "I was just getting up. First day of work today. I'm the new childcare worker for the man next door." She nodded toward Robert's door.

"It's only five o'clock. Those two won't be up for at least another few hours."

"Yes, I guess I'm just excited."

"You moved in yesterday, didn't you?"

"Saturday night after dinner." It hadn't taken her long to unpack. Her backpack held everything she needed for traveling, but it was still only one bag, so she had spent Sunday at the laundromat, and then at the grocery store, trying to find a few food items that didn't empty her bank account. As she thought of the teabags and bagels she had picked up for breakfast, her stomach growled. She hadn't eaten much the day before, and she was hungry, but she couldn't very well show up at 5:00 a.m. to cook. She didn't even have a key to their apartment yet.

"I'm Esther," the woman whispered, taking the last of the papers from Kiran. "Thanks for helping me pick these up and so sorry to bother you."

"Kiran. And don't worry, I was getting up anyway."

"Doris told me about you when she was in yesterday. She's so hoping you work out, especially since she left last night to go to California to nurse her brother." Esther glanced at the other door in the hall, the one where the dentist lived, and moved closer to Kiran.

"I hope I don't disappoint," Kiran said, wondering why Doris hadn't mentioned she would leave so soon.

"Shhh," Esther said. "Sorry." She tilted her head toward the other door. "That one gets mad if she wakes too early, and I hate being on the wrong side of her." Color rose in her cheeks. "I shouldn't have said that."

"It's okay. I won't tell," said Kiran. "As for working out, I'm aware I'm not their first nanny. But I really like Zack, and Robert seems like a good father." And not so bad to spend time with, once she got past first impressions.

"I have to go down to start baking," whispered Esther, "but I'm about to have coffee and a bit of breakfast. Could I tempt you to join me?"

"Let me just put on some clothes." She looked down at the prancing kittens and they both grinned. She liked Esther already, and it might be an opportunity to learn more about her new boss.

"Come by in about half an hour and knock at the back door. I'll have the coffee ready." said Esther.

"I'll be there."

Kiran waited until Esther was out of sight then stepped back into her apartment and into the shower. After living in hostels for the past few months, she had become efficient at getting dressed.

Twenty-five minutes later, she locked her apartment door and pocketed the keys. They were small things, keys, but for after living keyless and unhoused for so long as she traveled from place to place, it was huge. And the key tag on these was a tiny house with *home* written on it, which made it even more special. Doris had done everything she could to make her welcome, it was too bad she had left so soon. She ran downstairs and around the back of the building to knock on the bakery door. It opened only a moment later to a smiling Esther.

"You're right on time," she said. "I have a batch of muffins nearly ready, and the coffee's hot."

"I can't wait," said Kiran. "I confess I had one of your muffins on Saturday, and it was fantastic."

"Thank you. Would you also like an egg? I've boiled a few. I like a bit of protein to start my day."

"I would love that," said Kiran, coming into the back kitchen.

"Take those," Esther said, pointing to two cups of steaming coffee, "and sit down." She indicated a small table and chairs. "It's my break table. Gives me a place to put my feet up before facing the day."

Kiran placed the mugs on the table next to the cream, sugar, and spoons that were already there.

"Do you have a preferred seat?" she asked.

"I like to sit facing the clock so I can stay on schedule. Today is a light day. No tour buses scheduled to come through, and the locals won't start trickling in until seven or eight."

"Tour buses?"

"We get the occasional bus tour through here in the spring, and more during the summer. Sunshine Bay has become a destination of sorts. We're near the ferry route to the mainland and we have a lot of natural wildlife."

"I agree with that. It's beautiful here."

"And you arrived at just the right time of year to truly appreciate it."

"So it seems."

"Now, I want to warn you before I start that I have the very best intentions in telling you this. I don't want to sound like a gossip. But…"

"But?" Kiran shifted in her seat. She should have suspected that this wasn't just a friendly neighbor hoping to get acquainted. This woman had an agenda.

"I've known Robert since he was a kid. He and his sister, Nora, used to play in the park out back and come in here for muffins. They are like a niece and nephew to me. I never had my own children, you see, and I watch over them, though it's not my job."

Kiran took a sip of the coffee. Good coffee. She wondered for a moment if it was roasted locally.

"I was thrilled when Robert and April met. She was a painter, he's a musician, and though Rob had to give up his dream when she became pregnant, they were happy."

"What was his dream?"

"He was playing violin for the Vancouver Orchestra and had worked his way up to second chair when they found out they were expecting Zack." Esther lowered her voice, though no one else was around. "Neil, his father, was angry they got pregnant so soon and was sure that he was going to have to give up his music. But Rob didn't care.

He continued to play with the orchestra until Zack was born, and then they sold their condo and moved here so he and April could be closer to family. They managed to muddle through, with Rob commuting to the city to practice with the orchestra, until Zack was three. Then April got sick. That's when he gave up the orchestra."

"Does he regret it?"

"I don't think so. They built a life here and had happy times. Her treatment was successful the first time, and she recovered. They bought a small house where she set up an art studio, and he started teaching music lessons and helping his mother in the store. More than helping. Doris has been relinquishing control—as much as she can relinquish control." Esther laughed. "I think Robert's father has finally come to terms with it. Especially since April died. And I know Doris and Neil love having their grandson so close by."

"Do you think Robert regrets giving up the symphony?"

"Sometimes, when Zack is staying over with his grandparents, I hear him playing the violin. A lot of slow songs that are just plain melancholy."

"He must miss his wife."

"Yes, and he probably misses other things as well. Being a lone parent isn't easy. Even when the child is as wonderful as our Zack is."

"Does he have a girlfriend?" Kiran asked. Though he was too brooding and melancholy for her tastes, he was attractive enough in other ways. Women liked musicians.

"He's had some dates," said Esther evasively. Then she frowned and her eyes narrowed, making Kiran wish she hadn't asked. "Take some friendly advice," she said. "If I were you, I would steer well clear of thinking of him in that way."

Kiran felt heat rise to her face. "I didn't mean it that way," she said, hearing the defensiveness in her voice. "I was just trying to figure out if there was someone else in Zack's life I should be aware of. I'm not interested in another relationship anytime soon."

"Good, because he's gone through quite a few caregivers, and it's best to keep it professional," Ester's voice was flat and controlled.

Feeling chastened, Kiran said, "Maybe I should go."

"Oh no. Don't," said Esther. A buzzer sounded, and she got up to open the oven and pull out two large tins of piping-hot muffins. "I didn't want to say anything, but after what happened before, I thought you should be warned." She put the muffin tins on the counter and slid two trays of croissants into the oven.

What had happened before? Kiran wanted to ask but sensed it wasn't the time to pry. Instead, she watched as Esther returned to the table with the muffins, eggs, and a bowl of fresh fruit. "This looks wonderful," she said, waiting for her host to join her at the table.

"Eat up," said Esther, looking much more relaxed now that she had warned Kiran away from Robert. "I'll just grab the coffeepot and top us up. Then you can tell me all about yourself."

So that was the game. Kiran would get a little information about the family, and a warning to keep her hands off her employer, in exchange for her own background. Was Esther Doris's spy? Kiran took a bite of one of the morning glory muffins filled with coconut, walnuts, and raisins and decided that if this was the woman's weapon of choice, she would surrender any information Esther wanted.

As they ate, Kiran told her about growing up in Toronto, teaching in Sarnia—a city in southern Ontario—losing her mother to cancer, and losing her father to a new wife.

"You don't see your father?"

"Oh, I do. It's just that it's never been the same since he married again. His new wife is only forty-four, ten years older than me, and she has two young daughters. Rajani didn't want me to teach them music or crafts, or any of the things I learned from my mother. It was like she didn't want my father to be reminded of Mom." Though Rajani hadn't hesitated to enroll them in piano lessons elsewhere.

"Perhaps it causes your father too much pain to remember."

"Perhaps." Kiran took a bite of fruit so she wouldn't respond right away, and thought about Rajani's last tirade. Kiran had been showing Sima how to do a math problem. It was, after all, Kiran's job to teach children and she thought perhaps she could help. But when Rajani found them sitting at that hard-edged kitchen table, their heads bent together, she snapped. "Go to your room," she told Sima, and once the child had retreated, she charged toward Kiran, her energy enough to make Kiran jump up and put the table between them.

"Keep away from them," she hissed. "You're not their mother. I tolerate you being here because of your father, but you are not part of this family."

"I'm his daughter," said Kiran, dumbfounded. "Bhapa asked me to spend time with them."

"They aren't your girls."

"They're my stepsisters," said Kiran.

"I only agreed to have you stay in the suite because your father was worried about you after your breakup. And with the pandemic, I couldn't kick you out, could I? But women in my family don't live with men. They marry, or they stay home with their parents. I don't want you influencing my children."

"You didn't stay with your husband," Kiran blurted out.

"That is none of your business," she hissed.

"Seems like you are being a hypocrite. You know this is the twenty-first century, right?" Besides, did the woman want her to be living with Jacques for the rest of her life? The man had treated her like crap, cheated on her, and then didn't even feel bad about it.

"I don't care what year it is. You are not to spend so much time with them. Especially when I'm not here."

"If that's how you feel."

"If I had my way, you'd never be here."

"Fine," said Kiran. And, after a month of frosty exchanges and mutual avoidance, Kiran had given her notice at the end of the school year, packed up her backpack with all the things she really wanted, put the rest of her belongings into a storage cupboard in the back of her father's basement, and told her father goodbye.

"Where will you go, Beta?" her father had asked, concern etching his face.

"I've always wanted to travel across Canada, and there's still a lot of Europe I haven't seen."

"Kiran, what will you live on?"

"I have some savings from the last few months of work, Bhapa. And I can always find work tutoring kids or teaching English somewhere."

"Is it because of Rajani? Has she made things difficult for you?"

"She doesn't want me to interfere with your marriage. I am a grown woman, Dad, and she's right. I should be out on my own. Thank you for taking me in when things fell apart with Jacques. I really needed you, and you were there for me."

"That man was bad for you. You moved in with him too young. It was right after your mother—"

"Possibly." She had cut him off, unwilling to talk or even think about Jacques anymore. She often wondered what it would have been like if her mother hadn't died when she was twenty-one. Would she have moved to London, or in with Jacques? Would her father have taken a job traveling six months a year selling medical equipment? If she had stayed home, would he have remarried so quickly?

Or would she have stayed home, gotten married, and had children of her own? She would never know.

"You don't have to go. I'll talk to her."

"It's time, Dad. I need to try life on my own for a while."

He had nodded and said all the right things. "Yes. I understand. You have a lot of your mother in you. She liked adventure." Then he looked up the stairs to where Rajani was banging pots and pans, starting the cooking for the day, and she sensed a profound sadness. He had lost a lot when her mother died. And she couldn't blame him for getting involved with a woman who would give him the family he had lost when Kiran grew up and left home. She hoped her departure would decrease the tension in the house so he and Rajani could be happy.

"We can keep in touch through WhatsApp. Maybe we can meet up when you are traveling for work? You're always flying around the country."

"Yes. Let's do that," he said, brightening. And they had met up when she was working in Fredericton, and when she taught summer school in Newfoundland before heading off to Europe. Those visits had been just like the old days. Before her mother had died.

Before Rajani.

Before he had new daughters.

"How long do you plan to stay in town?" Esther asked, shifting Kiran's focus back to the kitchen.

"I'm not sure. At least until the end of summer. I'm hoping to find a teaching job, but I have to wait for the postings to come out."

"So being a nanny is temporary?"

"It's what I'm doing for now. And I have committed to stay until September."

Esther frowned. "You wouldn't take off before that, would you? If you found work elsewhere?"

"I'm not really applying elsewhere," said Kiran. "Though I may look at what's in Victoria."

"It's more expensive to live there," Esther said quickly. "And traffic. Much worse."

"As someone who prefers to bike, I can see the merits of a place with little traffic." That was all she said, but she noticed Esther's quick grin.

At least she had made a good enough impression on Esther, or perhaps it was Doris, to have them want her to stay. After so long not feeling like she had a home, Esther's comment made her feel warm inside.

Another timer went off, and Esther jumped up again to move pans between the oven and the counter.

"You'll be here to help with the MMFC, then," Esther continued when she sat down again. "I know Doris is feeling guilty about leaving Robert, but she's also worried about her brother, Jock. He's in hospital."

"I hadn't realized that."

"Nora, Rob's sister, is helping him. But she's going through a divorce, and Doris is concerned about her too."

"Well, I'll try my best not to give her anything to worry about at this end. And I've arranged fundraisers before, for the school where I last worked, so I can lend a hand."

"Robert will be pleased to hear it. I imagine he'll be a little out of his depth without Doris."

"Doris does a lot for him?"

"She does. Though, between you and me, I think she does it as much for herself as for him. It makes her feel needed. Her husband travels a lot, and she's always on her own, trying to make things work. Been doing it for years."

"Could she travel with him?"

"Perhaps, now that you are here to help and Robert has taken over the store full time. She wants to hand over the store, but at the same time she's feeling lost."

"When I've had that spare-tire feeling," said Kiran, "I know it's time to roll off to new trails."

Esther laughed. "That's a good way of looking at it."

"Is there any advice you can give me about working with Robert and Zack? You know, so I can help Doris feel more at ease while she's away?"

"Take an interest in their music."

"That won't be hard. I have an interest in music myself."

"Do you play an instrument?"

"Piano." Kiran took another sip of coffee and glanced up at the clock. She would have to go soon. She didn't want to be late.

"That's right. Doris said you were helping Zack the other day and that Zack really liked you."

"I also sing, though only in the shower these days."

"That reminds me." Esther took a bite of her breakfast. "There were three childcare workers hired before you. They didn't work out."

"You said something about that earlier," said Kiran. "Is there something I should be aware of?"

"I've never told Doris—or anyone—this, but I suspect they had a little help leaving."

"What do you mean?"

Esther leaned in and lowered her voice, though they were, as far as Kiran could tell, still very much alone in the bakery. "Yvonne, our neighbor, took them under her wing a bit when they first started and, well, she used her inside knowledge to find fault with the way they were caring for Zack."

"Did she want to do it herself?" asked Kiran, a sick feeling creeping into her stomach. She knew something about this job was too good to be true.

"I don't think so," said Esther. "She's a dentist and always busy. I don't even think she goes to the store much. No. I think she was having trouble with anyone other than April being in Zack's life. They grew up together. April used to use the apartment you're in for a studio, and I think Yvonne couldn't picture anyone else living there who might take her place."

"They must have been great friends."

"Yes, they were. I suggest you find a way to tell her right off the top that you are only here for the summer. Hopefully, if she knows that, she'll leave you alone. I think the last tenant also had a hard time living there. He was quiet, never caused any trouble, but Yvonne never liked him much."

"I'll see how it goes. Thanks for the warning."

"Oh, and if you decide to stay, think about joining the choir in the fall. The Belle Tones Chorus is an all-women's group, and we have a great time. Our next concert is part of the Robert's fundraiser. We do a sing-along and everyone participates. And then everyone goes to family activities later. So no alcohol—just music, good company, and, in another room, there are crafts and face paints and that kind of thing for the children."

"That sounds like fun. I was picturing a ball or something where people get all dressed up in formal clothes."

"People still dress up a bit, smart casual I suppose, just because getting out and having fun is worth getting dressed up for. But it's a family thing. The other men in the support group that started the fundraiser have children also, and the kids wanted to help. This year is Zack's first time playing with the band. He and his father are playing a duet."

"Yes, I was helping Zack practice the other day. No wonder he wants it to be perfect."

"I'm sure you can help him on that score," said Esther, rising again as another timer went off.

Kiran stood too and picked up her dishes. "Where should I put these?" she asked. "I should probably go back upstairs and let you get on with things."

"Just set them in that dish bin," said Esther. "We'll take care of it when my kitchen helper gets here."

"Thank you for breakfast," said Kiran. "I haven't had time to do a big shop for food yet, so I really appreciate it."

"Not a problem," said Esther. "I loved having the company. I just hope you'll join me again if I didn't scare you off with all my questions."

"It's nice that Robert and Zack have friends who care enough to ask," said Kiran.

"Robert has a lot of those," said Esther. "Though he still misses April. It's hard to get over someone who means so much."

Something in Esther's tone made Kiran think they weren't just talking about Robert and April anymore. "Have you ever been married?" she asked. When she saw the stricken look on the woman's face, she wished she hadn't. "I'm sorry. I shouldn't have been so forward."

"I was engaged. Years ago now. I lost him in Afghanistan. He was a cameraman on one of his first big news assignments. So excited to tell the story through pictures, he was. But he never made it back, and though I have had relationships since, I found no one to take his place."

"It's hard to learn to live with a loss like that," said Kiran, thinking of her mother and how her father must have felt. "It takes time."

"I was a right mess, drifting, getting myself into trouble. Rudderless. Then my father got sick, and my mom needed help here, in the bakery, so I took a baker's course, an apprenticeship, and eventually took over the business. Mom still works in the summer when they're in town, but right now they're doing the snowbird thing. It was the best thing for Dad to stop working when he did. Gave him a whole new lease on life. They'll be back in a few weeks. They're in Costa Rica this month."

"I've never been down that way," said Kiran. "I think that would be a lovely place to go in winter."

"Yes, though personally, I like staying in one place. Though I didn't start out wanting to be a baker, I've risen to the occasion." She chuckled at her pun. "And I've found the family business to be a good fit. Besides, I'm forty-nine now, and I have no interest in coming up with a new career plan. We make enough dough here for my needs."

"And you do it so well," said Kiran. "I'm in loaf with your muffins."

"Hah! You made a punny! My friend works in the book-shop down the street, and she's always coming up with them when she's here for her morning coffee. I should introduce you; I think you'd like her. Do you read much?"

"Oh yes, when I get the chance. Though I mostly listened to books when I was traveling, especially through the prairies."

"So you've traveled a lot?"

"For the last couple of years. But it gets tiring, not belonging somewhere. I'm looking for a place to put down roots." Her remark seemed to settle Esther's concern, and Kiran reminded herself that she was still on trial here in Sunshine Bay. She didn't want people to think she wasn't invested in the place.

"I know Doris is glad you landed here. She liked how well you got along with Zack."

"Speaking of whom, I'd best get to work. Thank you so much for the breakfast.

Esther walked with her to the door. "Have a good first day, Kiran. I'm glad you're here. And anytime you want company before dawn, you know where to find me."

Kiran stepped out into the cool spring air and enjoyed the first few moments of the sunrise. It was nearly seven, and Rob had said to be there around seven thirty. She had better get a move on.

CHAPTER 9

Robert finished dressing and went into Zack's room to rouse him—for the fourth time that morning. "Hey, time to wake up, buddy. You'll be late for school."

"Hmm," the boy murmured, and rolled over into his pillow.

"Zack." Rob raised his voice. "Come on!"

"I'm coming," mumbled the boy.

There was a knock at the door. "That will be Kiran," Rob said. "I'm going to let her in. You get dressed."

"Kiran's here?" Zack asked, sitting bolt upright.

"Yes, it's her first day today. You need to get up so you can tell her all the things you like for lunches."

"Okay." Zack threw off the covers, jumped out of bed, ran toward his dresser, and skidded to a stop to pull open the drawers.

Rob stood, staring at the boy's quick turnaround, until another knock sounded at the door. "Go open the door, Dad," Zack said. "You don't want to keep her waiting."

Rob chuckled and went to let in Kiran, who was dressed in a yellow top and blue jeans, like sunshine after months of clouds.

"Good morning," she said. When he didn't move to let her in, she asked, "Am I too early?"

"What? No." He stepped back to give her room to pass. "I was just waking Zack. He's slow in the mornings. Come on in." She smiled, and he was momentarily flustered.

"Where would you like me to start?" she asked, walking toward the kitchen and hanging her purse on the back of a kitchen chair. "Zack must need a lunch, but did you eat breakfast yet? Do you like continental, omelettes, porridge? I should have asked you the other night." She went to the sink and washed her hands, then dried them on a tea towel.

"Whoa, slow down," he said, holding up his hands and laughing. "One thing at a time."

She crossed the floor and looked up at him expectantly.

"For this morning," he said, "let's just have some toast and peanut butter. The toast and toaster are in there." He pointed to the cupboard just behind her.

"And bananas!" said Zack as he ran into the room, bumping into Kiran in his hurry to get into the conversation. Peanut-butter banana toast is my favorite."

"Well, good morning!" she said, twisting to catch her balance. Robert steadied her, then stepped back quickly when he noticed her flushed face. He hadn't meant to embarrass her.

She didn't look him in the eye, instead turning to Zack. "Why don't you show me where everything is, and we can get started?"

Zack grabbed her hand and pulled her toward the cupboard where they kept the toaster. "Come on, then." Kiran was nearly pulled off balance again, but she only laughed. A friendly laugh thought Robert. One he could listen to all day long. His eyes followed the pair, marveling at how grown-up Zack seemed to be, showing Kiran where they kept everything. Robert filled the coffeepot with water and measured grounds into the filter while he waited for the pair to complete the tour.

"Do you want a cup of coffee?" he asked Kiran, opening the cupboard.

"I've already had two cups more than normal this morning," said Kiran. "I can't have any more for a bit or I'll be jittery."

"Jittery?" asked Zack. "That's a funny word."

"Yes, as jittery as a jitterbug."

"There's no such thing as a jitterbug," said Zack.

"No? You're probably right." asked Kiran, grinning at Robert. "I would love a glass of water, though. And do you have any tea bags? I normally drink tea in the mornings."

"Yes!" Zack jumped up and opened the door to a small walk-in pantry. "We have tea in here." He pulled out a box of tea and presented it to Kiran.

"Why, thank you," she said. "But first we should find that bread so we can make you peanut-butter toast and a sandwich for lunch. What kind do you like?"

Zack was off again, opening the fridge and pulling out ingredients to make a sandwich.

Kiran laughed. "With all this, your sandwich will be as high as you are. Come here and tell me your favorites while the bread toasts."

She turned toward Robert, who had settled down at the table near the window to watch them.

"Would you like me to make you a sandwich too?" she asked.

"You can keep it in the fridge downstairs," said Zack.

"I could," said Robert. "If you would, please make me one of whatever Zack is having."

"Minus pickles. Dad doesn't like pickles."

"That's true," Robert said.

"Okay." Kiran pointed to Zack. "A sandwich with every-thing and"— she pointed toward Robert—"a sandwich with everything but pickles."

"Well, not everything," said Zack, proceeding to tell her all of his preferences and ending up with a much shorter sandwich than first expected.

The toast popped up. Kiran placed two more pieces into the machine while she spread the toast with peanut butter and listened as Zack explained the right way to slice bananas.

She put the toast on a plate and handed it to Zack. "Here you go. Do you want anything to drink?"

"Orange juice," said Zack, putting his plate on the kitchen table and climbing into a chair. She poured juice into a glass and brought it to him.

"Would you like peanut butter and bananas, too?" she asked Robert.

Robert looked at his son, who was taking his first bite of his toast. "Yes, I would. It's been a long time since I've had that."

"What do you usually like?" she asked as she brought the toast to him, along with the coffeepot to refill his cup.

"Dad eats oatmeal, or cereal, or sometimes omelettes," said Zack, speaking around a mouth full of gooey breakfast.

"Or yogurt with berries," said Robert. "Don't speak with your mouth full, Zack."

"Okay," Zack said, his mouth still full, and Robert rolled his eyes toward Kiran.

"Sorry," he said, apologizing for his son's behavior.

She laughed. "Don't worry about it. I teach kids this age."

"You're a teacher?" asked Zack.

"I am," she said. "I taught kindergarten up to grade four."

"I'm in grade four!" Zack screamed. "I'm going to be in grade five next year."

"Wow!" said Kiran. "Do you like school?"

"Yes!"

"Then you'd best eat up," said Robert, "or you'll be late."

Zack sat forward in his chair and dug into his breakfast, and Kiran returned to the table a few moments later with a cup of tea.

"What would you like for dinner?" she asked Robert quietly. "I can stop at the store on the way back from the school and grab some groceries."

"Why don't I come with you? I've got some help coming into the store this morning, and you and I can pick up groceries for a week at the mall. The stores at that end of town are less expensive than the ones down here, so I try to go out there every couple of weeks and buy in bulk."

She nodded. "That will give me some idea of what you might like as well."

Kiran rode silently beside Robert, focusing on the Bach concerto on the radio and looking out at the ocean as they drove. She was trying to get her mind off the driver. When he grabbed her that morning and set her back on her feet after Zack knocked into her, it had… awakened something.

She tried to tell herself that she was just grateful that he had saved her from a bump and a bruise, but she knew it was more than that. He was a decent guy. A guy who was the opposite of Jacques. A family guy. A guy who reminded her a lot of her father.

What she had felt—and was still feeling—was attraction.

And, she reminded herself as he turned the car onto a road lined with huge evergreens, he was her boss and her land-lord. And she had promised Esther not even to consider looking at him in any other way. This was a professional relationship, and she had to keep it that way. Otherwise, if

Esther was correct, her new neighbor Yvonne might find a reason to get her fired.

She needed the job, and she had already settled in to her new home. She could not risk all that for the alternative: going home to live with Rajani.

No, she would keep those feelings bottled up, avoid thinking of him in that way, and just get on with things. There were other men in the world she could date when she was ready. She didn't need to fall for the first man who had been nice to her in ages.

But her feelings did suggest that maybe it was time to try meeting someone. To date. Once she was established in Sunshine Bay, she would consider it.

About five minutes later, the road came out into a suburb, and they came upon a mall with a large grocery store.

"Here we are," he said. "It's a good time to come. Not many people here at nine on a Monday morning."

He got out and went to grab a cart, and she followed him. As they entered the store, she reached into her pocket to pull out the list she'd written the day before.

"You made a list?"

"I haven't had a chance to buy a lot of food yet for my apartment."

"Oh, of course. I should have taken you out yesterday to take care of that. But you can eat with us if you like."

"Yes, I know. But first thing in the morning, and sometimes in the middle of the night…"

"You may get hungry."

"Exactly. Though this morning I was rescued by Esther. She made me a lovely breakfast."

"And pumped you for information, I'm sure. She's one of my mother's informants."

"Your mother means well, and if I am plied with food like that, well, I don't mind sharing."

He laughed. "Remind me not to tell you any of my secrets if it's that easy to get information out of you." He turned the buggy toward the vegetable section.

She followed, wondering if he was joking. Did he believe she would divulge personal information she had learned about him to neighbors? "I wouldn't do that."

"Do what?"

"Divulge things I learned while working for you. I know how to keep confidences."

He turned and looked at her with a quizzical smile. "Don't worry. I don't have a lot of secrets left since April died. Her death eviscerated me, and, to cope, I attended a grief support group in a small town. I am now an open book."

"Still. If you share things with me, don't worry. I won't be telling others."

"Thanks. I appreciate that. Now." He pointed to the side of the store laden with fresh produce. "Let's start here. I'll let you know which veggies Zack absolutely won't eat first, then we can go around the rest of the store. There are only a few canned goods and spices I need."

She followed him and picked up a few items for a salad, careful not to add any parsnips or sweet potatoes to the cart. They were on Zack's no-go list, and she couldn't really blame him. Parsnips? Who liked parsnips?

"Were you serious about wanting curried dishes?" she asked after they had picked up the vegetables.

"Yes, I love curry. And if it's mild, we can get Zack to try it."

"Let me pick up a couple more things, then." She added two large garlic bulbs to the cart, as well as a piece of ginger root, a bunch of leafy cilantro, and a few green chilis. "I'll also need a few spices. I hope we can get them here."

"Sunshine Bay has moved into the twenty-first century in that regard," he said. "And there is a large South Asian population here. They even sell ready-made rotis and samosas in the frozen foods section."

"And fried onions?" she asked. "They are so much more convenient."

"I haven't looked, but when we're finished with the rest, let's see. There's a section that sells a lot of those items."

"If Zack doesn't like curry, does he like cheese? I can always make him a sandwich as a back-up if he hates it."

"Don't let my mother hear you say that." Robert grinned. "She is adamantly against making another plate just because a child doesn't like her cooking."

"Maybe I could compromise. Make some curry and a salad or sandwich he might like? If we want him to experiment, it's easier if he has a choice."

"That's a good approach. And if he doesn't like it, I get the leftovers." One side of his mouth rose in a shy smile, and she laughed.

"What would you like tonight? A lot of children like chicken curry. At least my little sisters seem to."

"How about we have that tomorrow? Start with something I know he'll like first, like spaghetti."

"I can make a pretty good spaghetti," she agreed.

"And tomorrow we'll start Zack's culinary adventure," said Robert. "Chicken curry sounds like a good dish for him to try first," he said. "What do we need?"

After another half hour of walking up and down the aisles, they had collected, among other things, all the ingredients for spaghetti, chicken curry, rice and rotis, and salad. It was more food than Kiran had seen in one place in months. How on earth were they going to get through it all? She would have to make things that could be frozen. She hated to waste food, especially after traveling on a shoestring budget—and seeing so many people living on so little.

When they got to the cash register, he paid for the lot. "I can pay for my own," she said, and he shook his head. "Once you've been paid. Don't worry about it right now."

"As long as you take it off my pay," she said. "This is expensive."

"I only do a big shop once every couple of weeks," he said, "and pick up a few necessary things in the interim."

"Some of these items will last several weeks," she said. "Like lentils."

"And I have a deep freeze in the back of the store," he said.

"So, we can freeze extra things," she said. "Are you okay with that?"

"Yes, of course. I don't have time to cook every day."

She relaxed about the extra food. He differed from her ex and a lot of other men she knew, who wanted a hot meal on the table when they arrived home and expected someone else to make it for them. She would try cooking a few days ahead so there were meals in the freezer. This would free up time during the week for her to apply for work, network with other teachers, find some friends. If she intended to stay here, she needed to people to connect with.

"Robert," a woman called out, and Kiran looked up to see a woman in her mid-fifties coming toward them. It had been a while since she'd been in any one place for long. She'd forgotten that in small towns, everyone knew each other.

"Hi, Louise," said Robert. "What are you doing here on a Monday morning?"

"Oh, I took the day off. I have some work to do getting ready for the concert."

"Louise, this is Kiran. Kiran is Zack's new caregiver. Kiran, Louise is the Belle Tones choir coordinator. We're working together to get ready for the fundraiser."

"Do you sing, Kiran?" asked Louise. "We're always looking for fresh voices."

"Kiran's a pianist. She's helping Zack with his music."

"Really? Have you ever accompanied a choir? Our pianist has broken her leg, so she can't work the pedals for a few weeks."

"No, I haven't ever done that," said Kiran—and then she remembered her promise to meet more people. "I'd be willing to give it a try, though, if I can fit it around my time with Zack."

"Not a problem there," said Robert. "I'm sure we can free you up."

"You'd be willing to help out?" said Louise. "Why don't you come this week to try us out, see if it's a good fit? I have a package of music in the car. I'll be right back."

"Louise is always organized," said Robert, when the woman was out of earshot. "And she can talk a desert flower into living in a rainforest. That's probably why she and my mother get along so well. Two peas in a pod."

"Are you sure you don't mind? I don't even know their schedule."

"Anything to help the choir," he said. "Besides, their practices are Thursday evenings with maybe two or three extras closer to the concert date. I'll be home."

She relaxed a little. "It'll give me an opportunity to meet some women in town. It's been a while since I've been able to settle in and meet new people."

"I think there are a few teachers in the choir as well," said Robert. "It might help you make contacts."

"Perfect," said Kiran, as Louise rushed back into the store with a red folder.

"Can you come on Thursday night to meet the choir and try us out?" asked Louise. "I called our director, and he says that this week will be very light on piano playing. Just a few chords and the first parts of the madrigal we are learning. It will be a good week to start."

"See? I told you she was organized," said Robert with a smile.

"I guess I have a new job," said Kiran. "Yes, if you give me the address, I can be there."

"We practice at the church downtown," said Louise.

"It's only a few blocks from the store," said Robert. "I'll show you where."

"Is it a church choir?" asked Kiran.

"No, just a community choir that practices in the church. A lot of groups use the church to hold meetings or activities. It even opens its doors during the winter to those who are unhoused."

"Sounds like a valuable community resource."

"Exactly," said Louise. "I refer people to programs there all the time."

"Louise is a social worker," said Robert. "The manager at the family services branch downtown."

"I see," said Kiran. "It's nice to meet you, Louise. I'll be there on Thursday."

"Seven o'clock at the back door. Don't come too much sooner than that—someone else uses the space until then."

"Seven it is," said Kiran, holding up the music folder. "I'll look these over in the meantime."

"Wonderful." Louise grinned. "See you then!" And she was off—before Kiran could change her mind.

"That's all wrapped up," said Robert. "I'm sure you'll enjoy them. They're a great group."

"And even if I don't, it's only a few weeks, I imagine, until their regular pianist is ready to play."

"Yes, though you may need to play at the concert."

"Oh, I don't think…" Committing to a performance in front of an audience wasn't what she thought she was doing.

"The choir does a sing-along at the end of the concert. A lot of people come out for that."

"But—"

"Mom says you can play, so I'm sure you'll be fine."

"It's just that I haven't played in front of an audience in years."

"I'll help you if you get stuck on any of the pieces."

"It's not that. I haven't played in front of an audience, other than elementary school kids in music class, since my mother died."

His eyes softened. "Yes, I understand she died of cancer. Maybe this is the perfect time to start again. It would be a way to honor her memory and help others going through the same thing."

"I hadn't thought of it that way," she said. And it felt better to think of playing on behalf of her mother.

"I'm sure she would want you to play if she invested that much time in getting you lessons and listening to your early efforts," he said. She laughed at his wincing expression, as though he could hear her younger self playing more wrong notes than correct ones.

"That's what my father says as well," said Kiran. "He always insisted that I continue, but Jacques, my ex, hated to hear the piano. He preferred to play his synthesizer and experiment with strange, atonal sounds. So I only practiced when he wasn't home." She should have known they were incompatible earlier in their relationship. Jacques had always liked dissonance, whereas she preferred harmony.

Robert looked as though he wanted to ask her something but seemed to think better of it. "Let's get these things into the car," he said, "before Louise comes back and ropes you into helping organize the silent auction and raffle."

"Do you sell raffle tickets?" Kiran glanced around, half expecting Louise to jump out from behind the display of jam jars.

"Of course, at the store. It's a community effort. Last year we raised five thousand for the cause. This year, we're determined to surpass that. I often auction off a free lesson or two as well."

"I suppose if she asks, I could offer to give a piano lesson. If I could use the piano at the store, that is."

"Of course. But you don't have to feel obligated."

"I know." But she rather liked the idea of being obligated to help someone learn music, of having someone rely on her—someone who would notice if she wasn't there to follow through. It had been a long time since anyone had counted on her for anything.

And now she had four people counting on her—Robert, Zack, Doris, and Louise.

oris finished packing on Saturday night and wandered around the house, watering plants, unplugging appliances, securing the windows and the back door. She walked upstairs and past his office to the bedroom—and then she turned back.

She edged open the door into his private office. He'd shared with Nora, Rob, and even Zack, but she hadn't spent time there in… how long? She couldn't even recall a time when she had come in to sit with him here. It was before April's death, certainly. That time in their life had been all-consuming. Full of pain and poignancy. And Neil had been her constant throughout.

She walked into the room to see what he had been working on lately. Though this was technically his office —there was a desk and a filing cabinet against one wall— the majority of the room was what Neil called Grand Central Station, or what the children called the train room.

Neil had set up a model railway in the center of the room, and another along the walls. Over the years he brought pieces back from his travels, and, with the help of the children, he'd built whole communities down here. When he learned new techniques or found new features he wanted to add, he simply updated or rebuilt sections or, in a couple of cases, broke down his model and started again.

She walked around, touching his collection of different scale models, the Amtrak train that was running up some mountains—was that the California Zephyr route he'd talked about?—and his special Christmas train that he used to set up around the tree when the kids were small. Why didn't he do that anymore? She tried to remember when he had stopped.

The current town he was building was more elaborate than she remembered. He had added a lake since she'd last been in. Using resin, perhaps? She would have to ask him. And there was the downtown area of Sunshine Bay with a model of her music store, painted green like she'd had it done only two years earlier.

He had placed models of people outside the stores, too. A boy with red hair running down the street; a tall brooding man with black hair, leaning against the store. Esther was in front of her bakery, and Armand was dancing the tango outside the dance studio. But where was she, and where was he?

She climbed under the platform that held the model and stood up in the middle to get a better view. And then she spied a figurine, with her signature spiky silver hair, in the square behind the store, holding a microphone and singing in front of a band. Max, her old friend and colleague, was playing saxophone. But it wasn't Max with the wild afro he'd sported in the early eighties when they were playing together. It was the Max from today, with his hair closely shaved. Max's husband, Joel—an older version of him as well—stood nearby, operating the lights like he had when they'd been on the road together all those years ago.

She scanned the space for Neil. In the process, she found members of the choir, staff from the other stores, and all the people who made up their lives, their community. But, try as she might, she couldn't find him anywhere.

Maybe she would look again tomorrow. She reached into her pocket for her cell phone and spent the next several minutes snapping pictures of the model from all angles, end to end on both sides.

But as she did, her heart pounded harder. If Neil didn't see himself here, in the town he had created, in the town they had made their home, what did that mean? And how would she help him find his way back here, where he belonged?

Scanning the model, she had other questions too. Of all the things she had done in Sunshine Bay—raising children, running a successful business, teaching hundreds of children and adults to make music, even working with the local college to advise on the creation of a music program

—why had he chosen to depict her as a singer in a band? She hadn't performed in years, and she only played enough piano and sax to keep up her skills as a teacher.

She had given up the dream of being a singer when she met Neil. They had moved to Sunshine Bay where his family lived, and, when she had taken the inheritance her father left her, built a store like the one she'd grown up in.

With all the ways he could have depicted her, why did he have her singing in the square?

She would have to ask him that, too.

But first she had to find him.

Doris checked into a hotel in Victoria on Sunday evening, close to where she would board the ferry to Washington and spent the evening searching for Neil on social media. He hadn't posted anything since a Linked In notice about a paper he was giving at a civil engineering conference in Brazil this weekend on laying rails. He hadn't told her he was presenting a paper this weekend. Had he? She would have remembered, surely.

Neil always talked to her about his work. Or at least he always used to. When had he stopped telling her things?

More importantly, when had she stopped listening?

She tried tracing a few of his Facebook friends, but couldn't find anything more. They were about as social media–friendly as Neil was. How was she going to find him?

She's searched until the early hours and had finally concluded she would just have to ask people. Nora might know how to reach her father. They'd had always had a strong bond.

Tears welled when she imagined admitting to Nora that she and her father were having marital troubles. Troubles that she hadn't even noticed. What kind of wife did that make her? She put her face into the pillow and ugly-cried until, exhausted, she slipped into slumber.

Three hours later, she was on the ferry, prying her eyes open with caffeine and trying to focus on the present. While in transit, there was nothing she could do to find Neil.

The day was warm, and only a few fluffy clouds dotted the blue sky. She stood on deck, the soft fingers of a breeze ruffling her hair, and watched the sea for whales and seals as they sailed past the islands. She might get lucky and see some wildlife today.

It felt strange to be traveling. She had not been off Vancouver Island in years, not since she'd helped Robert and April pack up in Vancouver and move back to Sunshine Bay. And it had been many years since she'd been to Washington state.

Seeing no whales, she took a walk around the deck and snapped pictures of the San Juan Islands as they passed. She would post this on Facebook so Neil, if he ever took the time to check his social media, would know she wasn't home.

She spent the remainder of the ferry ride thumbing through her pictures of the model train, but still she couldn't locate him.

Where was he?

When the ship docked at Port Angeles, she drove her old reliable Mazda 3 down the ramp and followed signs to the I-5. She had at least twenty hours of driving ahead, which she planned to break over three days. That was plenty of time to think.

And she did think. About how angry and panicked Robert had been that she was leaving so quickly, about how Sandy had begged her to come as soon as possible, and about how she hadn't made herself available for Nora after her separation—though, she reminded herself, Nora didn't want her help.

And she thought about Neil. Perhaps he wasn't leaving her. He'd said he needed time to consider what he wanted next. Or maybe he had already left, and she hadn't heard him correctly?

Best not to think.

She pulled over to the side of the road and sorted through the library in her reading app to find the next audio book in the series she was listening to. A feel-good fiction book was what she needed, and for the next three days, she would pretend she was on a vacation. *Fake it 'til you make, and everything might work out.*

The book she picked was about a woman starting over at sixty. Doris hoped she would get her happily-ever-after. She needed one right now.

CHAPTER 11

Four days later, at ten in the morning, Doris rolled into Cataluma, looking forward to seeing her daughter, Jock, and Jock's stepson Eugene. She was happy to stay in one place for a few days, and even happier to have something useful to do to distract herself.

Her first task would be to find Jock a place to stay while he recovered from his hip surgery. He couldn't stay in the apartment above the store due to the stairs, and Nora and Eugene had taken his two bedrooms above the store. And though Sandy was now visiting her sister for a few days, Doris knew she wouldn't stay there long. Sandy and Rose could only stand each other for a short time before they got on each other's nerves.

Besides, there were strings attached to staying at Sandy's, the primary string being that Virginia would not be allowed to darken her door frame. "I mean it, Doris,"

Sandy had said. "That woman can't know where he's staying. I'd have to fumigate."

Outside the store, Doris took a moment to call Sandy for her address. It had been a long time since she had been home in Cataluma, and Sandy had moved from a house to a condo since then.

"I'm at my sister's place. I left my key at the store. In the cash register. Ask Nora."

"Are you sure about this? I can find a hotel," said Doris.

"No, don't do that. I'd like to visit with you, even if I don't want to see that brother of yours ever again."

"Where are you staying?"

"Santa Barbara. Why don't you stop by when you go in to see Jock? Rose has extra room. You can stay here for a night or two. Say yes. Please."

"That sounds good. I'll stop by the store and the hospital and then come by. Could you text me your address and your sister's address as well?"

"Yes. As soon as I hang up. Looking forward to it." Then she yelled, "I'm coming!" Before she hung up, Sandy whispered into the phone. "You can help prevent a murder if you come soon. She's getting on my nerves, and I've only been here twenty-four hours."

"Okay," said Doris, but all she heard before the phone clicked off was "I said I'm coming!"

Doris shook her head as she put the phone back in her purse. She back into traffic and drove to the Cataluma branch of Making Sweet Music. She wasn't sure who she felt sorrier for, Sandy or her sister.

She walked into the store just as Jock's stepson, Eugene, was bidding a customer farewell. A barking dog rushed toward her.

"Well hello, Duke," she said, bending over to pat the bouncing Pomeranian. "How are you doing?" It had been nearly three years since she had seen the little dog, but he seemed to remember her.

"Mom? I was just going to call you!" Nora hopped up from where she was sitting and ran around the counter to give her a hug. Doris returned the hug with fervor. It had been such a long time since she'd seen Nora, but she looked good. Healthy. Happy. "What are you doing here early? Where's Dad?"

"Why? Were you going to call me? Has something gone wrong with Jock?"

"No. I just wanted the name of your supplier for guitar strings."

"Call Rob. He found someone local. We've been having a hard time getting supplies the past few months, too."

"Thanks. I will. Now, tell me why you're here so early. I didn't expect you for days yet."

"Sandy called. Told me she had to visit her sister and that you and Eugene would need help."

Eugene raised his eyebrows with a knowing look, and Nora smiled. "Did she say how long she'd be away? She left rather suddenly."

"No. A few weeks at least. But she said I can stay at her condo and that Jock can stay in the spare room for a few days until Eugene finds him a more permanent solution."

"Glad she's giving us some breathing room," said Eugene. "I'm having trouble finding a place to rent, but I have my feelers out. There's a bungalow a few blocks up that comes up mid-May." It was good that he was already looking. Maybe getting Jock settled would take less time than she thought.

"And Dad?" asked Nora.

Doris fought to keep her dismay from showing on her face. Not even Nora had heard from Neil. So, she found herself doing something that would have gotten her mouth washed out with soap when she was younger.

She lied.

"Your father's business trip has been extended. He's set up a few more meetings with clients." Better to skate away from the truth. The last thing her nearly divorced daughter needed was to think her parents were divorcing too, no matter how old she was.

"And where is he this month?"

"Brazil this past weekend, presenting at a rail conference. Now he's off seeing clients, so still in South America. I keep missing him when I call, but I'm sure we'll connect soon."

Nora looked at her quizzically. "Don't you ever want to travel with him?"

"I plan to—once I'm assured you and your brother are settled."

"Mom, you don't need to worry about us. We're adults."

"I realize that, but Rob needs help. Being a single parent isn't easy. And you… well, I feel bad I haven't been more available to help. So, after my trip, I'll come back and make sure Jock has things back to normal. Once your divorce is final, I can help you pack up."

"Pack up?"

"You don't plan to stay in Seattle, do you?"

"No, I don't think so, but—"

"Then come home. You can help Rob with the store until you get your accounting business up and running. We have room at the house."

"At the house? I'm not moving to your house."

"You can live in the cabin out by the lake if you prefer."

"No."

"Why not? You don't have plans. You've been living in your friend's basement since you left Crispin. Why would you want to stay down here?"

"Why are you so worried about me now? I've been on my own for nearly a year."

"I told you. I've been helping Rob look after Zack and the store. He needed me. I'm sorry if you feel I wasn't there for you, but…"

The door to the store opened then, and a group of young women walked in.

"Mom, let's not speak about this right now, okay? I have a store to look after, and you need to get yourself settled in Sandy's place. Maybe drive down to see how Jock is doing?"

"I'm sorry," said Doris. "I didn't want things to start out this way. I just want you to be safe."

"I know. But I'm not a child anymore."

"You're my child. You'll always be my child."

"I realize that, Mom, but I'm also a grown woman, and I need to figure out my life for myself."

Doris looked at her daughter for a moment, then nodded. "Yes, you're right. We can talk later. I've been traveling all day. If you give me Sandy's key, I'll go there first."

"Sandy's key?"

"She left a set in the till."

"Oh, I wondered what that was for." Nora walked around to the till and opened it, reaching into the back of the tray. She handed a key ring to Doris. "I'll see you later, okay? Maybe you can come around for dinner."

"I think today I'll drive over and visit my brother. I have a friend in Santa Barbara I haven't seen in years. I'll be back in a day or two."

"Friend? You never mentioned a friend in Santa Barbara."

"I had a life before you were born, dear." Then she squeezed Nora's arm, bent to pat Duke on the head, and exited the same way she'd come in, keeping the tears that were welling in her eyes from spilling in front of Nora.

Robert was right. Nora didn't want to come back to Sunshine Bay any more than Doris wanted to come and live in Cataluma. She was grown. Rob was grown. So now Doris could focus on Neil and her marriage.

Why did that make her feel so emotional?

She got in the car and located Sandy's house so she'd know what it looked like when she brought Jock there. Then she drove the hour to the hospital.

The woman at reception directed her to Jock's private room near the end of the hall on the third floor. At least he had that luxury. It would be horrible to stay in this place for long if you had to share a room. Still, knowing how active her brother was, she imagined Jock was anxious to get out.

"What the hell are you doing here?" Jock asked when she stepped into his room.

"Well, hello to you too," she said, walking right up to the bed and taking a momentary pleasure at being able to tower over him.

"Eugene and Nora have everything under control at the store and with the program for the strawberry festival."

"I know. I was just there. They've got things humming along well. I came to look after you."

"I'm staying with Sandy."

"Sandy says she quit her job. You can use her apartment for a few days, but we have to find another place to stay for the next few months."

"Sandy called you?" His face fell, and the normal cheerful spark in his eyes died. "What else did she say?"

"She said she's done. Something to do with your girl-friend—Virginia? I haven't had a chance to talk to her any more about it. I thought I'd stop here first. You know, see how my only brother is doing. If I'd known I would receive such a warm welcome, I wouldn't have bothered." She knew this side of Jock and wished for a moment she'd taken a week to get there, stopping to enjoy her trip instead of pushing through. She was exhausted, and she needed a friendly person to lean on.

"I told her. Virginia is not my girlfriend. She's just a student. A student that doesn't want anyone knowing she's taking lessons. It gave me a distraction while I was here."

"You've been conducting music lessons from your hospital bed?"

"Shh. Don't say it so loud." He motioned for her to step closer. "Just some vocal work. She had an audition, and I was coaching her."

"Coaching her?"

"Yes. It's boring in here. Besides, she offered to pay me double."

"But why help someone Sandy has such a problem with?"

"Weren't you listening? They were private lessons. No one, especially Sandy, was supposed to know. I promised Virginia I wouldn't tell anyone. She's nervous enough as it is about trying to get a new part."

"Is she an actress or something?"

"She's been taking voice lessons and is auditioning for a few musicals. It's all in fun, but she's nearly fifty-five and nervous about jumping into something new and untried, even if it is just amateur dramatics."

"Fifty-five? She's brave to try acting at that age."

Jock scowled at her. "I hate that attitude. I get it so much from students." He raised his voice to mimic what he'd obviously heard too many times. "Aren't I too old to try something new? Isn't this just for the younger people?" He scowled again. "If you aren't dead, then it's not too late to try something new."

"Okay, point taken." She looked at him more closely, and her frustration with him dissipated. Though Jock had a way of pushing her buttons, as only a sibling can, she loved him.

"I mean it," he said. "I'm thinking of changing my whole life. I was considering selling up and traveling around the country in a Westphalia van. I even talked to a guy about buying his. Until this happened." He waved at his hip. "Damned fool to try stretching so far. I lost my balance. I'd kick myself, but it's hard with this new hip." He tried to laugh, but his little joke splatted on the floor between them.

"You were planning to travel around the country in a van? Alone?" Even after her relatively short trip here, she couldn't imagine wanting to travel the country alone.

He blushed. "Well, no. Not alone."

"With Virginia?"

"Dammit, woman, I said she was a student. No. I was planning on asking Sandy."

"Sandy?"

"She's always on about wanting to see the Americas. We've joked about chucking it all, getting a van, traveling around. I was thinking of asking her if she would… you know." He shrugged.

"No, I have no idea what you're talking about, and I'm too tired to read your mind."

"I was going to ask her to marry me," he said, looking up at her in despair.

"Marry you? I didn't know you were that close."

"We spend nine hours a day together. Of course we're close. And that business would be nothing without her. I'd be nothing without her."

"No wonder she's so mad about Virginia. You've broken her heart, you stupid man."

"People who live in glass houses, Doris, should not be throwing stones."

"And what's that supposed to mean?"

"It means you should focus on your own life before reaming me out about my mistakes."

"What are you on about?"

"Neil came to visit a few days ago, on his way through to LA to some meeting. Emerging technology, I think. Then he was heading down to South America. He looked like he was barely hanging on. He doesn't know what to do, but he said he's not going home. Doesn't want to fold his tent and sit on the front porch or some such thing."

"What else did he say?" Neil had come in to see Jock. And told him about their marriage? Who else did he tell? How could he do that without talking to her first?

"Nothing much. He was figuring out what to do next. Decided to visit some of his old haunts around LA after he gets back, places he used to go when he was at school."

"Did he say where? We went to school together, remember? Maybe—"

"I'm not sure. He's traveling with a colleague. Joe somebody."

"It better not be Joanne," she mumbled. They'd all met at university. Joanne liked to dance too close to Neil when they were younger, even after it was clear Neil had chosen Doris.

"I doubt it," Jock said, though she could tell by the look on his face he wasn't so sure.

"I didn't know there was anything wrong until the day he left two weeks ago," she confided, sitting heavily on the chair next to his bed.

"You probably were just being you," he said, as though he didn't think that was a good thing.

"I really wish you would say what you mean instead of talking in riddles." She folded her arms in front of her and sat back, holding back the tears again. She hated to cry in public. Especially in front of Jock.

"My guess is that you've been so busy managing everything you forgot you had help. You can make a guy feel…" He waved his arm in front of him as though trying to conjure up the words. "Surplus to requirements."

"Surplus to requirements? He's away so much, I don't have much choice."

"Except now he's considering retirement, and he doesn't see how he fits into your life."

"Did he say that?"

"Didn't have to. Change is hard, Doris. And when a person gives up their career, well, it's a big part of their identity."

"You sound almost wise," she said, smiling hard, trying to trick her brain into not crying.

"I've had a lot of time to think in here. And a lot of time to feel helpless."

"It's only temporary. You'll be well again in no time."

"Maybe," he said. "I've got a bad infection, so they're keeping me in on heavy-duty antibiotics for a few more days. Then we'll see."

The seriousness of her brother's situation—and hers—started to sink in. She couldn't leave Jock now that Sandy had abandoned him. She would need to get Sandy's side of the story, and work on a way to mend the rift between the pair. Once she was satisfied Jock had the care and support he needed, she would find Neil.

If he wanted to be found.

"Do you know where Neil is staying?" she asked.

He looked at her with the same pity she imagined everybody would show when she told them about her rocky marriage. She didn't want his pity. She wanted him to be well and able to look after himself so she could track down her errant husband and make him talk to her.

"I don't know, but when he left, we were still speaking, so I don't think he's blocked me on Facebook yet. He said something about visiting rail museums after he gets back from South America. Or maybe taking a trip? To tell the truth, I was on some heavy painkillers that day and I probably missed something. I think he's just trying to figure out what to do next."

"I wish he would do it with me instead of on his own. I don't know what I want to do either. Who am I without the music store to look after?"

"You're great at solving other people's problems, Doris. I'm sure you can sort this out for yourself."

"That's why it's taken me so long to give the store to Rob," she said. "I don't know what I'm supposed to do if I'm not teaching or talking about music." As she said it, she realized that she too was at a crossroads. She really didn't know what to do next—especially if she had to do it without Neil.

"Once I'm out, I'll help you find Neil, and maybe you can figure it out together."

"Fine," she said, not daring to hope. It would be nice to rely on her brother to help her, but she was bad at relying on others. She didn't like relinquishing control.

"I think he's just trying to find his footing, Doris. I don't think he wants to leave you."

"Well, he's got a pretty strange way of showing it," she said. "He hasn't answered any of my calls or texts. For all I know, he could be dead. He's never gone this long without letting me know how he is."

"I'm sure he's fine. He'll come around."

"It wouldn't be the first gray divorce."

"Now you're just being dramatic."

"It happened to my friend. She and her husband were married for nearly forty years, and he went off to live with a younger woman. You sure he said Joe and not Joanne?"

"Yes. And he said Joe is a work colleague, so even if it's a woman, it only means that they are going to the same conference and project meetings. Not the same hotel room and the same bed."

She eyed him, considering his words. "You're right, of course. We've been together for a long time. I shouldn't jump to conclusions. But why doesn't he answer my calls?"

"Did he lose his phone?"

"Maybe." A man came into the room with a tray of food, and she realized it was nearly lunchtime. "I should get going. I'll come by and see you tomorrow."

"If you see Sandy, find out how she is. Tell her she's got it all wrong."

"I'll try. Meanwhile, have you been eating?"

"The food is horrible."

"But you need to eat. Think of it as building up your strength so you can come home and fight for her."

"How'd we end up like this?" he asked.

"Not sure, but we'll sort it out." She took the lid off the plate and pushed the tray closer to him. "The soup looks passable, at least."

He stared at it a moment then took a tentative spoonful. In a few moments, the bowl was empty, and he began polishing off the beef sandwich that accompanied it. He picked up the coffee and drank it, then glared at her. "Satisfied?"

"Yes. Just make sure you keep eating. I expect you to be well enough to get out of here as soon as I find a place for us to stay."

"I was going to stay with Sandy."

She raised her eyebrow at him.

"Right." He frowned. "Of course."

She bent over to give him a quick hug. "We've made a right mess of things, but don't worry. We've not yet begun to fight," she said, with a refrain they had recited as children when they played together. "We can fix this."

"I hope so," he mumbled. But he didn't sound very optimistic.

CHAPTER 12

When Doris arrived at the home of Rose, Sandy's sister, the door opened before she knocked.

"Am I glad to see you," said Sandy, pulling Doris into the wide entryway of the Spanish-style bungalow. "Look who's here, Rose. You remember Doris. We were in school together."

Rose, a slim woman in her early sixties, about five years Sandy's senior, glided forward to greet her. Doris looked between Sandy, a petite bundle of energy, and her calm, sedate sister, and understood why they had trouble being together. Their energies didn't match. Nor did their lifestyles, according to her surroundings. The off-white walls, blonde wood, and neutral furniture were a stark contrast to Sandy's home, with its bright walls hung with colorful framed posters.

Rose had gone to school to become a doctor, and then also married one. She divorced that same doctor and then got remarried, this time to a stockbroker who had passed on three years before, leaving Rose a very wealthy widow.

Meanwhile, Sandy had stayed in Cataluma, married her high-school sweetheart, and run the local hardware store. They had done well, but not, surmised Doris, as well as Rose. And, if she remembered Sandy's complaints correctly, Rose liked to compare herself to Sandy, highlighting what they had—or, in Sandy's case, did not have.

Sandy couldn't stay here long. Doris needed to either mend the rift between Sandy and Jock or hope Eugene's house-hunting leads panned out soon.

"Come in," said Rose. "We're just sitting down for luncheon. I'll have an extra place set for you." She walked ahead to the kitchen, leaving Rose and Sandy in the hallway.

"She's gone to give instructions to the cook," said Sandy, rolling her eyes. "Why would a single woman need a cook? She hardly eats enough to keep a bird alive."

Doris smiled. Best not to get into that. "I wish I had one," she said. "I'm a boring cook, according to my son. He thinks we should broaden our palates."

"Well, he's wrong," said Sandy. "When we were at college, you used to make great food. Neil raved about your cooking. Probably one of the reasons he married you." Sandy laughed.

"It's not much of a draw now." Now why had she said that? She was here to help Sandy resolve things with Jock, not unburden herself.

"What do you mean?" Sandy asked, lowering her voice. "What's wrong?"

"I think he's leaving me, Sandy." There, she'd said it. And it helped a little to say it to someone who knew her, who might understand and not judge.

"I don't believe you. That man's always been smitten with you."

"Believe it."

Sandy put her hand on Doris's arm, and Doris tried to shake it off without seeming ungrateful. The last thing she wanted was pity or compassion. She was close enough to tears as it was. And, she reminded herself, she was here to help Sandy, not the other way around.

"Tell me what happened," Sandy demanded, leading Doris down the hall to a dining table now set for three.

"He left on one of his trips, said he had a lot to think about and that he wasn't coming home after his work trip. He's taking a sabbatical. That's all I know."

"I'm sure there's more to it than that," said Sandy, lowering her voice as they became aware of Rose giving instructions to the cook in the next room.

"He said I was too busy with the children. Not enough time for him. And that he wants to retire now and doesn't want to do it alone."

"And he didn't ask you to give up the store? Or get Robert to look after Zack on his own?"

"To be fair, Robert needed a lot of help when April died."

"But does he need so much of your help now?"

"You sound like Jock."

Sandy frowned and sat back in her chair. "Don't ruin my meal by bringing up his name."

"Sorry."

"Does he have a release date yet?" Sandy asked in the next breath. With effort, Doris didn't point out that she had just been told not to talk about Jock. "I only ask because I need to know when he is likely to be using my house."

"Right, of course," Doris said, biting back a smile. Perhaps it would be easier than she thought to bring Sandy and Jock back together.

"Well?"

But she didn't answer because the door to the kitchen opened, and Rose glided into the room and sat at the head of the table. The cook trailed behind with a soup tureen.

"I hope you enjoy lobster bisque," said Rose. "It's richer than anything I normally eat, but I thought, since I have company, we would try it."

"It sounds lovely," said Doris. She glanced at Sandy, who was glaring at her sister. "Doesn't it, Sandy?" She kicked her friend under the table.

"Oof! What?" Sandy turned her glare on Doris.

"I said, doesn't that sound lovely?" Doris returned the glare with one of her own.

"Yes, absolutely," said Sandy. "It sounds like a real treat."

"And shrimp sandwiches," said her sister. "I have to admit they're one of my favorites, and I remember how much you liked them when we were younger, Sandra."

Sandy grimaced at the use of her full name.

"I love shrimp sandwiches," Doris said, before her friend could say something nasty. "I'm feeling spoiled."

The cook, an older woman who reminded Doris of Julia Child, set the tureen in the center of the table and ladled it out into three bowls.

"Thank you, Lena," said Rose. The cook nodded then returned to the kitchen, leaving the trio in awkward silence.

"Mmm, this looks good," said Doris, picking up her soup spoon. The others followed suit, dipping their spoons into the bowl and raising it to their lips, blowing gently before taking a bite. "Mmm," said Doris again. "My compliments to the chef. This is wonderful."

"Thank you," said Rose. "Now, how are you, Doris? I understand you have been to visit Jock."

Sandy glared at Rose again and shifted in her seat before dipping her spoon into her bowl.

"Yes. He's frustrated," said Doris. "He's not used to being laid up, and now he's contracted an infection, so his release date is delayed."

"Those are important to keep an eye on," said Rose. "Did they give an estimate of how long he will be in hospital?"

"A few more days, and then I may be able to take him home. Or at least to an apartment or room in Cataluma." Doris glanced over to see that Sandy was listening intently.

"Well, it's best to get up and go as soon as possible. Unfortunate about this setback," said Rose. "But he's a pretty strong man, from what I remember." She looked at Sandy for confirmation.

Sandy just nodded in the affirmative and took another bite.

"And he has some help at home for now," Doris said. "I'll be around until he gets back on his feet, and his stepson and my daughter are helping with the store."

"Eugene also helped put some grab bars in my bathroom," said Sandy.

Rose's eyebrows rose and just a trace of a smile emerged when she exchanged a glance with Doris. So this was the way the wind blew. Rose wanted Sandy back in Cataluma, too. It was nice to know she had an ally. And here she had always thought Rose had an icy disposition.

"Good to know," said Doris. "I'll have to ensure any rooms we rent have them too."

"Yes, that will be important to his recovery," said Rose. When Sandy didn't add anything more to the conversation, she pivoted. "How is your husband, Doris? Neil, isn't it?"

Doris glanced at Sandy, who was strangling a grin. It felt like they were back in high school. Really, her friend was behaving so badly.

"I'm not sure," said Doris. "He left two weeks ago for a conference in Brazil, and now he's traveling to see clients. I haven't been able to reach him. Wherever he is, he probably has questionable phone connections."

"Are the two of you considering retirement soon?"

"He said he would like to. But me? I love running my store. Love teaching music. I'm not sure I'm ready."

"I didn't think I was ready either," said Rose. "But I'm glad I left work when I did. I had three lovely years with Lee before he passed on."

"I was sorry to hear about your loss."

Rose nodded. "Thank you. It's been hard to adapt. We were very close."

"How do you do it?" Doris suddenly had a need to know. If she was going to be on her own, maybe Rose, and indeed Sandy, could give her some ideas about how to go on. Thinking about life without Neil made her chest hurt.

"I'll give you the same answer that Sandy gave me." Rose smiled gently at her sister. "The same way a person who's lost their limb goes on. One horrible, lonely day at a time, until you can find a new way of living. A new way of moving in the world. New interests. And, if you're lucky, new people and a new purpose."

"I can't believe you remembered that," said Sandy.

"It got me through the dark days at the beginning, knowing there would be light somewhere in the future. And maybe I'll find a new love, like you did."

"I was mistaken," said Sandy quickly.

"How can you be so sure?" asked Rose.

"I'm positive," said Sandy, rising from the table. "Doris, excuse me. I have to lie down. I'm exhausted. I'll see you in a few hours."

Rose and Doris watched her go. "She's hurting," said Rose.

"So is he," said Doris. "I assume you meant Jock when you referred to new love."

"She was sweet on him for years before she met Chad, and then Jock married as well. When they were both left on their own, it was wonderful to see how well they fit together. I don't know what happened."

"The usual. Lack of communication. I think if I got them into the same room and they had a civilized conversation, this would all be resolved." She smiled at Rose. "And you could have your peaceful life back again."

Rose laughed. "My life is anything but peaceful. When Lee died, a friend of mine demanded that I start volunteering. They needed help, and I needed something to get me going again. So in a few weeks I'm off to Kenya for the fourth time, to perform surgery on children with cleft palates. Such a rewarding thing to do."

"I can only imagine how much your patients' lives change. What a wonderful thing to be part of."

"And not something I would have done if Lee had lived. Traveling, unless it was in a cruise ship or a first-class hotel, just wasn't his thing. And the poor man wilted in the heat. So, you see, there is life again, however different. And it can be meaningful. But at night I miss him terribly. Though Sandy has kept me busy the last few days." She smiled widely this time, and Doris chuckled.

"I can only imagine."

They were interrupted then by the cook, who came to offer them coffee.

"Thank you," said Doris, watching the woman pour the dark liquid into white porcelain. The cook stepped back into the kitchen, laden with dirty dishes.

"She never quite got over being the youngest sibling," said Rose, picking up where their conversation left off. "And I suppose I never made it easy for her. She was the one who took care of our parents when they needed help in their later years, and I was a little jealous of their bond. I just wish we could work past it."

"Maybe her staying with you will help."

"Perhaps." Rose picked up her coffee cup to take a drink. "But I was rather hoping she would go home before I left, with her next steps resolved. I worry about her."

"I will work on her," said Doris. "I think the pair of them belong together, and I hope that in the next few weeks they will see it too."

"And what is next for you?"

"I wish I knew, Rose. Normally I have a plan and a plan B and often a plan C."

"You know what they say about plans, Doris."

"That when you make them, God laughs?"

"I was going to say plans change, but your version works, too."

"Yes, I'm finding that to be the case. And any time I help others make plans, I seem to be thwarted or ignored." She thought of Nora's reaction to the idea of going home and cringed. Maybe Neil was right. She meddled too much.

"I used to do that with patients," said Rose. "Tell them what I thought they needed to do." She laughed. "But one day when I was on an oncology rotation during my residency, I met a woman with cancer. She was forty—only fifteen years older than I was at the time—and we were recommending an aggressive treatment that would give her a fifty-fifty chance of getting it all. She refused all treatment. I was devastated because I knew my recommendation was right. But I didn't consider that it wasn't the right decision for her. It wasn't even my decision to make. She taught me a lot, that woman."

"You're right, of course. It isn't my life, and it isn't my decision."

"So I suppose you need to ask now, what does Doris want to do next?"

Doris bit into one of the chocolate biscuits the cook placed beside the coffee and pondered that thought for a moment. "I'm still going with my plan A, Rose."

Rose laughed. "And what, pray tell, is that?"

"I'm going to find Neil and discover if there's anything left of our marriage to save."

"I would do the same. I did do the same, in fact. Unfortunately for me, my first husband needed to dedicate himself completely to medicine. Still does. He never married again. We still see each other from time to time, but that man broke my heart."

Doris sent her a look of commiseration.

"It's okay. I had a good life with Lee, and we have a daughter who is happy living out in New York. I visit several times a year. I doubt I would have had a family with my first husband. So life worked out."

"And it will continue to work out if you keep going forward," said Doris. "That's what I tell my children."

"Good advice." Rose finished her coffee. "Now, can I show you your room so you can settle in? You must have had a long day. I understand you drove quite a way this morning."

"Thank you for lunch, Rose. And for having me to stay."

"It's a pleasure to have company. That is something I miss since Lee passed. He always brought people home. It was why I hired a cook. And now I have a hard time letting her go. Lena is like family."

"Well don't, then. Maybe you'll find a reason to start entertaining again."

Doris followed her host down the hall to the guest room, told Rose she was going to take a quick nap, and sank into a deep slumber, knowing that even though plans change, she still preferred to make them with Neil. And in this case, for all her talk, she didn't have a plan B.

She had to find him and make him see sense.

But first she needed Jock and Sandy to reconcile. Judging by Sandy's obstinate avoidance of the subject, that wouldn't be easy. None of her plans these days were working—except, thankfully, Kiran. When she had spoken to Rob the previous evening, he had shared that Zack adored her and was very well-behaved.

At least that was working.

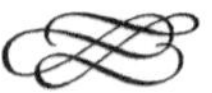

Kiran and Zack set off after breakfast to walk the few blocks to the school.

"Why do you have to come with me?" said Zack. "Grandma doesn't come with me anymore."

"How far does she walk with you?" asked Kiran.

"She lets me meet Josh and we walk in together."

"And your father is okay with that?"

"Dad worries too much, but he knows Grandma is usually right."

"He loves you," said Kiran. "But I understand what it's like. My mom used to hold my hand when she took me to school. I was glad when my grandmother moved in to stay with us. She understood."

"Your grandma lived with you?"

"Yes, after my grandfather died. She lived with me from when I was about your age until I was sixteen."

"And she walked to school with you?"

"She did. Though she would stop when we got outside the schoolyard and let me go in by myself." She had forgotten how her grandmother had encouraged her independence when she was younger.

In fact, her grandmother had done more than that. She had advocated for Kiran to always have the freedom to try new things, and had funded some of those opportunities when her parents were struggling. Kiran wished she could properly thank her grandmother now, but she had passed when Kiran was in high school.

"I'm not a baby," said Zack. "I don't need anyone to walk to school with me."

"No, but I promised I would walk with you, and I don't want to risk my job."

"Dad wouldn't fire you for that," said Zack, but he looked uncertain.

"How about we compromise?"

"Compromise?"

"I will walk with you until you are a few feet from the school. Then I'll stand on the sidewalk until you meet your friends on the playground."

He frowned, and she laughed.

"One thing about me being so short is that from a distance, people think I'm another student."

His eyebrows shot up, and he laughed. "You are pretty short."

"Yep. I didn't eat enough veggies when I was little, I guess."

"My dad says it has to do with genes," said Zack. "I got my red hair and freckles from my mother." He frowned. "Was someone else in your family short?"

"My grandmother was four feet eight." Kiran held her hand up to her shoulder. "Really tiny, but really mighty."

"My grandma is a giant compared to your grandmother."

"Yes, she is," said Kiran. They were approaching the school, so she decided to put their agreement into action. "Let's cross the road here." She pointed to a nearby cross-walk that was over a block from the school. "Then you can walk the rest of the way on your own."

"Thanks, Kiran," he said, as they got to the other side of the road. "There's my friend Josh." He pointed toward a boy with dark-brown hair about half a block ahead. "I'm going to run."

"I'll meet you here at three?" she asked.

"Okay," he said, resigned to the fact that she would be doing her job no matter what he said. Then he ran ahead. "Josh, wait up!" The boy ahead turned around and stopped, waiting for Zack, and the pair continued the short way to the school together, heavy in conversation.

Kiran watched them go into the schoolyard then walked back across the street and started to retrace her steps. The breeze from the ocean wafted up from the waterfront and coaxed her to alter her route a little. She walked three blocks toward the water and along a shorefront path through the park.

Seagulls rested on the wind above her head, and she stood a moment at a railing overlooking the beach, watching as a gull dropped a clamshell onto the rocks below. It then landed, ate its fill from the broken shell, and lifted off to hunt for more.

Kiran walked back, taking in the scent of flowers that lined the path. When she'd returned to her new home, she tidied the kitchen and took chicken out of the freezer for dinner. She hoped Zack would like chicken curry. But what child didn't?

Robert came upstairs as she was finishing making Zack's bed. He frowned. "Thanks for doing that, but I think he needs to learn to make his own bed from now on."

"Oh, sure. That makes sense," she said, looking around at the tidy apartment. "Is there anything you would like me to do now?"

He was still frowning. "Robert?"

"Huh?" he said, startled back from wherever his mind had wandered.

"I was asking what you would like me to do now."

He looked around the apartment and saw nothing was left to do. "You could practice the piano pieces for the choir. The first classroom downstairs is free until about two."

"That's a good idea."

"Or go and explore town, go to the gym, whatever you like. As long as you pick Zack up at three and work with him on his music and any homework."

"I'll start with the music," she said. "I'll just grab it and come down so you can show me which room to use."

"I'll see you downstairs," said Robert gruffly.

What was that about? thought Kiran. This man's moods were hard to gauge. One moment he was friendly, the next he was critical of her making a bed. At least there was a classroom below that would keep them separated. The less time she spent with him alone, the better.

She retrieved the music folder and went downstairs to find the room. She had seen the front of the store but never the back.

She arrived, to find an older giant of a man standing behind the counter, ringing up a sale. When the customer left, she said hello as loud as she could so the sound would reach his ears at that altitude.

He turned toward her and smiled. "You must be Kiran," he said. "I'm Max. Rob said you would be looking for a piano to practice on. Let me show you the way."

He ushered her down the hallway past a series of closed and labeled doors: an office, two classrooms, the bath-room, and a storage room. He opened the door to the second classroom, and she stepped inside. The room was large enough for a class of about ten, along with a beau-tiful grand piano.

She gasped.

"It's Doris's pride and joy," said Max. "She used to play classical. Years ago. Before we met and I ruined her."

"What do you mean?"

"We met when we were in high school in LA. During a summer music master class."

"And?"

"We hit it off, and I introduced her to jazz. She took to it like a bird to flight. She's got a great voice, Dayo does."

"Dayo?"

"It was the band's nickname for her. The only other Doris any of us had ever heard of was Doris Day, so we called her Day, or Dayo."

She chuckled. "So what do you play?"

"Saxophone. I put together a band after that, and Doris came to spend the summers with her aunt in Los Angeles, much to her father's chagrin. He wanted her to stay in Cataluma and run the store, but since Jock—that's her brother—was off playing music, he couldn't say no, especially since she had free room and board with her aunt and a job for the summer.

She played with us through college and found us contacts —kind of doubled as a manager. She has a way of not taking no for an answer." He chuckled at an old memory. "She was the one who got us the first gigs, kept the band together for the first couple of years, but when we became regulars on the circuits, she stayed in LA to finish her degree and met Neil.

"Then how did you end up here?"

"We played for a lot of years through the States and Canada, but when I got tired of traveling, and John, my partner, got sick, Doris gave us a home. She's a good woman."

"Sorry to hear about your partner."

"Oh." He laughed. "All John needed was a place to settle. Road life didn't suit him. When we moved here, he started learning to clog at the dance studio down the street. You know, Riverdance stuff. He lost about sixty pounds and got fit again. His cardiologist calls him a textbook success." He chuckled. "My only complaint is that now he's nagging me to do something about my health." He patted his ample belly.

"I'm sure he docs it out of love," said Kiran.

"Or self-preservation." Max's booming laugh filled the room. "He doesn't want to nurse an old sicky, and—between you and me—I don't want that man to be my nurse. So I've been seeing a dietician. Even gave up bacon and fried food to get him off my back." He let out another booming laugh.

Kiran giggled.

"Anyway, darlin', here's the piano. No classes today until two. Enjoy! I have to get back out front."

"Thank you, Max," she said to his retreating back. She closed the door behind her, set the folder of music onto the piano, and pulled out the first song.

She dragged the bench closer so she could reach the keyboard and pedals, then stretched her hands and began to play. The sound that came out of the instrument made her smile. What a treat this piano was to play.

She practiced the first song three times, each time becoming more confident. When she was done, she moved on to the next, and within the next hour she'd gone through all five songs that would be part of the perfor-mance: a couple of ballads, a pop song, a jazz piece, and a madrigal, all on the theme of hope and love. The selection had something for everyone.

In between songs, she could hear sounds from the front of the store, most frequently Max's laugh. Every time she heard it, she smiled. It was nice to have a friendly, constant presence nearby. It brought her grandmother to mind for the second time that day.

Every morning her grandmother would walk with her to school and stand in the background, much like she was doing with Zack. But Kiran had never been anxious to test the world beyond parental bonds like Zack. Instead, she had been shy, reticent, eager to stay close to home.

Her grandmother had been the one to push Kiran to try new experiences, to adapt, to see the world from many sides, just as she had when she'd moved from India to England for university, and then to Canada when she married Kiran's grandfather.

Kiran smiled as she remembered the stories her grandmother had told of her adventures and challenges becoming a nurse in Canada. Her grandmother had been a tiny woman who overcame any obstacle set in front of her. And she had taught Kiran to look at life the same way. To say yes to a world of wonder, even when times were tough.

At noon, there was a knock on the door, and she stopped practicing the fifth piece to call out, "Come in."

The door opened, and Robert poked his head inside. "I'm going next door to the Whisk to grab some lunch. Do you want to come?"

"Yes, I'd like that," she said, gathering up her music and closing the piano keyboard. "Let me put my music upstairs and grab my wallet."

"You can leave the music on my desk in the office, and don't worry about your wallet. It's on me today. We can call it a working lunch." He grinned. "I want to see how things went with Zack this morning."

"Sure," she said, following him down the hall to the office, where she lay the bright red folder on top of a pile of paper. "You have a lot of paperwork," she said.

"It's a mess. I've been preoccupied by the fundraiser. My mother did the taxes but hasn't been paying a lot of attention for the past couple of weeks. I guess she was more worried about her brother than I realized."

"Is there anything I can do to help?"

"Do you know anything about accounting? Or ordering?" he asked as he held open the front door for her.

She turned to look up at him. "I worked in shipping and receiving while I went to college. So I can help with that part."

"Really?" He considered her with what she thought might be renewed interest, then shook his head. "No. I can't ask you to do two jobs."

"I'm not doing anything until two thirty. The music is straightforward, and if I practice an hour each day until

Thursday, I won't embarrass myself in front of the choir. I'd be happy to help if I can."

"All right," he said. "I'll take you up on that. Though I warn you, the storage room is a mess."

"I've been living in hostels for two years. I'm sure I'll manage."

"You'll have to tell me about your travels," he said. "April and I talked about traveling, but then we had Zack and she got sick. So it never happened."

"Traveling is fun, interesting. But it's nice to stay in one place and really get to know it. It's been a while since I've done that."

"You'll be able to stay here for the summer at least," he said, with lopsided half smile. "I hope you like staying in Sunshine Bay. It's a little dull after traveling, I expect."

"Everywhere has something to offer," she said, walking under his outstretched arm as he held open the door to Whisking Love. She could get used to having a man to open doors for her, she thought, then realized she was once again thinking about Robert as a man and not an employer.

She had to keep that all straight or she would be inviting trouble—and, judging by what had happened to her predecessors, unemployment. She could not afford that right now. Not unless she wanted to go home with her tail between her legs and beg Rajini to take her in again.

But as they stopped at several tables to greet patrons while Robert introduced her, she found herself wanting to learn more about him. He had a side that was so different from her first impressions. He was confident. Friendly. And people sought him out. He seemed interested in them, and in what they had to say.

"You know a lot of people," she said when they finally got to a table at the far side of the room.

"Comes from growing up here, I suppose." He handed her a menu. "I've been on a couple of committees for the Chamber of Commerce recently. Mom encouraged me to get involved and develop a network of business-people. It's important to keep up with what's going on in town."

"How do you find time to do that while running a store and raising Zack?"

"Mom helps with Zack, and Max has been with us for years."

The server came, and Kiran ordered the roasted veggie sandwich she'd had the week before. It was perhaps the first time in years she'd been able to order from the same menu more than once.

"Tell me about your travels," Rob said. "Where did you like visiting best?"

She told him about Europe and her trek across Canada, and he listened avidly, laughing at her anecdotes.

"I'd like to travel more one day," he said. "Try some of the foods, see how people live."

"It was interesting, and I learned that I could do hard things on my own and figure things out along the way." It had been a great confidence builder after the Jacques years.

"I can only imagine," he said. "One day maybe I'll see what it's like."

"I'm glad I did it, but after living out of a backpack and not knowing where I would be staying the next night, I'm looking to settle in one place and build a life. A community."

"And you think you might want to build a life in Sunshine Bay?" He was watching her closely, as he had been doing for their whole meal, as though what she had to say really mattered to him.

"I think so," she said softly, but she didn't add what she was really thinking.

Especially if I had someone like you to build a life with.

CHAPTER 14

"Have you been down to the waterfront yet?" Robert asked Kiran when they were leaving the restaurant. It had been an enjoyable lunch. He wanted to extend their time together, listen to more of her funny stories about her travels. She was easy to be with.

"I have. I walk this way in the mornings on my way back to the shop," she said. "I like watching the seagulls."

"Ah, but have you stopped by Gertie's gelato place yet?" he said.

"It's not open when I come this way," she said.

"Could I tempt you with a cone? It's one of Zack's favorite places to go, and I feel like you should test it out before you take him. Get the lay of the land."

"A behind-the-scenes scoop?" she suggested, with an impish grin.

"Exactly." He fell into step beside her as they strolled. "He also enjoys the climbing bars, though he's almost too old for them now. He's growing fast."

"He is taller than many kids his age."

"Did you never want children?"

She didn't answer right away, and he immediately regretted the question. "Sorry, that sounds like something my mother would ask. Please forget I said anything."

"No, it's okay. I did want them when Jacques and I got together, but it turns out he didn't. After living with him for ten years and understanding that he was more interested in Jacques than anyone else, I finally left."

"Not all relationships work out," he said.

"I wish I had realized that earlier. I could have saved myself a lot of pain." She smiled sadly. "But, as my grandmother would say, every experience is valuable if you learn from it."

"That's true," he said, as they turned a corner toward the beach. "And even sad times are worth living through if you get the joy." He thought of all the times he and April had laughed together. They almost balanced the pain of her loss in the end.

"I try to focus on the positive things in life," said Kiran. "I find more of them when I do that."

"That's a good theory," said Rob. He liked the way she could find a ray of sunshine on a cloudy day.

"I like to think it's a fact," said Kiran. A woman walking a golden retriever passed them, and Kiran asked the woman if she could pat him. Rob watched as she bent over and spoke to the dog, rubbing it behind the ears. "You're a good boy, aren't you?" She stood and wished the woman a good day before resuming their conversation.

"What else does Zack like doing?" she asked.

"My dad has a train set—actually, a train room. When he's in town, Zack goes over to help him build model houses and lay track and talk about trains. Dad's a civil engineer who specializes in railway systems. Tracks mostly. It's quite an involved subspecialty."

"Trains and piano. Anything else?"

"Every July I send him to the local music camp in Parksville, down the road from here. They have master classes, and at the end of the two weeks they put on quite the production. And he reads a fair amount, stories about dragons and dinosaurs. And trains, of course."

"I'll keep that all in mind. Just trying to think of ways to keep him busy over the summer months."

"He also swims. Which reminds me, I have to enroll him in lessons again." He pulled out his phone and made a note, then steered them both toward the gelato shop.

As they stepped inside, Kiran's face lit up. "There's so much to choose from."

"I generally start with anything chocolate and then work my way through by the end of summer," Rob joked. "Zack likes the peanut butter and strawberry flavors best."

"Hi, Rob," said a woman from behind the counter. She wore a colourful apron that clashed with her multi-toned hair, though the look kind of worked when you took it all in. She was looking at Kiran, her eyes bright with delight.

"Hi, Gertie. This is Kiran, Zack's new childcare worker. Kiran, this is Gertie, owner of the best gelato parlour on the island. She's also an alto in the Belle Tones choir."

"Nice to meet you," said Kiran. "Which of these do you recommend?"

"Depends on what you're in the mood for, love." To Rob, she said, "I've sold almost all my book of tickets. Do you think I can get another one from you? I know Louise has some, but I won't see her until Thursday."

"I can drop them off tomorrow," said Rob. "Will that be soon enough?"

"Yes, that will be fine." Then she turned back to Kiran. "Have you decided?"

"Maple Walnut," she said. "I haven't had that in years."

"And I'll have the Chocolate Delight," said Rob.

A few minutes later they stepped out with their cones, and Rob watched Kiran eat hers happily while they strolled toward the store. She had a way of making even the simplest things seem like an important event. He found her, what? He licked his cone and thought about it as she rushed to the railing to point out a harbor seal.

Charming. She was charming.

"That's Fanny," he said. "She's a local seal that hangs around here where the fish boats unload their catch. She's also been known to steal crabs from crab traps if you aren't careful."

"People go crabbing near here?"

"Right off the pier."

"I'd love to try that," she said.

"Mom has some traps in her garage. I'll take you and Zack one of these weekends if you like."

"That would be so fun."

"And Zack would enjoy it. He hasn't gone crabbing for a couple of years, but when dad took him, he seemed to have fun."

While they finished off their cones, they watched as Fanny dove around the boats in the marina. Then Kiran turned toward him. "Thank you for the walk and the gelato. Should we get back and tackle the storage room?"

"Yes—and relieve Max for his lunch break," said Rob. "John will be expecting him home."

"He goes home every day for lunch?"

"It's John's way of monitoring what he eats."

"The way Max told it, he was his own instigator of his healthy diet."

"That's only an illusion," said Rob. "John is a bit of a control freak when it comes to health-related things. And Max goes along with it."

"The things we do for love, eh?" said Kiran.

"Ha. Exactly."

"We'd best get back, then. John doesn't sound like someone I want to get on the wrong side of."

"He is a big pussy cat, really," said Rob.

"But even pussy cats scratch sometimes," said Kiran, picking up the pace.

When they arrived back at the store, Rob took out the list of orders and found a bucket for the soap and water they'd need to dust off the shelves.

Leaving the storeroom door open so he could hear the bell, he climbed to the top shelves and wiped them down while Kiran tackled the ones below. When they were done, she started sorting what had arrived, and shelving any items she could while he went to help customers.

Max returned an hour later and took over with the customers, all of which were looking for a beginner's book that was being used in a local parks and recreation class. His mother's doing, of course. She worked hard to make sure they had relevant stock, and she did it by networking. He would need to ask who her contact was at parks and rec so he could do the same.

He walked to the back room and found Kiran had arranged the stock on the labeled shelves. The place looked so much better, and the dust was gone.

"Thank you for doing this," he said, and she squeaked before turning around to face him.

"Sorry, didn't mean to startle you." He looked at her shirt, where it seemed all the dust had migrated. "You're almost finished in here, and I've only been gone an hour."

"I'll need a ladder to reach those shelves." She pointed above, to shelves he could easily reach.

"I'll get those," he said stepping closer to her and picking up the first box.

She stepped back, though not far, and watched as he made quick work of shelving what was left. "There." He turned toward her and caught her looking at him before she quickly looked away.

He knew that look. He's seen it many times since April had died. It was the look a woman gives a man when she is attracted to him. And up until now, that look had only irritated him. But today, he wasn't irritated, or even wary.

"I should get changed," she said, looking down at her clothes. "I have to pick up Zack soon." But she didn't make a move to leave the room, and he didn't want her to leave. And that should have bothered him. She was his employee, his son's caregiver. He had fired Christine for showing an interest in him, and yet he wanted Kiran to stay.

Which meant she had to leave.

"Sounds good. I'll try to tackle some of the paper in my office." He didn't move out of her way, though, and they looked into each other's eyes until she finally broke eye contact.

"I'll let you get to it, then," she said, stepping around him.

He followed her out to the front of the store and watched her walk out into the sunshine, and around the side of the building, taking that sparkle with her.

Max stood at the other side of the room, shaking his head and tsking.

"What?" said Rob.

"Better watch out, boy. That girl's got that somethin'-somethin'."

"Somethin'-somethin'?"

"You know what I mean. Be careful, or she'll have a place in your heart before you know it."

"She's my employee."

"Keep telling yourself that, Rob," said Max. "But I don't think she's a girl you should trifle with. She's the kind you take home to meet your mom."

"She's already met my mom."

"And your mom already approved." Max laughed. "You are in trouble."

"She's not interested in me. We're too different."

Max raised his eyebrows at him. "Really? I must have misunderstood."

"Misunderstood what?"

"The way she was looking at you just now. Like she wanted something more." He tapped his chin with his finger and looked at Rob. "A whole lot more."

"You're mistaken," said Rob. "And did I mention she's my employee?"

"John was one of our roadies for years," said Max. "But maybe I have fewer scruples than you do." His laugh filled the room, and Rob scowled and retreated to his office, where he counted the minutes until Zack and Kiran returned.

Kiran stood under the warm water and washed away the grime. But she couldn't wash away the tingles she felt when she remembered how Rob had looked at her.

He had wanted to kiss her. She hadn't imagined it.

Which meant she had to stay on her guard and avoid being alone with him. Because if he had touched her, or even crooked his little finger, she would have been in his arms in a heartbeat. And then she would be out of a job, out of this apartment, and back home, where Rajani ruled the roost and she lived in a basement.

She turned off the water, stepped out of the shower, and toweled off, letting her imagination play the "if-only" game. If only she wasn't working for him. If only she wasn't living in his apartment. If only she met him under any other circumstance. What would she do then?

The answer to that was simple. She would not play it safe. She would see where this could go.

But under the current circumstances, she had to stop her feelings for him from growing. Period.

She could do it. She had done hard things before.

If only she didn't have to.

CHAPTER 15

On Thursday, Kiran finished up the supper dishes, happy that Rob and Zack had both enjoyed the lasagna and salad. It was fun to cook for others, especially people who appreciated the effort she made.

"Well, I'm off to choir practice," Kiran said. "Wish me luck."

"They're a good group of women," said Rob. "And I've heard you practice. You've got this."

"Thanks," said Kiran, turning to put the last glass into the cupboard and pleased he had noticed her practicing and hadn't focused on her mistakes. He was making it so hard not to think about him. So hard not to want to get to know him a whole lot better. Wiping any signs of longing from her expression, she turned back toward the pair who were sitting at the table Zack had helped her clean off. "I'll see you tomorrow?"

"Yes, we'll be interested to hear how it goes," said Rob.

"And while you're gone, I'm going to beat Dad at rummy."

"Sounds like you've been challenged," said Kiran to Rob. "Have fun, you two."

She let herself out of their apartment, reluctant to leave them, and went next door to grab her music, just as a tall woman with long blonde hair exited the apartment next door.

"Oh, hello," said Kiran. "You must be Yvonne."

"And you're the new nanny," said Yvonne with a frown. "Hope you're better than the last one." Then, without saying anything else, she walked to the end of the hall and exited down the stairs, leaving Kiran to stare after her.

"As a matter of fact, I am," Kiran whispered under her breath, as she unlocked her apartment door to pick up a sweater and the music folder. She glanced at the daisies on the table, now withered, and peered out the window to the square below. In the dusk, the view wasn't as cheerful as it had been the day she arrived, and the flowers had seen better days, but she would not look at the dark side. And she would not let that woman's comment make her doubt herself like she had when Jacques would pick on her faults. She was good with children. Great. And Zack and Rob seemed to like her.

In the end, their opinion was all that mattered.

She took the daisies out of their vase and dumped them into the compost bin under her sink. She would find some new ones, or maybe a plant, to replace them. Then she locked the door behind her, walked to the church, and knocked on the back door five minutes before she was expected. The door opened, and she found Yvonne staring back at her. *Great.*

"Did you follow me here?" Yvonne said.

"No, I'm here for the choir practice." She concentrated on keeping her voice calm in the face of this accusation. "Louise is expecting me."

"I don't know how you'll catch up this late in the season," said Yvonne, stepping aside to let her through. "Maybe you should wait until September."

"I'm not here to sing," said Kiran, relieved to see Louise rushing toward her.

"You're right on time," said Louise. "Welcome. Come in." She motioned for Kiran to follow her into the church. "We're starting soon." When Kiran caught up to her, Louise leaned closer. "Did the music all make sense to you?"

"Yes. It's straightforward. I just need you to tell me what you need me to do. Do I play along with the different sections?"

"We'll have you play some of the introductory sections and Ben, the director, will find you the music for the sing-along portion of the show, in case our other pianist isn't back on time.

"You think you'll need me to play the sing-along for the audience?"

"It's simple music. You'll be fine."

"How bad is your pianist's leg?"

"Hard to tell. Turns out it was her ankle joint, and she had an operation a few days ago. She probably won't be better until September."

"September?" Kiran hope of getting out of a public performance deflated faster than a parasail attached to a stalled speed boat.

Louise patted her arm. "You'll be fine."

"But the concert. I don't want to let you down. I haven't performed in a long time."

"Oh, not to worry." Louise waved away her concern. "The choir only has two songs you would need to accompany. There's a harpist coming to do the other three."

"And the sing-along?"

"No one in the audience notices the piano when they are singing along. They're a very energetic crowd."

"Good to know," said Kiran. Louise's words calmed her, but something still made her uneasy. Like she was being watched. Judged. She looked around to find Yvonne glaring at her from across the room. What was the woman's problem?

Louise patted her arm again, returning her attention back to their conversation. She had let Yvonne distract her and missed what was being said. "But today," Louise continued, "I believe we're all learning the madrigal. We'll just need you to play each of the parts as we go through them. Come, let me introduce you to Ben."

Kiran tried to ignore Yvonne, shook hands with Ben, and assured him she had practiced the pieces a few times already. That seemed to put him at ease. He appeared highly agitated, and she put it down to nerves about the performance to come. Maybe that was an indication of how poorly the choir was performing, and the fact that they had yet to learn two pieces. Any decent director would want their choir to succeed, and it was only a few weeks until the performance.

When Kiran moved to the piano and sat down, Ben rapped on the top of his music stand and the buzz of conversation in the room stopped as the women gathered at the front of the church. When she was introduced, the choir all clapped—save one. They were happy to have a replacement.

She spent the next sixty minutes picking out the parts Ben asked her to assist with, and each of the three sections— altos, sopranos, and second sopranos—sang their parts separately. Then she played the first chord to start them off from the top—and sat back, marveling at how well the different pieces fell into place. Though the choir was made up of women from all walks of life, they sounded so good together it was clear some had been singing for years.

By the time the break came an hour into practice, Kiran was relaxed and enjoying her new task. Louise took her into the kitchen where the choir was gathered, made sure she got some tea and a biscuit, and introduced her to a few of the members. They asked her the questions people usually did when she went to a new town.

"Where are you from?"

"Ontario," she answered.

"What brings you to Sunshine Bay?"

"I was traveling," she said. "Always wanted to visit Vancouver Island. My mother spent time here as a child, and I wanted to experience it for myself."

"Where's your mother now?" asked a woman named Jayne, who sang in the alto section.

"She passed more than ten years ago," said Kiran. "Breast cancer, which is why I'm glad to contribute to the fundraiser."

"Oh, I'm sorry about your mother."

"I've been living with the loss a long time," said Kiran.

"Glad you can help with the fundraiser, though. It will be a great one this year," said Jayne. "We had to do the first and second one virtually. We all got instructions from Curtis's son and learned to record ourselves. Then he took all our voices and did his magic. He's a recording genius, that kid. He has a brilliant future. We sold the recordings, and it helped us raise money after the show."

"Ingenious."

"Yes, it was. Last year's concert was our first in person. It was small. A lot of choir members were still concerned about the virus no one wants to recall."

"So, this one is the fourth show? And that's why it's bigger than in the past?"

"And we all want to help Curtis and Rob hit their ten-thousand-dollar target. It's a stretch goal, but if we sell the recordings, make some money on the silent auction, and sell enough tickets, we think we can do it."

"That would be fantastic."

"April was our friend, and it's a way to keep her in our hearts."

"She must have been a special woman," said Kiran, thinking of how often Robert zoned out when he was looking at one of her paintings or the family picture in the front room.

"Yes, she was."

"And a particular friend of Yvonne?" Kiran asked. Perhaps Jayne could explain why Yvonne had taken such a dislike to her.

"Yvonne and April were like sisters," said Jayne.

"That would explain why she seems so protective of Zack and Rob."

"Yes, and…"

"And?"

"There's more to it, but it's not my story to tell," said Jayne. "I happen to know because Yvonne was distraught one day and I was there to listen. People tend to share, sometimes overshare, with me. Probably why I became a counselor."

"I wouldn't want you to betray a confidence," said Kiran, wishing the woman would do just that. It might leave a clue as to Yvonne's attitude toward her.

"Thanks for understanding," said Jayne. "Yvonne means well, but she's still grieving April's loss. She's a bit of a loner, so losing April was hard on her."

"Thanks for sharing," said Kiran, placing her cup into the dishwasher, following Jayne back inside, and taking her place at the piano. She understood now how important April had been to Yvonne, but it still didn't explain why Yvonne was so hostile toward her.

The rest of the practice passed quickly, and Kiran continued to be impressed by the choir. Ben seemed to know how to pull the right notes and tone from each member, and they all worked hard for him.

As she was placing her music back into the folder and closing the piano lid, Gertie from the ice cream parlor walked up to thank her and welcome her to the group.

"You really bailed us out," said Gertie, pulling on her coat. "See you next week?"

"See you then," said Kiran, rising and tucking the stool under the piano just as Esther approached.

"Great job," said Esther.

"Thanks," said Kiran, putting on her sweater and picking up the music folder. "The choir sounds wonderful. You've all been practicing. It's like you're professionals."

"Well, many of us have been singing together for years. Betty—she was the one in the front row with the robust voice—helped found the group twenty-five years ago. We'll be having our silver anniversary concert in November."

"And Ben is easy to work with."

"Yes, though I suspect we'll lose him soon. His wife was transferred to Vancouver, and they only see each other on weekends now. He was telling my friend Curtis that he'd have to leave his job at the college or figure out another way to make their marriage work long distance."

Kiran winced. "Not an easy choice unless you hate your current job."

"Which he doesn't. He's teaching in the music program, and he's been successful, by all accounts."

"Don't tell me—another friend told you. Is there anywhere you don't have a connection in this town?"

Esther blushed. "You make me sound like a gossip."

"No, just a well-informed resource," said Kiran, giving Esther a quick smile before following her out of the church and back into the kitchen, where they found Louise and Ben deep in discussion.

"Thank you for your work today," said Louise when she saw Kiran approach.

"You caught on quickly," Ben added.

"It was fun," said Kiran. "I'll see you next week."

She and Esther pulled on their coats and set out for their apartments.

"How are things going with Zack?" asked Esther.

"So far, so good," said Kiran. "He's an easy kid to be around."

"That's great to hear," said Esther. "And thanks for being such a good sport about the choir. I know Louise probably roped you in."

"I've enjoyed meeting people outside the store. Particularly women. Everyone at the store is male."

"Yes, that's true, isn't it? Max, Rob, Zack, and I think even the two students they hire for the summer are men. They should be starting soon."

"All the more reason to find women to talk to," said Kiran. "It's one of the things I miss most about working in schools. I used to have some good friends in Sarnia when I taught there."

"I'm sure you'll meet people here soon."

"I hope so. The choir is a good start, I think. Jayne seemed nice."

"Oh, she's a kind soul. She works with families. She and Louise work together in the same agency." They crossed the street to their building.

"I suppose there's a lot of overlap in a town this small. People who know each other from other aspects of their lives."

"Yes, and they're often related in the strangest ways, so best not to say anything about a person you wouldn't want to say to their face."

"Wise words," said Kiran, unlocking the door to their shared hallway and holding the door for Esther.

When Kiran got inside her apartment after wishing her friend a good night, she hugged the sheet music and danced around the room for a moment. The evening had gone better than she expected. She had played competently and had been able help right away. She enjoyed working with musicians again. More than teaching, she had missed playing music.

The choir members she'd met had been friendly and help-ful. She wished she understood Yvonne's sour attitude toward her but decided to forget about the woman And she did—until the following Monday when she and Zack were walking to school.

Zack bounced ahead, excited about his class's upcoming unit on dinosaurs. "You know they lived over sixty-five million years ago?"

"I did know that, yes."

"And they were huge, Kiran." He held his arms wide and turned around in the street in front of her.

"Yes, as high as the tree over there," she said, pointing to a cedar across the street.

"Wow." Zack looked up at the tree in wonder. "That's gigantic!"

"Yes, though the blue whale is bigger. The tallest dinosaur was about seventy feet high, and blue whales can be up to a hundred feet long and two hundred thousand pounds."

"Really? I'd like to see a blue whale."

"So would I," said Kiran. "I think they come as far as California. Perhaps one day you can go and see one there."

"I want to go to Drumheller, where they have dinosaur bones," said Zack.

"It's pretty impressive," said Kiran. "I stopped there for a day when I was traveling through Alberta this year."

"Really?"

"Yes. Did you know one tooth of a Tyrannosaurus rex would be as long as your forearm?"

"Wow!" said Zack. "I'm gonna tell my teacher."

Kiran laughed at his excitement. What was it about dinosaurs that always caught the imagination of children?

They approached the crosswalk, and Zack saw his friend Josh waiting for the light to change.

"Kiran, can I go with Josh today? You can wait here?" He turned to her with pleading eyes.

"Yes, but make sure you watch for traffic and go straight to the school."

"Where else would I go? We're talking about dinosaurs today."

"Of course," said Kiran, shaking her head as he ran to join Josh. The traffic stopped, and the pair went across the street, talking loudly about dinosaurs. Zack pointed to the tree they had seen earlier, and both boys stood under it, looking up into the air.

She watched a few more minutes until the boys got into the schoolyard. then she turned toward the beach, only then noticing a yellow Volvo like the one parked outside the front of the store at night. What was Yvonne doing at the school?

There wasn't time to think much about it because her cellphone rang.

"Kiran? This is Doris. I'm calling to see how things are going. How is Zack?"

"Zack's doing well. I just dropped him at school. They're talking about dinosaurs today."

"He'll like that," said Doris. "And his music?"

"He's got both pieces down pat. He's more than ready for the concert. How is your brother?"

"He's still in hospital, but hopefully he'll be released in a couple of days."

"That's good news," said Kiran.

There was a pause at the end of the line, and then Doris said, "Yes, it's good he's healing."

"When do you think you'll be back?"

"It's hard to say. Depends on Jock's recovery. I'll know more in a week or so."

"Well, things are going well here, so you don't need to worry."

"Thank you, Kiran. And thank you for filling in with the choir. Rob said it's been helpful."

"I'm glad to pitch in," she said. "And Zack is a great kid."

"I should go. I just wanted to see how you were doing. Thanks again."

They hung up, and Kiran walked home, silently thanking Doris for giving her this job. In only a short time, she had been made to feel like perhaps, for the first time in years, she was home. In time this home might include a partner, too, but meanwhile she would be thankful for what she had: a house, a job, and budding friendships—all the ingredients for a meaningful life.

CHAPTER 16

$\mathcal{D}$oris hung up the phone, feeling relieved and redundant at the same time. Everything was going fine at home without her. Was that how Neil felt when he called home? Like an outsider? Sighing, she went to take a shower, then changed into clothes she hadn't traveled in. She was feeling much more herself by the time she opened her bedroom door and wandered into the kitchen to find her hosts.

There she encountered the cook, who was busy scrubbing out the oven. Lena rose and pointed her toward a doorway. "They're on the patio," she said. "And thank you for coming. They're getting along better now."

"I'm not sure I did anything."

"Happy coincidence, then," she said, shrugging her shoulders and squatting down in front of the oven to continue her work. Over her shoulder, she said, "There's tea and coffee out there. Fresh."

"Thank you," said Doris.

When she stepped out onto the deck, she found the pair close in conversation, but they stopped when she sat, and Rose poured her a cup of tea from the teapot.

"Thank you," said Doris, picking up a small pitcher of milk to add to the tea. "You two seem to have a lot to talk about."

"Actually, we were thinking we should go out." Sandy looked at Rose expectantly.

On cue, Rose picked up the conversation. "We know you haven't been on vacation for a long time, and since it's a beautiful day, we thought we could take you shopping at some little boutiques not far from here."

"Shopping? It's nearly three."

"Shops are open until nine here. This isn't Sunshine Bay."

"True." Doris hadn't shopped for clothes in person for a long time. She ordered them online.

"I need a new look, Doris," said Sandy. "One that says I am fun, interesting, adventurous."

"You're already all those things," Doris said, picking up one of the small sandwiches on the table and taking a bite. She had a feeling she would need some sustenance.

"My boring retail outfits fail to impress that fact on people. Apparently, they say I'm a steady, dependable doormat."

"Sandy," Rose admonished. "Don't put yourself down." She focused her gaze on Doris. "Help me get this one out of her funk. She's starting to slide into the doldrums again."

Doris noticed Rose's pleading tone, and glanced down at what she was wearing. "I guess I could stand to find a few new items," she said, realizing the wardrobe she had brought with her, though her best, had seen better days. Her clothes were serviceable, comfortable, and made of sustainable natural fabrics. But Sandy was right. It couldn't hurt to have one outfit that suggested she was fun, that she had a little life left in her. No wonder Neil had given up on her. She looked like a mom—and not the "yummy mummy" variety either.

"Excellent," said Rose. "And after we go shopping, we want to take you out to dinner. I picked up three tickets to a dinner theatre downtown."

"And there's a jazz club nearby we can go to afterward for drinks," said Sandy.

"I'm glad I had a nap," said Doris. "Sounds like we have a lot to do in the next few hours. I haven't gone out to a play or listened to jazz in ages. The last opportunities were when Neil was away, and I hate to go alone."

"Well, that sounds like a yes," said Rose to Sandy.

"Let's go." Sandy rose from her seat.

Doris snatched another finger sandwich from the tray before running to catch up with the pair, pleased the sisters were getting along so well.

After an enjoyable two hours browsing shops—many of which, Doris noticed, had been for taller, bigger women such as herself and not for petite Sandy or willowy Rose —she was beginning to smell a plot. While the sisters had each managed to find an outfit, they'd joined their considerable forces to put together outfits that flattered Doris, with long flowing lines and tasteful colours that also screamed, "I'm a musician, an artist, a free spirit."

"This one is perfect," said Sandy, as Doris modeled their latest creation.

"You've said that about all those as well." Doris pointed to a collection of items piling up on a rack nearby.

"Yes, but this one reminds me of something you used to wear in college. Back when you were singing."

Doris turned to assess herself in the mirror, trying to see what Sandy was talking about. Clothes were not her forte, and she appreciated the help. These palazzo pants were not something she would have chosen, but they had big pockets and they fell in a flattering line. And the jacket the sisters had chosen to go with it made her seem, well, vibrant. Like she was ready to take on anything. Her shoes would need to be changed to sandals, perhaps, and a large statement necklace would help round it out, but she loved the colours.

"I like it," she said.

"And you need to get a few of those others," said Sandy. "A capsule wardrobe."

"I do have a capsule wardrobe," said Doris, thinking of her suitcase of dull clothes again.

"You have a capsule storekeeper wardrobe," said Sandy. "You need a capsule traveling-for-fun-and-frolic wardrobe."

Doris considered the pile of clothing. How many of these items would she wear again in her regular life?

"If you're worried about the cost, it only looks expensive," said Sandy. "This is a second-time-around shop. The clothes are designer, but either they didn't sell at the shops this year or they're on consignment at a fraction of the cost."

"They are pre-owned?" They didn't look pre-owned.

"That's the way we shop these days," said Rose. "It's one of the things Sandy and I agree on." She tapped her sister on the arm playfully. What had happened to this pair in the past few hours? Whatever it was, it gave her hope. If Sandy could solve her rift with her sister, maybe she could forgive Jock too.

Then Doris would be free to find Neil and bring him home where he belonged.

She looked at the outfit she was wearing. "I was just wondering where I would wear these again after this little trip." She assessed the pile of clothing they had amassed. Four tops, another two pairs of slacks, and a cropped pant, all selected to be mixed and matched.

"They always say you should shop for the job you want," said Sandy. "I think that goes for the life you want as well."

"I like my life just fine," said Doris, "or at least I did two weeks ago."

"But right now, your life is a bit in flux," said Rose. She looked at Sandy. "I think, whether you want to admit it or not, you are at a crossroads. You're considering leaving the running of the store to your son, and you need to explore what else is out in the world for you."

"And I want to find Neil and bring him home," said Doris. Sandy and Rose glanced at each other. Was that sadness in Sandy's eyes?

"Yes, of course you want to find Neil," Rose quickly added, "but in the meantime, you have an opportunity to discover possibilities for your future if you aren't running a store. And maybe even have a little fun."

"And these clothes are fun," said Sandy. "When you're wearing that outfit, you exude relaxation and confidence."

"So you're saying the clothes make the woman?"

Sandy shrugged. "Well, it can't hurt to try."

Doris glanced at her reflection. She did look more relaxed, less rigid, like someone who didn't have a care in the world. She turned to Sandy. "The way I see it, I have two problems here."

"And what are those?" Sandy's eyebrows raised in question.

"One, do you think they have a shopping bag big enough to hold all these? And, two, what am I going to do for shoes?"

"Oh, shoes!" said Rose. "There's a little shop up the street that doesn't close for another hour or so. Let's all change into what we'll wear to the show and get you some shoes on the way."

Doris left swinging a full bag and feeling like she had taken an important first step toward a new life. One perhaps Neil would want to be a part of. She would try anything.

Ninety minutes later they entered the restaurant. Doris was wearing her new outfit and dressy sandals, Sandy was sporting a flirty floral dress Doris wished her ridiculous brother could see, and Rose wore a new-to-her black shift and floral shawl that complemented it. It had turned out to be a pleasant first day in California. It felt more like a holiday than a duty call, Doris thought, as they were seated at a table with a crisp tablecloth and candlelight. They ordered cocktails and their choice of the four prepared menu options.

Settling in to listen to the first comedy act of the evening, she was transported into laughter. When the act was over and their appetizers arrived, they talked about the comedian, a woman who had made jokes about the dubious pleasures of menopause, Doris wondered why she didn't do this more often. When was the last time she went out with a group of girlfriends?

She didn't know, which meant it had been far too long. What else had she let go of? What else had she missed out on by marrying Neil and moving to Canada to run a store? By settling down?

More important, what did she want more of now?

As the empty appetizer plates were removed and the entrees arrived, the main act, an improv group, mounted the stage and soon had them all laughing so hard it was difficult to eat. And Doris knew that for today, all she wanted was to enjoy the show and the company of women friends. And for today, that was enough.

She could try to find Neil tomorrow.

CHAPTER 17

Tomorrow came too early. The alarm on Doris's phone blared, and she patted the bedside table before realizing it was on the dresser across the room. She struggled to her feet to stop the persistent ring and, once she was vertical, gave up on the idea of going back to bed. Instead she searched her purse for ibuprofen and got ready for the day.

After donning a new outfit and applying some makeup, something she hadn't done in a long time, she walked down the hall to the kitchen.

"They're out on the terrace again," Lena said, nodding in that direction, and Doris followed the laughter.

"Good morning."

The pair stopped laughing, giving her the distinct feeling that she had interrupted a private moment.

"You look better, Doris," said Rose. "A lot more relaxed already. Coffee?"

"Please." Doris took a seat. "But I'm not used to such late nights—or the wine." She touched her head. "I took some ibuprofen."

"Well, I hope it's working, "said Sandy. "Rose and I have another outing planned. We hope you can come too."

Doris took the coffee Rose poured for her and added cream. "And what is this outing?" she asked cautiously. Her head still hurt.

"Just to the local park. There's music, and an afternoon tea nearby. I think you'll enjoy it," said Sandy.

"Sandy tells me you used to sing in a band. Do you still sing?" asked Rose.

"I sing in the shower sometimes," said Doris. "Though it's been a while since I even did that."

"We have a treat, then. Rose has found a group that gets together to do sing-alongs once a week. It sounds like a blast."

"Sing-alongs?"

"It's called Still Singing," said Rose. "A friend of mine told me about it after my husband died. It wasn't something I was looking for at the time, but I looked them up and they're still around. And they still sing every Wednesday afternoon at one of the local seniors' centers."

"I'm not a—"

"It's okay. We don't like to think of ourselves as seniors either, but this one is for anyone over fifty-five."

"Oh," said Doris, deflated. She hadn't thought of herself as a senior before. She worked, she contributed.

"Just because you're a senior doesn't mean you're decrepit, Doris." Sandy was laughing. "You should see the look on your face."

"Aging is just living," said Rose. "Everyone ages if they're lucky."

"And in that outfit, you look like you have an awful lot of living left to do," said Sandy again, laughing.

"I'm glad you find my old age amusing," said Doris, glaring playfully at Sandy. "It seems to me you are only six months younger than I am."

Sandy stopped abruptly, and Rose and Doris roared. "Your face doesn't look much different from Doris's right now," said Rose, and soon they were all grinning.

"What time does this event begin? I should go to the hospital first."

"Why don't you just call him today? He's just resting anyway," said Sandy.

"And we have an appointment at the salon and spa," said Rose.

"Spa?"

"We're going to get our faces and hair done and get mani-pedis," said Sandy.

"My treat," said Rose.

"I can pay my way," Doris protested. How could she accept such an expensive gift?

"You would be doing me a favor," said Rose. "I haven't done anything like this in years. It's fun to spend time with you and my sister. Please?"

"I know. You can pay us back with a song later," said Sandy.

"You want me to sing for my supper?" Doris said in mock horror.

"Exactly," said Rose and Sandy together.

"Deal," said Doris, feeling a twinge of guilt about not going to visit Jock. She would go tomorrow. "Do I have time for coffee this morning before we go?"

Sandy poured another cup of coffee from the urn and handed her a plate of pastries and another of fruit.

"Eat up. You're going to need your strength today. We're going to have a blast."

The day whirled by faster than a hummingbird's wings. The spa visits left her rejuvenated and looking better than she had in a while. Then came the haircut that left her spiky hair softer, lighter, more playful. By the time they arrived at the seniors' center, Doris felt like a different woman.

There were about twenty women gathered when they walked in, some alone, others milling around in pairs or trios. While the sisters went off to the bathroom, Doris joined the throng, interested to see who would be leading this ragtag group.

She didn't have long to wait. A man strode in dressed in a polo shirt and khaki slacks, and a flash of anger overtook her before she realized that though the outfit was like one Neil had worn hundreds of times, and the man wearing it was fit, at least six feet tall, and sporting gray at the temples of an otherwise thick black head of hair, this man was not her missing husband. Her anger plunged to sadness, and she lost focus, missing the instructions. She glanced around and realized Sandy and Rose were still not back.

They'd abandoned her—a situation that was becoming far too familiar.

"So," the man was saying, his eyes alight with mischief and his smile vibrant. "Let us all move into a circle. Come, come." He motioned for everyone to come to the center of the room and stand in a semicircle.

The women rushed to do his bidding, and Doris smiled to herself. Perhaps they were here for him as much as for the music. And then her amusement turned to worry. Neil had that effect on women too. He was what her mother had once referred to as "a catch."

It had never bothered her before because they had been so close. And, until now, she hadn't worried about him looking elsewhere. But now…

A strong clear voice brought her thoughts back to the task at hand. "My name is Raul," the man said, "and today we arc here for singing." He motioned for her to step closer. "Come, don't be shy. Join us."

She moved into place, and he smiled with delight, then turned to everyone in the room. "Let's get started."

The sisters still had not returned so she turned her attention to the class. Raul was entertaining, and she might learn some tips for working with groups.

But instead, she learned something else.

The class started with the usual stretching, deep breathing, priming the pump: exercises meant, as Raul said, "to get our instruments ready to play."

Doris threw herself into the fun and laughed along with the others who felt just as awkward doing Raul's moves. "I feel ridiculous," said the woman beside her as she loosened up her chest by pretending to draw and shoot an arrow.

"You're trying something new. Try to have fun with it," Doris said. The woman nodded and tried the breathing exercise again. "See? That's better."

"Thank you. I wouldn't even be here if it weren't for my sister. But she caught the flu, and now she's too sick to come."

"Sorry to hear that," Doris said, before taking another deep breath, counting to four, holding it in for four, and releasing for a count of four. "My friends have abandoned me, too. But now that we're here, let's enjoy it."

The woman beside her, who introduced herself as Rebecca, nodded, then followed along, breathing in to the count of six.

By the time they sang, Raul had them relaxed, smiling, laughing, and surprised that they could make sounds that were pretty good. By focusing on the process instead of the outcome, he had made many of the women forget their concerns and just do it.

They sang a few songs as the words were flashed up on the wall by an IT assistant from the center named Jasper. Jasper sat in the corner, beating on a drum that gave them a rhythm to focus on, and soon they were all singing. Doris let out her voice, the one that had been hiding for years behind the businesswoman she had become, and felt, for the first time in a long time, like she was fully awake. Renewed. All the massages and pedicures and makeovers in the world wouldn't have been able to do what this sing-along had done.

She was singing in a group. In harmony with others. Making music with strangers. She had come home to who she was, who she was always meant to be. She was a singer. How had she forgotten the joy it brought her?

When the class was over an hour later, Rebecca, too, was smiling. "That was so fun. Will I see you here next week?
"

"No," said Doris, disappointed. "I'm only here for a short time, but it was great to meet you."

"You too," said Rebecca. "You should sing more often. You have a wonderful voice."

"Thanks," she said. "See you." Then she turned to find the sisters standing just inside the hall, watching and grinning.

"You were great," said Sandy. "Just like the old days,"

"And where did you two get off to?"

"I'll tell you later," said Sandy. "Let's go to the park. There's music there, and we're going to have hot dogs for lunch. When was the last time you had a good hot dog?"

Doris followed along, thinking of the last time Zack had asked her for a hot dog. She had told him no, that they weren't as nutritious as vegetables, but she had to admit that the scent of cooked onions and barbecued wieners was tempting. She was on vacation today and would go back to reality and responsibility tomorrow.

The music in the park comprised a group of college students who came every week for practical performance experience. Rose had brought along a blanket, and they sat down, unpacked the hot dogs and drinks they had purchased, and enjoyed their meal and the music.

"They're very good," said Doris when the first set was done. "They have quite a future, I should think."

"If we're going to stay for the next set," said Rose "I'm going to grab some coffee. Do you two want anything?"

"No, I'm good," said Sandy and Doris shook her head. They watched Rose walk toward a nearby food truck and step into the gathering line of customers.

"Speaking of futures," said Doris, turning back to Sandy. "What are you planning to do next? Or have you thought that far ahead?"

"I'm thinking of moving here," said Sandy." It's been good to visit Rose. We're finally getting along."

"Is that what you really want? How would you spend your time?"

"What I really want is to travel more. Maybe I can help Rose with her work. Or find a solo travel club. I've read about those. Women traveling alone but in a group of other solo travelers, so it's safer."

"I'll help you find one," said Doris.

"Or, if things don't work out with Neil, maybe you and I can travel together. Like we did that time we went to New York. Do you remember?"

"That was fun," said Doris, though she also remembered that she had gone to New York because her relationship with Neil was on the rocks. Max had called to ask her to fill in for their new lead singer, who had come down with laryngitis just when they had finally booked a prestigious venue. She returned to the band they had started in high school, and it had felt like coming home then, too. But she had missed Neil, and when he showed up in New York to see her perform—and begged her to come back to him— she had done it without a second thought.

They had spent the next week in New York with Sandy and Max, and she sang until their lead was well enough to join them again. Then she had followed Neil back to the west coast. She hadn't looked back much on that opportunity, believing it had only been temporary, but now she wondered. Would she have been able to make a go of it?

Instead, they'd married. Her father helped her set up a store, and when he died three years later, leaving her mother alone, Doris had taken on the responsibility of helping her mom through her grief. Her mother had traveled between Sunshine Bay and Cataluma, helping run the stores and caring for her grandchildren until she, too, passed on a decade later.

By then Doris was raising her children, experiencing all the trouble and triumph a small business brings, and working to build a thriving music community in Sunshine Bay. She taught, she worked, and she took care of things while Neil traveled for his job. Only now did she realize she had lost something along the way: her voice, and the joy singing brought to her life.

Neil was right. There was more to life than what they had. She just wished she could talk to him about it.

"Have you thought about what you'll do if Neil doesn't come around?" asked Sandy, as the musicians came back to the stage for another set.

"No. I've never considered being alone before." She eyed her friend. It was almost as though Sandy wanted Doris's marriage to fail.

"My advice, for what it's worth, is to find a plan B. Find something you are passionate about that you can do or share with the world. Something to get you through if Neil doesn't return—or even if he does. We all need something for ourselves that we love to do."

"For me, it's music, of course," said Doris. "But I've spent so many years managing the store, I hadn't realized that I missed performing."

"I was hoping you would say that," said Sandy. "I loved hearing you sing today. It took me back years. We had so much fun then."

"We did, didn't we?" said Doris. Before children and business and marriage. Before adulting, as Nora once called it, took over.

Rose returned just as the band was starting their next number and half an hour later, after the final note was played, the three of them clapped enthusiastically. Sandy even put her fingers to her mouth to whistle. The performers smiled—one blushed at the attention—and bowed. "We should do something like this in the park near the store," said Doris, and Sandy frowned.

"No more talk about work. You are on vacation!" Sandy admonished.

"All right, I'll stop thinking about work. Where to next?" asked Doris as she helped Rose fold up the blanket.

"It's four. We thought we would go home for a bit, change, and go out tonight for dinner at a great Indian restaurant I know. Do you like Indian food?"

"Absolutely," said Doris. "I don't have it often as only one restaurant in Sunshine Bay serves it, but when I go to Victoria or Vancouver, I have it there." She didn't look Rose in the eye when she said this. She hadn't been to Vancouver in years, and her last trip to Victoria, besides the one to get the boat to Seattle, had been at least a year before. Her life had become so narrow, and she hadn't even noticed.

"Then we're going to a jazz club," said Sandy.

"I love jazz," Doris said. The sisters beamed in response. "Thank you both. I so appreciate this little break."

That evening, decked out more new outfits and full from their chicken curry, kabobs, and samosas, the trio walked into a little club Rose knew. The owner, a grateful patient of Rose's, gave them front-row seats.

They ordered wine, and Rose excused herself. "I'll be back in a moment."

"This is nice," said Sandy. "I love the ambience. It's like a club from the forties or fifties."

"I see what you mean," said Doris, taking in the plush seating, intimate round tables lit by candles, and vintage posters hanging on the walls. A server approached with her wine, and she nodded a thank-you.

"Where did you get off to yesterday when I was in the singing class?"

Sandy made a big deal of swirling the wine and taking a deep whiff of the aroma. "Ever been to a wine tasting?" she asked in response. "I went to one last summer, with…" She frowned. "Well, it doesn't matter who it was with. It was fun, and I learned a little about what to look for. Like the legs." She demonstrated as she swirled the red wine. "See, what you're looking for is—"

"I've been to a tasting," Doris interrupted. "It was for a new winery on the island. Why are you avoiding my question?"

"I'm not," said Sandy, blushing. "Besides, you don't tell me everything—like when Jock is getting out."

"He's getting out the day after tomorrow. The antibiotics are apparently working, and they need his bed. I'm going in the morning to make sure I talk to the doctors and his physiotherapist. I'll get everything arranged."

"And has Eugene found another place for him yet?"

"No. But when I texted him earlier, he said he had a lead."

"That's good. I think I can stay with Rose for another week. Hopefully that will give you the time you need."

"What went wrong between you, Sandy? I know he misses you."

"Oh, look," said Sandy. "The band is back. And here comes Rose. We'll talk about it later."

Doris glared at Sandy, who had the good grace to blush again. If that was the way she wanted it, Doris wouldn't ask any more questions. Where she and Rose had snuck off to the day before was likely family related. But if that was the case, why not say so?

Then it dawned on her. It had to be something to do with Sandy's breakup with Jock. And, because Doris was Jock's sister, they didn't want to share. She could respect that, though it was obvious how much Sandy missed her brother. But she wouldn't think about it now. She was here, listening to her favorite music, and having a drink again. She was on vacation for one more day before she had to go back to the hospital for Jock. Tomorrow she had to return to reality, responsibility. Tonight, she intended to enjoy every drop of wine and every moment of this wonderful evening.

The band finished forty minutes later, and the lights went up a little as another group came onstage and the host stepped up to the mic to announce the next set. But instead of introducing a band, he explained that they had four intermission acts and an open mic from the audience. And then she heard her name being called.

"What did you do?" she asked Rose and Sandy, who were both laughing.

"You said you'd sing for your supper," said Rose. "Now's your chance."

"And you can't say you aren't warmed up. I heard you this afternoon."

Doris rose, pretending to be annoyed for a moment, but a frisson of excitement went through her as she walked toward the stage and spoke to the band. And when the host handed her the microphone and the band played the first few notes of "Unforgettable," she opened her mouth, took in a breath, and crooned to the audience just as she had over thirty years before.

The audience quieted, and the host's mouth hung open a moment before he remembered to close it. She was not what they had expected. Smiling to herself, she poured even more emotion into the song, caressing the lyrics and seducing the audience with the smokiest tones she could muster.

When she finished, the audience applauded, and a few got to their feet in appreciation. As she smiled at the audience, bowed, and set the mic back on its stand, she was shaking. Neil was right. There was more to life than just working in retail. She was a performer.

She had lost that part of herself in the weeds of responsibility, but now she owed it to herself to find out what else life offered.

Robert could take over the store and, with help from Kiran and others, care for Zack. He was a grown man, and she had to remember that.

CHAPTER 18

*R*obert walked into Whisking Love and sat at the table near the window. Yvonne was waiting.

"Thanks for meeting me," she said. "I ordered you a coffee."

"Thanks," he said, taking the seat across from her, ignoring the drink, and getting straight to the point. "What's this about? You said you wanted to tell me something that concerns Zack?"

Yvonne looked down at her cup of green tea and Robert waited, his leg vibrating under the table.

"I'm trying to figure out the best way to say this," she said, and a heaviness settled on his chest. What had gone wrong now?

Robert rested his hand on his leg to settle it and broke into the lengthening silence. "I find the direct approach works best, and I've got a lot on today, Yvonne. Just say it, okay?"

"It's about your new nanny."

The weight on his chest doubled, just as it had the last time they'd discussed nannies. It was Yvonne who always caught their questionable behavior and saw things he didn't. She had warned him Christine was getting things wrong weeks before that nanny had tried to kiss him. She had been right to bring her concerns to him those other times, but he thought he was getting better able to judge people. And he thought Kiran was different. He *needed* Kiran to be different.

"What about her?"

"She's not walking Zack to school."

"She leaves with him every morning."

"And she leaves him several blocks from the school. Then she goes for a walk to the beach, sits there scrolling through her phone, staring out at the sea, and takes a long time to get back here."

"Zack's never said anything. He seems to like Kiran." He thought of the times Kiran and Zack did homework at the table, and how much time she spent with him on his music. How attentive she was toward him. This didn't sound like the Kiran he had grown to know and trust. But then, he had only known her a short time.

"I'm sure he does. She seems quite likeable," said Yvonne, in a tone that suggest she didn't think Kiran was likeable at all. "I'm just concerned about Zack's safety, as I know you are."

"Who told you this?" Was someone gossiping about Kiran, and if so, why?

"I saw her do it myself," said Yvonne. "She left him to cross the street without her. I happened to be driving past his school the other day."

"Are you sure?" But he could tell by the look on her face that of course she was sure.

"I thought you should know after…"

"Thanks." He cut her off. He didn't want to revisit his earlier mistakes with childcare. "I'll speak to her about it." He rose to leave.

"Like I said, I didn't want to bring this up." Yvonne's expression belied this comment. "If it wasn't for Zack's safety… But I promised April I would watch out for him."

"Thanks," he said again, desperate to get away. Yvonne always had a way of reminding him of his shortcomings— and the fact that it was his fault April had gotten so sick. Every time she noticed something about the women he hired to care for Zack, or even the three women he had tried to date, it reminded him of what else he had missed.

He didn't need her reminders. If he hadn't continued to spend weeks in Vancouver with the orchestra, and had instead been around more, maybe April would have been less distracted, less busy with Zack. If he had been more attentive, she would have found the cancer sooner. He could have convinced her to get treatment earlier. And she would still be here. "I have to go. I'll see you later. Thanks for the coffee."

He glanced down at the rapidly cooling brew and grimaced. He probably should have at least tried to drink it, but his stomach was in knots. He had trusted Kiran. And now Yvonne, whom he also trusted, was telling him he shouldn't.

When would he be able to rely on his own judgement?

As he walked away, he wished he could talk to April about this, but of course, if she were here, this wouldn't be an issue.

He would check it with Zack.

Checking things out with Zack proved difficult because Kiran was always around.

She picked Zack up after school, and that evening, when Robert closed the store, he came upstairs to find the two of them working on Zack's homework. He watched from the doorway, not wishing to interrupt them yet. He liked to watch them together. She was so easygoing. Funny yet firm. When Kiran was around, he felt lighter, more relaxed. Happy.

"I don't understand," Zack said, running his hand through his hair in frustration.

"Which part are you having trouble with?" she asked.

"I hate decimals," said Zack.

"You liked fractions, though," said Kiran.

"They're easy."

"Well, decimals are just another way to write fractions."

Zack looked at her in disbelief and sat back in his chair, arms folded.

"Do you want me to show you what I mean?" She pulled a pad of paper closer to her and picked up a pencil.

"Okay," Zack said reluctantly, leaning forward on crossed arms to see what she was writing. "But I don't understand how they can be the same."

Robert watched as she drew pictures to illustrate what she meant, and smiled when Zack's face lit up as he grasped the concept.

"Oh! So one quarter is the same as point-two-five."

"You've got it," said Kiran. "Now you do the rest, and I'll get the dinner."

Zack bent over the paper and worked, dashing through the list, and Kiran went to the stove. She had made Indian food again, and a tossed salad was sitting on the counter.

His mouth watered, and his stomach coaxed him into the room.

"Hello," said Kiran. "You're just in time for dinner."

"Dad, Kiran is teaching me decimals," Zack said excitedly, looking up from his now-finished page of exercises. "Josh and I couldn't figure them out today. Wait until I show him."

"That's great," said Rob. "Now off you go to wash your hands."

Zack scampered down the hall to the bathroom, and Rob cleared his pages off the table.

"Thank you for working with him."

"It's good practice for me." She came to the table with a cloth and wiped it down before setting it with cutlery and glasses.

"Yes, I imagine so. How's your hunt for a substitute job going?"

"I'm pretty low on their on-call list, but I have an interview tomorrow for a job in September."

"That's great." Though he'd known this was coming, had even encouraged it when they'd met, he was disappointed. He would miss her if she left. He brought three glasses and the jug of water to the table.

"It's at Zack's school, but for the grade three students," she said. "So at least I know the neighborhood."

"They will be lucky to get you," he said, as Zack returned to the kitchen.

"Who?" asked Zack.

Kiran looked at Robert, and he shrugged. He hadn't said anything to Zack about Kiran looking for a teaching job. He hadn't considered how to broach the topic.

When he didn't answer, Kiran did it for him. "I'm looking for a teaching job, Zack. For September. "

Zack's face fell. "You're leaving?"

"No, not exactly," said Kiran. "If I get the job, I will still see you most days because it would be at your school, but for the younger kids."

"But you wouldn't help me with homework anymore?" Rob felt his son's disappointment like a punch to the gut. Kiran looked at Robert with an expression that said, "Help me out here, buddy."

He tamped down the gut punch. "Zack, Kiran is new to Sunshine Bay, and she agreed to help us this summer while Grandma is away."

"But what if Grandma doesn't come back?"

"Grandma will come back. She always comes back." Though he had to admit she'd sounded happy when he'd talked to her that morning. She was enjoying her freedom from the store. Maybe she'd be gone longer than he thought.

"But she doesn't know how to explain about decimals and dinosaurs like Kiran does."

"Kiran is here for the summer. Afterward, she is hoping to find a teaching job. But that doesn't mean she won't see you anymore."

"And if I get the job at your school, I'll find a house near here, so if you have trouble with math, I can tutor you sometimes," assured Kiran.

"You mean you would move away too?" wailed Zack. Robert walked over to put his hand on his shoulder, but the boy shook him off.

Robert turned toward Kiran. "You wouldn't need to move right away. I'm sure we could come to some arrangement if you wanted to rent the apartment. My mother will be back in September."

Kiran smiled gratefully, and he basked in the glow. He enjoyed seeing her smile, especially if he caused it.

"So you could still live next door and still see me after school?" said Zack.

"Sometimes," said Kiran. Rob could see she didn't want to promise what she couldn't deliver, and he appreciated her for that.

"Okay," said Zack. "Can we eat now? I'm hungry."

Robert and Kiran both laughed, and their eyes met with mutual gratification that Zack was placated. But when

Robert held her gaze a little longer than necessary, she flushed and turned to pick up the salad from the counter.

He focused on pouring water into their glasses, and she blushed when he looked at her. He averted his gaze and focused instead on the plates full of food Kiran was bringing to the table. Zack's eyes widened. "I liked this last time. What's it called again?"

"Biryani," she said, sitting down at the table.

"It smells great," said Robert, looking at her—and then past her, to the framed picture of him and April and a much younger Zack. His stomach knotted a moment as he realized he was thinking of another woman while looking at a picture of his wife.

And his thoughts were inappropriate for a boss. Kiran might be a temporary employee, but she was an employee all the same. He had to keep reminding himself that.

He was attracted to his son's caregiver in a way he hadn't been attracted to a woman since April died. But he could never act on that attraction. At least not while she lived under his roof. But Max was right. She did have something special.

Unless Max was just as blinded as he, and Yvonne was right—again. When it came to his caregivers, Yvonne, so far, had not been wrong.

The three of them spent the evening together playing board games and laughing, until Zack started to yawn, and

Kiran suggested it was time for bed.

"You go ahead. I'll put the game away," said Robert. Kiran nodded, placed their glasses in the dishwasher, and bade them good night. He watched the door close behind her and realized he already missed her.

"Go get ready for bed, Zack. I'll be there in a few minutes to read to you." He put the game away, reflecting on their evening. He appreciated that Kiran had suggested games tonight. Kiran and Zack both played to win, constantly one-upping each other, and he had laughed so much his stomach had hurt. It had been a long time since he and Zack had made their own fun instead of sitting in front of the television listening to laugh tracks. Even if Kiran moved on, he would try to make this a tradition at least one night a week.

He knocked on his son's door to start their next book when he remembered his conversation with Yvonne. He wanted to assure himself that in this instance Yvonne was wrong and that he and Max, who was also an excellent judge of character, were right about Kiran.

"Hey Zack, can you tell me something?" he asked, sitting down on the bed.

"What?" Zack asked, standing beside the bookshelf.

"When you go to school, does Kiran walk you all the way to the door?"

Zack didn't answer. Instead, he was taking an inordinate amount of time to choose the next book when they both knew he was going to ask Robert to read the Harry Potter book he had purchased for him the day before.

"Zack?" Robert got up and put his hand on his son's shoulder, turning him around.

Zack looked up at him from under lowered lashes, his face as red as his freckles. "Kind of," he mumbled.

"What does that mean? Kind of?" Was Yvonne right after all? The heavy stone was back on his chest, and he had to labor to take a breath.

"She takes me to the school," said Zack, turning back toward the shelf.

"But she isn't taking you all the way to the door?" His voice rose, and Zack backed a few steps away from him. How could Kiran do this when he had promised his wife he would keep Zack safe?

"She takes me to the school," said Zack, "and I walk into the school with Josh."

Something in the way the boy avoided his gaze told him this wasn't the entire truth.

"How close to the school?" he asked.

"A block or so," said Zack, picking up the book. "Can we read now?"

"Does she let you cross the street alone?" He watched Zack's eyes closely.

"No. Not alone."

"Does she walk across the street with you?"

"I already told you I don't walk across the street alone," Zack yelled.

"Okay, I was only asking," said Robert, taking a step forward and reaching toward Zack to pat him on the shoulder.

"I'm ten and three quarters, Dad," said Zack, stepping away and holding the book like a shield in front of him. "I'm not a baby."

"No one said you were a baby, Zack."

"Well, stop treating me like one. And don't get rid of Kiran too."

"I don't treat you like a baby," he said, dropping his hands to his sides. Did he? He didn't think he did. It was his job to keep Zack safe. "And what do you mean, *too*?"

"You get rid of all my sitters. Even Grandma left."

"Grandma went to help Uncle Jock. She'll be back."

"No, she won't. She's going to go traveling with Grandpa. I heard her tell Esther."

"You must have misunderstood. She'll be back in September. She said she would."

"Leave me alone," said Zack, angry tears springing to his eyes. "You always make them leave."

"You don't want me to read the book to you?"

"No. I can read it myself."

"You sure?" Robert stared at his son, who climbed into bed, opened the book, and focused on the first page. "I thought we were going to read it together."

Zack didn't answer, simply turned the page. His body language screamed for Robert to go.

So Robert walked quietly out of the room and closed the door behind him. He wanted to scream or go for a run to release his frustration, but he couldn't leave Zack alone. Instead, he went to his room, took out his violin, sat in front of a picture of April, and began to play. But after a few notes, he stopped. He didn't want to play music. He didn't want to sit here looking at April, who kept smiling back at him as though everything was okay.

"It's not okay," he said to her. "Why did you leave? What am I supposed to do next?"

The picture didn't answer—it never answered—so he walked to the front room and got lost in a Jack Reacher film, feeling like the loner Reacher was. His mother was gone, his wife was dead, his nanny had disobeyed a direct instruction and was probably leaving for another job, and his son hated him.

What was he supposed to do now?

~

*R*ob was dragged from his dream the next morning by someone shaking him. It was a good dream, with Kiran on the dock, pointing out seagulls; Kiran playing the piano; and Kiran in the stockroom, staring into his eyes.

In his imagination, he pulled her into his arms and she came willingly, clinging to him as he picked her up and set her on the footstool, bringing her to his height. All the while she said nothing, just looked at him with those eyes, so close he could see the specks of gold in their depths.

"Robert?" Kiran said.

"Mmm." They were sharing a kiss now, one that he wished were real.

"Robert?" Dreams were funny. weren't they? In this dream, she could talk and kiss at the same time. She really was special.

"Robert, wake up," she said, and he reluctantly opened his eyes to find Kiran standing over him, shaking his shoulder. "Wake up. You slept in."

"What? Why are you in my room?" he demanded.

"I, um… I'm not," she said, waving her hand toward the rest of the living room. "You must have fallen asleep in front of the television."

He blinked and scanned his surroundings. "Right." He rubbed his eyes. "What time is it?"

"Seven twenty," she said. "I came a little early because I promised Zack pancakes this morning and I need to make the batter."

"Where's Zack?"

"I imagine he's still asleep," she said. "I just got here and haven't had a chance to look yet."

"Right," said Rob, swinging his feet around to the side of the couch and standing up. "I'll go wake him up while you make breakfast."

"Sure," she said, watching him warily. Did he look that frightening in the morning? If he did, April never had a problem with it.

He walked to Zack's room, knocking on the door before opening it. Zack was asleep, his bedside light still on and the book flat on his chest.

Robert picked up the book—Zack was on chapter two already—and placed it on the bedside before shaking Zack. "Hey, you're going to be late for school."

"I don't want to go to school," mumbled Zack, snuggling back under the covers.

"I thought you were going to show Josh how to do decimals today," said Robert, calling on his son's sense of responsibility.

Zack opened one eye and closed it again.

"You don't want to let him down, do you?" he chided.

"Let me sleep," mumbled Zack.

"I'll be back in a few minutes. Hope you wake up before I return. Kiran's making pancakes today."

Zack's eyes opened again, and Robert smiled to himself. Appealing to his son's sense of responsibility didn't work as well as appealing to his stomach. He'd have to remember that in the future.

Satisfied that Zack was getting up, Rob went to shower. Under the warm water, he relived some of his dream, and realized that for the first time in years, he hadn't dreamt of a woman with green eyes. He had dreamt of a woman other than April, and he hadn't felt guilty. What he felt when he thought of Kiran was not guilt.

It was longing.

And he had to stop that. She was off-limits, and she worked for him, and she had probably put his son in danger. And he really wanted none of that to be true.

Twenty minutes later, showered and dressed, Robert returned to Zack's room to find him packing up his schoolbag.

"Ready for breakfast?" he asked.

"Yeah," said Zack, grinning, their words from the night before seemingly forgotten.

"Well, I smell pancakes."

"Coming," said Zack, and Robert walked to the kitchen to find Kiran at the stove, adding a pancake to the growing pile beside her on the counter and pouring more batter onto the griddle.

She turned as he entered and asked if he wanted berries or syrup.

"Berries," he said, "but only one pancake." He walked to the coffeepot to pour a cup. "Do you want some?"

"Sure," she said, shifting one of the pancakes from her pile to another plate and adding a ladleful of cooked berries from a pot simmering on the stove.

He added cream to both cups of coffee and set them on the table, then walked to the cutlery drawer to grab spoons, forks, and knives.

"Whipping cream?" she asked.

"No, but I'm sure Zack will enjoy it," he said, taking the plate from her and bring it to the table.

"Is he okay?" she asked.

"Of course," he said, taking the plate from her and sitting down at the table.

"I worried yesterday that the news of my job hunt unsettled him."

"He's okay," said Rob, wanting to ask her about walking Zack to school. But after the blow up with Zack the night before, he decided to wait.

"That's good," she said, flipping the pancake and preparing a plate for Zack with berries and whipping cream. Zack appeared in the doorway, dressed, with his shirt tucked and hair combed.

Kiran set the plate on the table and Zack whooped loudly, proving that though he was growing up, he was still a kid —and still someone Robert needed to look out for.

Which meant he needed a caregiver he could trust. Not someone who only followed some of his instructions. Maybe he should find out for sure if what Yvonne said was true. The only way he could do that was to follow them.

He had asked Max to come in early so he and Curtis could discuss the progress of the fundraiser over breakfast. But breakfast wasn't until nine. That left plenty of time for him to follow her and get back for the meeting.

CHAPTER 19

*K*iran tidied up the kitchen while Zack went to brush his teeth and grab his school things. She was glad Robert had gone to open the store.

Something was disconcerting about the way he had been watching her today and yesterday, like a spider watching a fly and waiting for it to wander into his web.

Though she hadn't known him long, something about finding him asleep on the sofa felt off, and it wasn't like Zack to sleep in. Something had happened the night before, and though Robert said it was nothing to do with her looking for another job, she didn't think he'd told the whole truth. Either that or she had gotten this family all wrong. Were the past couple weeks about them both being on their best behavior? And now they were relaxed enough to show their true personalities? If so, they were good actors.

But then, so was Jacques.

She would ask Esther about it later. Maybe it was nothing to do with her. Perhaps a significant anniversary was approaching, or something had happened she wasn't aware of. At least Esther could give her some advice. She seemed like a kind woman who cared about both Robert and Zack.

But she didn't have time to think about it right now. She had to walk with Zack to the school and come home and get ready for her interview. She wanted that job. It would mean she could afford to stay here, even save for a down payment on a house. It would help her set down roots.

Zack was more silent than normal as they walked to school, and when they got to the place where she normally dropped him off, he touched her on the arm and said, "Can you walk with me across the street too?"

"Sure, but what about Josh?"

"Josh isn't here yet," he said, looking furtively up the street.

"Okay," she said, wondering about his change of heart. They waited together for the light to change, and she saw that he looked nervous. Should she pretend not to know him, or should she step closer and protect him? She decided on the former when, as the light changed, he hurried to catch up with a friend as soon as they got to the other side of the street. He didn't even look back at her.

She stood beside the school gate and waited until he went inside, then continued to the shore for her regular morning walk, feeling again, as she had for a few days now, that she was being watched.

But she didn't see anyone, so she shook off the feeling and, when she got to her favorite rock on the shore, pulled out her phone and scrolled through her phone messages.

There were two calls from her father's house, and she felt guilty. It had been several days since she'd called him and decided she would have to do so later that morning, after she spoke to Esther and went to the interview at the school board office.

She wanted to have something positive to share with him. If he knew she had an interview, it would hopefully take some worry off his shoulders, and he would stop asking her to come home.

She went to Whisking Love and found Esther up front, serving customers.

When she got to the front of the line to order a coffee and a morning glory muffin, she asked, "Do you have time to join me?"

Esther looked at the line behind her. "Give me a few minutes. I'll meet you at the staff table." She pointed to the small table tucked up near the counter.

But instead of Esther, it was Rob who joined her.

"Good morning." His face didn't look friendly.

"Hello," she said. "Is there something you need?"

"I need to know if you've been walking Zack all the way to the school. I was told that you drop him off across the street and let him walk by himself."

"I take him to the school, and most of the time I walk across the street with him and up to about a block away. He goes the rest of the way with his friend Josh."

"I gave you strict instructions to take him all the way." His voice quavered, and she pulled away from him.

"You told me to walk him to school. Perhaps I should have confirmed that the agreement Zack had with his grandmother was something you also approved of. If it's not, I'm sorry. "

"What agreement with his grandmother?"

"Zack told me that his grandmother lets him walk with his friend Josh when they get a few blocks from the school. I've been watching him. He's very careful. He told me he walks home alone sometimes as well, but when you hired me you asked me always to pick him up."

"I would appreciate you following my instructions in the future," he said. Then he got up and walked out of the cafe.

"Are you okay?" asked Esther, who joined her, carrying a cup of coffee. "That looked intense."

Kiran swallowed hard and put both hands around the cup to stop from shaking. "He was angry that I didn't walk Zack all the way to school. I have been watching him go into the school with his friend. I drop him a couple of blocks away and wait until he gets in. I don't know why he's so angry."

"How does he even know you weren't walking all the way?"

"I'm not sure, but I saw Yvonne drive by the school yesterday, and she saw me waiting across the street while he went across with Josh. There is a crossing guard, and Zack is careful. I didn't think it would be a big deal."

"That's what Yvonne was in here talking to him about yesterday. I was wondering about that. He looked upset when he left."

"Why does she care so much? Is she interested in Rob?"

"I don't think so." Esther pondered for a moment. "No, I would say she was more interested in April. She likely promised her she would look out for Zack."

"But when April died, Zack was what? Six? He's nearly eleven now. He needs to be allowed to grow up."

"I think Doris was starting to see that. She even let him walk home with his friends sometimes."

"That's what I told Rob, and he got so angry. Esther, what if he fires me?"

"I don't think he'll fire you. You're good with Zack, and he needs you."

"I've never seen him angry until today. It was a little frightening."

"Rob wouldn't hurt you. You are safe there."

Kiran smiled, accepting Esther's reassurance. "Still, I hope I get the job I've applied for. It will give me the means to leave if I need to."

"You feel trapped?" asked Esther.

"Let's just say this reminded me not to become complacent. Not to trust a man too much."

"Did you trust another man too much, Kiran?" asked Esther. "I've fallen into that trap myself a time or two."

"When I caught my ex cheating on me and ended it, he cleaned out our bank account before I even knew what was happening. All I had was a hundred-dollar bill my dad had given me for my birthday. I had to go home, or I would have been out on the streets."

"What a horrible thing to do."

"Especially after ten years. The only good thing about the lockdown was that I could complete the rest of that school year from my father's basement and save six months' salary."

"Thank goodness for parents, eh? My mother was there for me when my last relationship broke down, too."

"Yeah?"

"Dirk wasn't a nice guy, but he had me so convinced it was all my fault. Everything that ever went wrong was because I had done something wrong."

"It's good you got out, then," said Kiran.

"Turned me off men permanently," said Esther. "And then my mother needed me to help with the bakery. The rest, as they say, is herstory."

"They say that, do they?" Kiran laughed.

"It's good to see you cheerful again," said Esther. "What time is that interview?"

"One o'clock." Kiran glanced at her watch. "I should get going. The school board office is at the other end of town, and it'll take me time to get there on the bus. I don't want to be late."

"Well, I wish you luck," said Esther. "And I'll see you tomorrow at choir practice?"

"Yes, I'll see you," said Kiran. "Thanks for listening."

Kiran didn't go to the store to practice piano as she had every other day. Instead, she went upstairs to her apartment, got ready for her interview, practiced answering questions in the mirror, and tried to appear the excited, engaged teacher she wanted to be.

She would not let her encounter with Robert bring her down. She was excellent with students. She had a lot of great ideas, years of experience, and she was going to show them she was the best person for the job.

By the end of summer, she would never be reliant on a man for money or housing ever again.

⁓

Robert wrenched open the door to Making Music and set the bells over the door jangling loud enough that everyone in the store turned to see.

He nodded to Max and the woman he was helping. "I'll be in the office." Once inside, he called his mother, who answered on the second ring.

"Rob? How are you?"

"Mom, I have to ask you something, and I want you to tell me the truth."

"Sure, but I don't have long. I'm picking up Jock from his physiotherapy appointment in a few minutes."

"Have you been letting Zack walk home from school by himself? Letting him cross the street alone?"

"Just a minute. Let me go somewhere so I can hear you better."

He paced up and down the office, scrubbing one hand through his hair and holding the phone to his ear with the other.

"Zack and I discussed this," said Doris. "He made the case that he is growing up, that his friends walked home from school, and that he could walk with some of them. As for the crosswalk, there is a crossing guard who stops the traffic."

"How long has this been going on?"

"Since January."

"January? And you never thought to tell me?"

"I didn't think it was such a big deal. You walked to school alone when you were ten. You were looking out for your sister when you were twelve. Zack is responsible. He's careful. He knows not to do things that are dangerous."

"I wish you had said something," said Rob, remembering Kiran's stricken expression and Zack's angry words from the night before.

"Why? What happened?"

"Yvonne told me Kiran wasn't walking with Zack, and so I asked her—no, I accused her—of not following my explicit instructions."

"I thought she was working out well. Zack always sings her praises when I talk to him."

"She is doing well. Helps him with his music and his homework, and she's a great cook, too."

"Then why was Yvonne concerned?"

"I don't know, but I'm going to get to the bottom of that."

"You're also going to apologize to Kiran. She's a keeper, son. And with your track record with childcare workers, you'd better do everything you can to keep this one."

"I'm messing this up." He had blown it by going off on them without all the information. Why hadn't he questioned Yvonne more closely? Why hadn't he talked to his mother before he accused Kiran of not keeping his son safe?

"Rob, I have to pick up Jock. You can do this. Go apologize." Then the line went dead, and Rob flopped down into the office chair. He had to make this up to both Zack and Kiran. He had to let Zack know he trusted him to cross a street alone, and he had to let Kiran know how important she was to their family. And he needed to find out what was behind Yvonne's actions. Was she just trying to make trouble? If so, why?

CHAPTER 20

Doris hung up the phone with a trace of guilt for not telling Rob that Zack was walking home with friends. But she didn't have time to dwell on it.

She walked back into the hospital and down to the physiotherapy department, arriving as Jock came out to the front desk to book his next appointment. Two weeks after being released from hospital, he was walking better, but she wished he would heal faster.

It had been two weeks since she'd last heard from Neil, when he texted to say he was in the U.S. and would be in touch soon. She wanted to text back to thank him for letting her know he was still alive. But she couldn't think of a way to say it without sarcasm. Instead, she let him know she was in Cataluma, that Rob had help with Zack, that Nora was doing well, and that she missed him. He had responded with a thumbs-up. Texting was an impossible way to communicate. Did the thumbs-up apply to one of those four pieces of information or all of them?

A therapist dressed in scrubs approached her, pulling her aside and back to the present.

"Mrs. Kelly? the therapist asked.

"No, my name is Hudson. Jock's my brother. I'm staying with him until he gets back on his feet."

"Do you know how he's doing with his exercises? I'm concerned he isn't progressing as quickly as he should be."

"He does them in his room," she said. "I haven't watched him. He doesn't want his sister policing him."

"Could you ask him if you can help? As I say, I am concerned he isn't progressing as much as she should. How long does he walk?"

"About ten minutes or so. Around the block."

"How often?"

"Once a day. Sometimes twice."

The therapist's face told Doris she had just learned something. "He should be walking ten to fifteen minutes four times a day. And working on increasing to twenty or twenty-five minutes three times a day. He needs to build endurance."

"And he knows this?"

"Of course. I've been telling him for the past two weeks."

"I'll get him out more often," said Doris, tamping down a rage that was building. How dare he impede his own progress, keep himself from healing? What was going on with him? "Leave it with me."

"Thank you. Let's see if it helps him improve within the next week. I'll see you back here next Monday."

"Do you have a list of the exercises he should do?" asked Doris, her eye straying to locate her brother. He was across the room, watching their exchange with a surly expression. He was being a stubborn brat. It was like when they were kids and he wanted his own way. She'd forgotten how passive-aggressive he could be.

"Yes," the therapist handed her a pamphlet and opened the page to show her what he was expected to do the first two weeks. "If you could encourage him, I feel confident his recovery time will improve."

"Thank you. I'll do my best," said Doris. When the therapist walked away to take her next patient, Doris glared at Jock. Oh, she would encourage him, all right.

When they got in the car, Doris rounded on him. "You've been lying. You said you were doing everything the therapist asked you to do."

"I'm doing the best I can, Doris,"

"It sounds like you need to double down," she said. "How are you going to get well if you don't get moving?"

"Without Sandy, what's the point?"

"Jock, I thought you were going to fight for her."

"You stayed with her for two days. You said she didn't talk about me, and you two were best friends. She's not interested."

"Just because she didn't talk about you to a friend she rarely sees anymore—who is also your sister—doesn't mean she isn't interested." She put on her seat belt.

"She hasn't visited me."

"Oh, for pity's sake," said Doris, "why would she? You haven't done anything to reach out to her."

"I messaged her on Facebook. She answered once or twice."

Well, that was promising. Doris turned the car on. "What has she been saying?"

"She asked if I was getting better. But she still doesn't want to see me."

"Then you need to go to her."

"I can't like this."

"Then you need to work harder to improve. Sandy nursed her husband until he died, Jock. Do you think she wants to be stuck nursing you for the rest of her life? She wants to travel. See the world. She's looking into solo trips she can do with other solo travelers."

Jock didn't answer her. He just turned his attention to the passenger window.

"Well, do you?"

Jock shifted away from her, winced at the pain in his hip, and turned his face further away. Exasperated, Doris turned on the car to drive home and picked up her phone to scroll to the book she had been listening to.

If he wanted to give her the silent treatment, two could play at that game. But he was as bad as two-year-old Robert had been during one of his tantrums. Jock needed to stop, because at this rate she would never find Neil. And the last thing she wanted was to live out her last days looking after her brother. She'd rather be home looking after Zack. She would have to call Robert back when she got home, make sure everything was going okay. Though what she could do about it from here was anyone's guess.

She glanced again at her brother, and he still refused to look at her. Fine. She scrolled through her list of audiobooks again, chose a spicy romance, then cranked up the volume so she could hear it over the busy traffic as they headed back to Cataluma.

They had driven about half an hour and were well out of the city when Jock leaned over to the console and turned off the volume. "How can you listen to that stuff?"

"Hey! It was just getting good," she laughed. It had taken a while, but she could still get a rise out of him.

"Sex, sex, sex. Love, love, love!"

"You don't like love and sex?" she teased.

"I… I… It's rubbish," he sputtered.

"Love makes the world go round," she said.

"Well, you don't find love among the tomatoes in the produce section like that couple did." He pointed toward the car speaker.

"True. You're more likely to find it online now," she said.

"Love at first sight. It's not even realistic."

"No? Why not?"

"Love is friendship first. All that claptrap is, just… lust. Just passion."

"Nothing wrong with a little lust and passion," she said, smiling as she signalled her move to the left lane and passed the car ahead. "It adds spice to life."

"You're telling me you believe in love at first sight?"

"Of course. The first time I met Neil, I knew he was the one." She stepped on the accelerator and got well ahead of the car before moving back into the right lane.

"Which is why you left him to play music in New York?"

"That was a blip. He loved me. He just needed to remember that. Absence makes the heart grow fonder."

"Out of sight, out of mind."

"Why are you being so grumpy?"

"Because…" Then he turned his head toward the passenger window again, as though he'd just remembered he wasn't speaking to her.

She toyed with whether she should turn up the book again and decided to leave him to stew in silence for a few minutes. They were almost home.

"You know, if you want Sandy back, you're going to have to do a damned sight better than you have been at your exercises."

He crossed his arms and said nothing.

"If you want her, you need to show her you still have some kick left. Sandy is young at heart. She doesn't need an old fuddy-duddy."

"Fuddy-duddy? You sound like Grandma."

"Well, you're behaving like you are decrepit and have no life left in you. What did you say when I first came to see you in the hospital? If you aren't dead, it's not too late to try something new,"

"Okay. Okay. You have a point."

"Yeah, I hate it when people throw my words back at me too." She laughed.

"It's sore." He mumbled. "When I do my exercises, I ache."

"Yep. And it will continue to be sore for a while, but if you don't use it… Well, you know."

"I wish she would talk to me."

"I think you need to give her some time. But there's nothing wrong with posting places you'd like to see on Facebook and tagging her sometimes. Show her you're still interested in life, Jock. You can't live like this anymore."

"Not with you nagging at me."

"Well, if you think this is nagging, keep doing what you're doing. Imagine how happy I'll be if you continue not to get better, and I can't go and find Neil. You may be stuck with me for a long time."

"Holy crap!" he said, bug-eyed. "That's incentive in itself."

"Ouch, that hurt." She laughed. "But I'm glad I could help."

She pulled onto the exit to Cataluma. "Want a burger today? I can't face cooking if I don't need to."

"Sounds good."

They sat in the parking lot of the burger place a few minutes later, munching their meals.

"Have you heard from Neil?" he asked.

"Nothing. I now know what it's like to be ghosted."

"He has tickets to that train show this week. I think it's for four days."

"I thought of going to see if I could find him," she said. Sandy and her sister even asked a private investigator to help me." She had been surprised when Sandy finally sat her down to tell her why they had been so secretive. The man they had hired was friend of Rose's who was just starting out in the business.

"And?"

"I'm still waiting. I don't know how effective the guy is, but he's apparently doing what he can to find him. And he's cheap."

"What's Neil going to think of you getting a PI to investigate him?"

"I don't need him investigated. I just need to find him. Sandy knows that. I didn't even know they'd done it until a week later. I told Sandy I didn't want to follow him, just find out where he is so I can meet him." But even that made her uncomfortable, if she was honest. Is this what their marriage had become?

"And how is it going with Robert? He got the store under control without you there?"

"There's been a blip with his childcare, so I'm not sure."

"He's a grown man. He'll figure it out. I did."

"You know, I forgot you were a single parent for years. You did okay."

"I relied a lot on friends. And Sandy."

"You two need to get in the same room and talk," she said. "Maybe even find some of that passion you hate so much."

He scowled at her. "Not until I can walk into the room without a walker. You were right. I need to get better."

"What was that?" She cocked her ear and put her hand behind it. "Did I hear you correctly?"

"Yes, you heard me. You were right. You may as well appreciate it for a bit. Doesn't happen very often."

"Ha! Sounds like the old Jock may be back sooner than we thought."

He chuckled before taking the last bite of his burger. "Yep, I'm back. Watch out world."

"Good, because I should get back to Sunshine Bay and make sure things are okay."

"I'll work harder at my hip, but you have to work on letting go. You're addicted to worry. It's no way to live. Let them make mistakes and learn to cope. They'll be fine."

She nodded as though to agree with him, but she couldn't help thinking about Kiran and Rob and wondering how things were going.

CHAPTER 21

Kiran emerged from the dark building where she had been interviewing for the past hour and blinked at the sunshine. She wanted to punch the sky but thought better of it. Instead, she went over the interview step by step in her mind. The trio of interviewers on the panel had been pleasant and attentive. And when she left all three smiled, nodded, and exchanged pleasant looks with each other as well as with her. They said they had a few more candidates and would tell her next week, but she could feel it in her bones that she had done well. At least something was going right for her.

She had to tell someone, so she fished her phone out of her bag and dialed her father's number. He would be happy for her, and she would be glad to give him this news so he wouldn't worry so much.

But instead of hearing his friendly voice, Rajani answered.

"Kiran, is that you?"

"Yes, is Dad there?"

"Did you get my messages?"

"I haven't checked them. My phone's been off. I've been busy today."

"Your voice mail is full now, so I couldn't tell you more," she said irritably, and Kiran considered that likely was true. She had not listened to any messages the past two days because of choir practice and interview prep, but why was Rajani so frustrated—and why was she answering her father's cell phone?

"Can I talk to Dad?"

"No." And then Rajani started to cry.

"What's wrong? Where's Dad?" Fear grabbed her throat.

"Kiran?" A man was talking to her now.

"Vijay Uncle? What's going on?"

"Your father is in surgery." Kiran swallowed hard at the sound of Rajani sobbing in the background. Rajani wasn't a crier.

"What kind of surgery?"

"He had a heart attack," said Vijay. "They're performing surgery on him today. He needs a quadruple bypass operation. Can you come? I promised him just before he went in that I would get you to come home."

"I'll get a flight home as soon as I can." She mentally calculated the cost and the balance on her credit card and decided she could do it if the price wasn't too high.

"We got you a ticket for today. It leaves from Sunshine Bay in four hours and connects with the flight out of Vancouver. I sent it to your email address."

"Just a second. Let me make sure I have it." She scrolled through her messages until she found one from the airline. "I've got it," she said. "I'm coming."

"Thank you," her uncle said. "I'll pick you up. You can stay with me. Rajani's sister and her family will stay with her when they arrive."

"Okay. I have to go."

Kiran grabbed a cab home and asked the driver to come back for her in an hour, making a list in her mind of what she had to do now: pack, contact Louise at the Belle Tones, and tell Robert she was leaving. He would need to find someone else to help him. She hoped he found someone he trusted, because he obviously didn't trust her.

Max was at the counter when she came through the front door of Making Sweet Music.

"Whoa, where's the fire?" he said, joking. Then she looked at him. "What's wrong?"

"Where's Robert?"

"In the office, tackling paperwork."

Kiran rushed down the hall, knocked once, and didn't wait for an answer before bursting in.

Robert looked up from his desk in surprise and then concern. "What's wrong? Is it Zack?"

"No, it's my father. I'm going home. He's had a heart attack." As she said it, the reality hit her. Her father, her wonderful father, was on a table under a surgeon's knife, fighting for his life right now.

"Do you need a ticket? I can help you get one while you pack."

"No. The cab will be back for me in an hour. I'm going to pack. I'm sorry. You'll have to find someone to pick up Zack."

"We'll be fine. Max is here, and I don't have any lessons to teach until four thirty. I'll pick up Zack. Go. Don't worry, we can manage for a few days."

"It's open-heart surgery, Rob. I'll be gone for a few weeks. In fact, I'm not sure I'll be back at all. My dad needs me." She turned away from his stricken face. She didn't have time to worry about him right now, but after she took a few steps, she turned back. "Can you tell

Louise? They'll need to find someone else to play for them."

He nodded, and she ran upstairs to shove everything she owned into her backpack. Forty minutes later she checked one last time under the bed, in the cupboards, and in the closets. Yes, she had everything, and the cab would be back soon, so she just had time to return her keys.

"Hello again," said Max when she walked into the store. "Rob's gone to pick up Zack, but I'm sure he'll be back soon."

"My cab's here," she said, pointing out the window. "Can you give these to him?" She handed him the keys. "And could you tell him I didn't have time to clean out the fridge? Maybe his cleaner can do it?"

"I'll tell him," said Max. "So you aren't coming back?"

She shook her head. "I don't know. My dad needs me, and he's all I've got left."

He smiled in sympathy then reached down to hug her. "If you're ever back this way, come on by. You're going to be missed around here."

"Thanks, Max." She hugged him tight. "Say goodbye to Rob and give Zack a hug for me. I'm sorry I can't wait until he gets home."

"I will. Now you'd best go. You've got a plane to catch."

She ran out to the cab and pushed her backpack onto the seat behind her. It was sad to leave Sunshine Bay just as it was beginning to feel like home. She would miss it.

As the cab pulled away from the curb, Robert and Zack came into view, and Zack saw the cab. "Kiran!" he yelled, and ran along the sidewalk.

She turned and waved at the boy standing on the sidewalk with his father's hand on his shoulder. They both waved back.

She would miss them most of all.

CHAPTER 22

Rob watched Kiran's cab drive away, and a profound sadness descended. His old companion, grief, was back, but this time it wasn't April he was thinking about. It was Kiran. When she was around, she made him feel like things were easy again—like there was hope, a purpose, a future.

But now she was gone.

"Where did she go?" asked Zack.

"I told you. She had to go home to see her father. He's sick."

"But she didn't even say goodbye!"

"She had to catch a plane, Zack."

"You always make them leave. I hate you." Zack ran into the store, and Robert went after him.

"He's gone upstairs," said Max, when Robert came in. "Kiran was here. She asked me to give you these." He handed him the keys to her apartment. "And to tell you she's sorry she didn't have time to clean out the refrigerator."

"That's it?"

"She was in a big hurry. The cab was here, and her plane leaves soon."

"I thought maybe…"

"Maybe what?"

"I don't know, a note or something. I'd like to know if she arrives home safe." And that she had forgiven him for their earlier conversation.

"I'm sure she'll let you know when she finds out more."

"I messed up. I accused her of not being careful enough with Zack. It was a stupid thing to even question, but I listened to someone else's opinion instead of trusting my gut."

"You could always apologize. You have her phone number, don't you?"

"Yes. I do. Thanks." He pocketed the keys. "I'll be back in a few minutes so you can go home. I just need to talk to Zack first."

"I'm going home to tofu burgers, so take all the time you need." Max grimaced.

"Still working on keeping you healthy, eh?"

"Yeah, and with Kiran's dad having a heart attack, it hits close to home, so I do appreciate it. But tofu? There's gotta be a better way."

Rob chuckled and walked upstairs to see his son. But before he did so, he thought of his own father. It had been a long time since they'd talked, and the last time he'd seen him, he had seemed more distant than normal. He pulled out his phone and sent a text. *Hey Dad. Hope you are doing well. Sorry I haven't reached out. Things are a bit wild here.*

A text came back immediately. *How's the new childcare worker?*

Rob: *She's gone home. Her father had a heart attack. Need to find someone else to help for a few weeks.*

Neil: *Your mother's in Cataluma. So who have you got lined up?*

Rob: *No one right now. It just happened.*

What did his dad expect? Childcare was hard to find.

Then his father texted again. *What about me? Could I help?*

Rob: *Do you know someone?*

Dad: *Let me see what I can do.*

Rob: *Okay. Thanks, Dad. Talk to you soon. Customers.*

There wasn't much his father could do from wherever he was, but it was nice that he offered. His father was rarely around to help.

Robert trudged up the stairs to face Zack. He would need to put an ad in the paper again. That seemed to work the last time. And he would need to rearrange schedules so there was someone around after school until then. With Kiran gone, Max had offered to do more hours, and the students, Paul and Jorge, were coming back soon. He could do this. They could make it work until he found someone for the summer.

He found Zack in his room, deep in his Harry Potter book. The boy only glanced up, tears still staining his face, then looked back down again at the book.

"She had to go, Zack. Her father was sick."

"Is he going to die?"

"I hope not," said Rob. "He's having surgery."

"Dad, what happens to me if you die?"

Robert sat down beside him and resisted the urge to say, *Don't be silly, I'm not going to die.* Because it wasn't silly at all. Instead, he said, "Well, you would live with your grandma and grandpa."

"But if they travel all over, how will I go to school? I'll never see Josh."

"They wouldn't travel all over."

"That's not what Grandpa said. He travels all the time, and he hopes Grandma will come with him one of these days."

"Zack, I'm not planning to go anywhere for a very long time. And Grandma and Grandpa would stay home with you. They wouldn't travel all over."

"Mom didn't plan on leaving either," said Zack.

"No, she didn't." Robert put his arm around Zack. "And we can't predict what will happen to us. That's true."

"What if Grandma and Grandpa are gone too?"

"Then you have your Aunt Nora. She would look after you."

"I don't know Aunt Nora. I want Kiran."

"Zack. I'm going to miss Kiran too. But she had to go."

"But she did things Mom used to do. She took care of me. I love her."

"I know. She is a very special woman."

"Do you love her too?"

"Well, I am fond of her." But love? He hadn't known her long enough to fall in love with her. Had he?

"Then you have to make her come back."

"Zack, she's where she needs to be right now. Her family needs her."

"Why can't she be our family?"

"I'm sorry, Zack. She had to go home. I'll find someone else to look after you."

"I don't want anyone else," sobbed Zack. "Go away." He flung himself across the bed and cried.

Rob patted him on the shoulder. "Zack, it'll be okay. Then he immediately regretted his words. It would not all be okay, and he hated it when people said that. But they *would* make it through. Together.

"Go away," said Zack, and Rob stood up.

"I love you, Zack," he said. "We'll get through this. You have me."

But Zack didn't answer. He just hugged his pillow and sobbed.

Rob went out to the kitchen to start dinner. He looked in the fridge and freezer and found several meals prepared. Kiran had been organized, and that meant he and Zack would enjoy chicken curry tonight. All he had to do was make rice and a salad. He could manage that. He took the curry out to thaw and went downstairs to take over for Max, close out the cash register, and get ready for his student, thankful there was only a forty-five-minute lesson today. He wanted to be close in case Zack needed him.

As he was closing out the till, he ran through the other things he had to do that week. The tickets were sold out for the MMFC, and Curtis had confirmed the catering and the harpist.

The choir. He had forgotten to call Louise. He picked up the phone and dialed her number to give her the bad news.

"I hope her father is okay," she said. "And I have someone in mind who can help in a pinch. We'll manage."

He thanked her and sent a quick text to tell Kiran he had let Louise know and that he hoped her father was okay. He needed to apologize for jumping down her throat, but that could wait. Kiran had more important things to worry about.

The back door to the store creaked open, and in walked one of the part-time music teachers and the students they were expecting. He would connect with Kiran again later. Right now, he needed to work.

CHAPTER 23

Kiran tried to focus on the movie streaming from the screen on the seat in front of her. She'd given up all thought of trying to sleep, though the child sitting in the seat beside her had managed. He was sprawled out as much as he could be given the restrictive space, and his head kept falling halfway to her shoulder. The boy's parents were oblivious, having both also succumbed to sweet oblivion.

The boy wriggled in his sleep, and she tried to shift herself away, ignoring the memories that being near him evoked: Zack falling asleep as she read to him, Zack cuddling between her and Rob on the couch when they watched shows together, Zack smiling up at her as if she meant as much to him as he had come to mean to her. That was before Rob's accusations.

The accusation that she would not have Zack's best interest in mind was a betrayal. She had done so much to hold their little home together while Doris was away. She had even given her free time to help with a cause that was, though close to her heart, not hers. It was his cause. His boy. His house. And she had done all she could to support him.

And he wasn't grateful.

The more she thought about it, the more her anger surfaced. It was emotion she usually pushed down. Kept buried deep. But as she sat with the child sighing against her, the anger bubbled. She was remembered all the times people had wronged her. Jacques had been the worst, but Rajani had pushed her way into their family and forced her to choose to leave her father for his happiness. And there had been others.

And what had she done?

Nothing. She had walked away, let them have their win. Disappeared from their lives as though she had never been there.

And what had it got her? Nothing. She had no partner, no job, none of the things she had always wanted. She had given it all up to leave Jacques so she wouldn't need to see him. She had given up her little home with her father because of Rajani. And now she had given up on Zack because Rob listened to someone dripping poison in his ear.

Well, enough was enough. She had every right to be near her father. She had every right to have a job she loved in a town she adored. She had every right to demand her share.

By the time she got off the plane—it was three in the morning in Toronto—and ran into her uncle's arms, she was determined that no one was going to push her away again. Not without a fight.

"Thanks for coming," her Uncle Vijay said as he hugged her. "We have missed having you around."

"Thanks for picking me up. You must be exhausted."

"I haven't slept much," said Vijay. "But the surgery was successful, and now you are here. That is all that matters to me."

"How is Dad doing?" she asked.

"He is tired. And he has a way to go before he will be back on his feet."

"When can I see him?"

"We'll go in the morning. They asked that we let him rest until then. Meanwhile, let's get you home. Your aunt is looking forward to seeing you."

Kiran smiled at the mention of her Aunt Kamala. It had been several years since they had spent much time together. "I'm all set," she said, patting her backpack.

"You brought an awful lot for a few days," he said.

"I wasn't sure how long it would take, so I brought everything," said Kiran.

"Don't you have a job to go back to?"

Kiran shook her head and shrugged. "It's complicated. Let's go, shall we?"

They arrived at her uncle's house forty minutes later, and Aunt Kamala was there waiting for them. Before Kiran could take off her shoes, Kamala folded her into her arms and gave her a big squishy hug. "It is so good to see you."

"You too," said Kiran, stepping back to get some air and finding herself pulled back against her aunt's large bosom for a second round.

When Kamala had finally tired of hugging Kiran, she stepped back and said, "Are you hungry? Come eat."

"I ate a big meal in Vancouver, and I had something on the plane," said Kiran, slipping her feet from her shoes and wiggling her toes in freedom. "And I'm not hungry."

"It's almost four," said her uncle. I think we all need a few hours' sleep."

Her aunt's face fell, then she smiled again. "Okay. Come upstairs and we will get you settled in. Later we will have breakfast together." Kamala bustled ahead and Kiran followed her up the stairs, settling into her cousin Meera's old room, which had been redone for company. She was soon fast asleep. She had missed this. She had missed home.

The next morning, after five hours of sleep, Kiran awoke to cooking smells from the kitchen. Dressing quickly, she joined the couple, who were drinking chai and eating freshly cooked parathas. "Oh, I love these," said Kiran, sitting down at the table in front of a paratha stuffed with potatoes. "I haven't had them in years."

"Whenever you were here, you and Meera used to pester me to make them for you."

"How is Meera? I haven't seen her since she moved to England after her wedding. Was that five years ago?"

"They're moving back in a few months," said Kamala. "And I'm going to be a grandmother in October. And now you are also back, so I hope we have a lot more quality family time together. I have missed you girls."

"Meera is pregnant? She didn't say." But why would she? They had drifted apart in recent years, and a lot of that was down to Kiran. She had allowed Jacques to control her life, tell her who she should see, who she should stay in contact with. And later she had been so busy traveling, she hadn't had time. Even when she had been in Europe, she hadn't managed to make her way to England. It had been so long since she and her cousin were together it would be difficult to bridge their time apart. How would she ever bring back the easy ways they had shared?

If you don't try, how do you know? she asked herself. She had to stop blaming Jacques and correct things. She had let her cousin drift out of her life, but she could do something about it. She would make it up to Meera starting today. She would send her a text. Tell her she was staying here. Tell her about her dad. And congratulate her. She was part of this family, and she had to fight to belong.

On the drive to the hospital, she pulled out her phone and sent Meera a WhatsApp message. She didn't receive an answer, but with the time difference, she hadn't expected one. Meera would be working. As a project manager for a consulting company, Meera worked long hours. But Kiran was proud she had taken the first step to reconnect with family and erase the isolation she had felt while living with Jacques.

When they arrived at the hospital, Kiran's buoyant mood immediately crashed. Her mother had spent much of the last year of her life in this building, and Kiran felt the weight of those memories as she walked into her father's room.

He smiled when he saw her, and she rushed across the floor. She wanted to hug him, but remembered his surgery and merely squeezed his shoulder carefully. "Bhapa," she said. "How are you?"

"Sore," he said, grimacing as he struggled to pull himself up in bed.

"No." Kiran put her hand on his arm and urged him to stay put. "You can get up when you feel better."

"But I want to get a good look at you."

"I'm right here. I'm not going anywhere until I know you are well again."

"You will stay at home," he said.

"I'm staying with uncle. He lives closer to the hospital, and I didn't want to impose on Rajani. Her sister is there. She doesn't need me as well."

"When I go home, you will come home too. Get a job nearby."

"Let's get you well first."

"I have already told Rajani to get your bedroom set up."

"Bhapa, don't worry about me. Concentrate on getting better, okay?"

"But you will think about it? And come home?" He looked at her intently.

"I will think about it," she said. *Home.* Where was her home these days?

"Ah, good," he said, lying back into the pillows and closing his eyes.

Rajani walked into the room then, and when she saw Kiran there, her face crumpled into tears and she fled from the room.

Kiran lifted her eyebrows at her uncle in a silent question. What had that had been about? Vijay shrugged and nodded toward the door. Seriously? He wanted her to go after Rajani? The woman hated her.

She shook her head no, but her uncle glared at her.

Sighing at the silent reprimand, she relented and stood up. "I'll be back in a few minutes," she said to her father. "Uncle will keep you company."

"Okay," he said, his eyes still closed. "I will rest a bit. It is so good to see you home."

Kiran patted her father on the arm and went out to the hallway and down to a waiting room designated for families. Rajani was there with her older sister, a woman in her late forties whom Kiran hadn't seen since her father's wedding.

"Thank you for coming," the sister said, patting Rajani on the shoulder as she cried softly. Kiran wracked her brain trying to remember the woman's name. *Naya? Radha? No, Shyla!*

"I'm sorry I didn't get the message until late. I was at a job interview."

Rajani sobbed louder, and Kiran looked to Shyla for answers. Getting none, she said, "Rajani, you must be happy he came through the surgery so well. Bhapa's going to be okay." She hoped it was true. It would be just like her father not to tell her everything. "Unless you've heard something I haven't?"

Shyla shook her head. "No, it's not that," she said. "Your father's surgery went well. He's expected to make a full recovery."

"Then what's going on?"

Rajani was sobbing on her sister's shoulder, making her lovely blouse all wet.

Finally, Rajani raised her head and looked at her. "It is all my fault."

"What's your fault?"

"The stress your father was under. The diet. I made him have a heart attack."

"I don't think you can make someone have a heart attack, Rajani," said Kiran. *Unless you scare them.* She had heard of people dying of fright. But she wouldn't voice that thought. The woman was already miserable.

"I came between you and your father. I made him do too much with the girls. I expected so much of him. He was exhausted."

"Dad doesn't always eat properly, and he's diabetic. And he's a grown man. He is the person who drives himself too hard. He's always been like that."

"But I cook all the food."

"Except when he's traveling. When he's traveling, you don't know what he's eating. And he doesn't get enough regular exercise. You know that's down to him." It had been a topic of conversation between her parents when she was younger. The irony was that her mother, who had always been fit and ate healthy food, had been the one to get sick.

"But I know he is stressed about you. He worries about you all the time, and I drove you away." A whole new floodgate of tears burst open, and Kiran found herself perching beside Rajani on one of the comfortable couches, patting her on the arm. What was it about hospitals and patting people?

"Can you ever forgive me? I was being so…"

"Selfish?" asked Shyla.

"Protective?" asked Kiran.

"Jealous," admitted Rajani. "I was so afraid I would lose him. Every time you were around, you reminded him of your mother. I was competing with a ghost."

"Not competing with a ghost," said Kiran. "Though perhaps living alongside one."

She thought of April, and how Rob was always thinking of her. She could understand a little of how Rajani felt. Zack's red hair came from his mother, as did his winning smile. Robert would be reminded of April every time he looked at his son, and anyone new in their lives would always be second. But second didn't need to mean worse, or second best.

"I'm going to see how your father is," said Shyla, and she rose to leave. "You two have a lot of talking to do." Rajani nodded toward her sister and turned toward Kiran. They were alone now, and Kiran was immediately on edge. Rajani cared about appearances, and she Kiran wondered if the last few minutes had all been an act for the benefit of her sister and her uncle. She braced herself for vitriol, and was surprised when Rajani looked up at her, eyes brimming with tears. The woman looked truly distraught.

"Your father thought the world of your mother," Rajani said in a whisper. "She was the love of his life. The way he tells it she was exciting, beautiful, perfect. And you always used to tell me if your mother were alive your father wouldn't have noticed me."

"I said that?" Kiran cringed as she thought back to some of their earlier conversations. Yes, she decided upon reflection. She had been that mean.

"Your father said you were lashing out. Angry because he and I started to spend time together only six months after your mother passed away. He was helping me get back on my feet after I left my husband, and I was helping him work through his loss. You found out when you returned from college that first summer."

"I remember," admitted Kiran. "I was horrible to you." Yes, the problems in their relationship were not only Rajani's fault. She had a role to play too.

"And then you got the job in Sarnia. Moved in with that… that…"

"Jacques."

"Kiran, I never knew how he treated you. Maybe I didn't want to know. He only came to our house one time, and he was so standoffish, as though we weren't good enough for him, and when you stopped visiting so often, I felt we weren't good enough for you either."

"No one was good enough for Jacques," said Kiran. "I wish I'd figured it out earlier."

"I wondered about that," said Rajani. "My first husband… Nothing was good enough for him either."

"When I left Jacques and moved home, Dad hinted that your first husband had been unkind."

"He was not unkind, Kiran. He was cruel. Very cruel."

"I know, but back then I didn't care. I was so absorbed in my pain. I acted like my breakup was the worst anyone had ever had in the history of breakups, and I think I was grieving all over again for my mother. I'm sorry I was so horrible to you. None of that was your fault."

Rajani shook her head. "I didn't help. I was jealous. You look so much like your mother, and I knew every time he looked at you, he remembered her."

"My mother was his first real love, and I know I remind him of her. But I am learning that love isn't limited. Love grows and expands. You just have to let it."

Was she talking to Rajani or to herself? She thought of the times she had noticed Robert looking at photos of April, April's paintings, or something in the house that she had used and loved. His gaze softened, and he seemed to drift away to a better time. A time that didn't include anyone new. Didn't include her.

"But I was awful to you," said Rajani. "And I was the one who was supposed to be the adult."

"We can get past it," said Kiran, remembering the promise she had made to herself in the car. "If we fight to keep Dad happy, we don't have to fight each other."

"He wants you to come home and live. I promised him you could. But how can you, after everything I've said? I was even jealous you got along with the girls and could explain schoolwork better than I could. Your own sisters." Rajani let more tears fall.

"Why don't I plan to stay for a few weeks first, see how things go? I can help you until Dad gets back on his feet. Then we'll see. I don't know if I will stay for much longer."

"You have to stay."

"Rajani, I don't think Dad has thought this through. He wants to see me more often, and I need to make sure that happens. But I also need to make my own way in the world. Build my career. Make friends."

"You have friends here. Family," said Rajani. "You can't leave again. And I am truly sorry for telling you to go in the first place. I know how hard it is to leave a man who isn't good, and I was jealous your father took you back home. My own father didn't support me when I left my daughters' father." She looked up at Kiran. "He refused to let me come home. He refused to let my mother contact me. If Shyla and her husband hadn't taken us in, I would have been forced to go back."

"I didn't know."

"Who talks about that?" she said. "I felt like I failed. That I invited his harsh words, his punches."

"How did you get away?"

"I moved to Toronto from Kitchener. I had to. He was well known there. Had powerful friends."

"I had no idea," said Kiran. She had been the selfish one, wanting her father for herself and not caring what Rajani had gone through.

Rajani looked sideways at Kiran. "That's why I'm so ashamed I let my jealousy get to me. I knew you had gone through similar pain. I knew you needed help. But I did it anyway."

"Where is your ex now?" asked Kiran. Her father had never told her.

"He is remarried and has two boys." She smiled wryly. "The girls never see him. They see your father as their father." She began to cry. "And now they nearly lost him too."

Kiran reached out and patted Rajani on the arm. "He's going to be fine. He has a lot to live for."

"But I need to put this right between us. He wants you to move back home. You could have the suite again. We could work on this. Please stay."

"Okay," said Kiran, thinking of how comfortable it had been to stay with her uncle and aunt. She had missed family. Maybe she did belong here. She could look for a job nearby, reconnect with friends. She didn't have anything anywhere else. "When your sister goes, and Bhapa comes home, I'll move back," said Kiran. "Give you help with the girls and Bhapa until he is back on his feet."

"And then what?"

"And then we'll see. I'll apply for jobs and see where I find one I like." She didn't remind Rajani about the job she had applied for in Sunshine Bay. Nor how much she liked it there. How much small-town life suited her.

"Your father will not like it if you leave again."

"Perhaps. But if I move out of Toronto again, you can visit, and I will make it a point to visit more often. We could spend holidays together. If I were married, he wouldn't think anything of it. And at my age, with my experience with men, I'm not sure marriage is something I want anymore."

"Oh, don't say that," said Rajani. "My second marriage has been wonderful. Don't let your experience with that man ruin your chances of finding happiness with someone else."

"I'm trying to keep an open mind. But meanwhile, I need to find my own way in the world. Find my way to serve others. You know?"

"Yes. And if you decide to go away to pursue your career, I'll help you explain it to him. But don't feel you have to leave again."

"I can't stay home forever," said Kiran. "I've been out of the house too long."

"You are a determined woman. Almost as determined as me," laughed Rajani. "I'm sure you will find what you are looking for."

If only she could feel as confident as Rajani that this was true. First, she needed to decide what it was she was looking for. Her mind drifted back to a dark-haired man and his little boy, waving to her from the sidewalk, but she shrugged away the thought.

Robert was still living in the past with April, and he didn't even trust her to walk his son to school. She needed to think of other options for her future because he wasn't one of them. Still, she couldn't help wondering how he was getting on and if he had found a new caregiver for Zack.

CHAPTER 24

Three days after Kiran left, Robert rose early to make breakfast and plan what to make for dinner. They had three days left of Kiran's pre-prepared food, and the evening before they had finished the last of her chicken curry. He missed her cooking, missed the way she made order from their chaos, her music, her ability to fill in and help with all the things that needed doing, but it was more than that. He missed the delight she showed in small things: the way she watched seagulls and found fun ways to engage Zack in learning. She had a way of making even boring things like decimals fun.

He missed *her*. And, for the first few days she was gone, he wondered if she would ever consider coming back. She had responded to his only text with a *thanks for letting me know*. Polite but distant. He couldn't blame her, and he knew that he had to apologize by phone, but she was with family and her father was ill. So he had simply left the communication open in the meantime. She could contact him when she was ready.

Meanwhile, he had to find someone to look after Zack. So, after taking his son to school, he went to Kiran's apartment, armed with a garbage can and organics bag, determined to clear out her fridge. He found the place as empty as the day she moved in, but now void of sunshine and daisies.

He gazed at April's painting, but the cheerful hues failed to brighten the space. He had a sudden urge to leave but forced himself to do what he came to do. He dumped the milk down the sink and the expired food into the organics bag, then exited as fast as he could. He would ask his cleaner to do the rest, to get it ready for when Kiran returned.

He shook his head. She wouldn't be back. The last contact they would have would be when he sent her last paycheck and severance papers. He locked the door and turned, startled to find Yvonne standing behind him.

"Did you really fire her?" She looked exhausted. Dark circles under her eyes emphasized her pale skin. "Esther said I got it all wrong, that she was good with Zack and that now she was gone."

"She quit."

"I'm so sorry." Yvonne's hands were shaking, and Robert stepped a little closer, though he didn't want to. Listening to Yvonne had been the reason Kiran had left on bad terms.

"Esther said I was wrong and I need to stop, but she doesn't know the truth. You deserve to know what happened. If you want me to move out afterward, I can go and stay with my sister. But you have to understand that all I have ever done is try to make things right again. Well, as right as they can be."

"What are you talking about?"

"April. I should have stopped her."

Robert glanced up and down the empty hallway, and though he was reluctant to take much more time with Yvonne right now, he could tell something was wrong. If she was going to unburden herself, they might as well be comfortable. "Come with me." He led the way to his apartment. "Sit down in the kitchen. I'll put on a kettle, and you can tell me what's wrong."

She sat at the table, perched on the edge of the chair nearest the door, and waited until he had filled the kettle and sat across from her.

"What do you want to tell me?"

"I knew," she sobbed. "I knew, and I didn't do anything."

Robert was stunned. Yvonne never cried. "What did you know?"

She clasped her hands and stared down at the table as though she were a child admitting to cheating on a test. "I knew about the cancer."

"We all knew."

"No. A year before she got the diagnosis, April told me she had found a lump. I told her to get it checked. I even offered to go with her, and she said she would go on her own. She promised."

"April found a lump a year earlier?" he whispered, not daring to believe what he was hearing. After all the guilt he had felt about not being there, about not supporting her enough, about putting his career first, she had known something was wrong?

"I'm sorry I never told you, but it wasn't my story to tell. I thought she would go. When I found out she hadn't, I forced her to go. But I should have asked sooner. I should have followed up."

Robert glared at her, anger rising like bile. He wanted to shout, to shake her, but it wasn't Yvonne's fault.

It was April who had been stubborn, had thought herself invincible. Even when she finally admitted she had cancer, it took him weeks to convince her to get treatment. She believed that if she didn't acknowledge it, the cancer would go away. She was only twenty-nine, and she didn't want to admit she could die. She wanted to paint, raise Zack, spend time as a family. Cancer messed up her plans.

Their plans.

Cancer took her away and locked him into a new life he and Zack hadn't been ready for. And now, according to Yvonne, April had known something was wrong and hadn't said anything.

And he was so angry.

"I'm sorry. I've tried to help since. With the childcare workers. To make sure they're good. Qualified."

"What do you mean?"

"The earlier ones weren't suitable. I found them doing all kinds of things wrong, as you know." Her voice trailed off, and she avoided his glare, seeming to gather courage to face him again. "But this one. Kiran. She's done a lot for Zack, and she even agreed to help the choir after Louise—a stranger—asked her for help. Zack seems so sad since she left. I shouldn't have said anything."

"You mean you've been driving them away?" he asked.

She looked up at him, shocked.

"Not driving away. Just making sure Zack was safe."

"Why?"

"Because I failed to keep April safe."

"Leave," he said, as he remembered all the times he had gone to her with his problems. "I need to be alone right now."

She stood and walked to the door but turned around before she left. "I'm sorry I drove Kiran away too. She was nice. Different. Maybe that was the other reason I was upset."

"Different?"

"You've been different. You looked happy with her. Zack was happy. And I was upset you were moving on when I can't seem to. I still miss her so much. She was my best friend."

"Kiran didn't leave because of you."

"She didn't?"

"She left because her father is ill."

"When will she be back? I need to apologize."

"I don't think she's coming back," he said. "I haven't heard from her since she left."

"Maybe Esther can get a hold of her," said Yvonne. "She and Kiran got along well."

"Yvonne, stop trying to make it better. Some things can't be fixed, and I need to be alone right now."

"If there's anything I can do to help, let me know," said Yvonne.

"What you can do is get some help working through your grief. It's not your fault. You are not responsible for April, or Zack, or me. You are responsible only for yourself."

"I'm going to ask Esther to give me Kiran's address so I can send her a card. And an apology. I feel so bad."

He didn't answer. He just walked to his bedroom to stare at the picture of April he had been looking at for four years.

"Why the hell didn't you say anything?" he asked her, tears in his eyes. "It could have been caught early. You would have had a fighting chance." Then he put the picture in his bedside drawer, angry at receiving no response, no reason, nothing. He had to go. Max needed to take a break, and he had work to do. Maybe that would help him forget all the pain.

He wished his mother could come back and help so he could… What? Run away for a bit? But no. His mother was in Cataluma, and he was going to deal with this on his own.

Doris walked beside Jock as he made his way around the block for the second time that day. He was still using his walker, but he wasn't leaning on it as heavily as he had the previous week.

"You're doing much better," she said, though his progress wasn't enough to allow her to leave him without support and go in search of her errant husband.

Jock paused for a moment. "Did the block get longer?"

"Do you want to rest? There's a bench just over there." She pointed down the street.

"Yeah." He walked over and sat down.

"You really are doing much better."

"I just wish I could go home. I'm tired of this. But I suppose Eugene and Nora have taken the place over anyway."

"They'll move once you're ready. They're already looking for places."

"Well, tell them not to look too hard," he said. "This may take a while."

A woman walked by with a poodle wearing pink booties, and they exchanged grins. "But you'll have to keep going if you want to travel around the country."

"Not on my own. What would be the point in that?"

"She'll come around."

He glared in her direction. "Don't worry about me so much. You need to stop using me as an excuse and go and save your marriage," he muttered. "I'll be fine on my own."

"Oh?" she asked, "And how are you going to manage?"

"I'm doing better. You said so yourself." He hoisted himself up again and leaned a moment on the walker before continuing. "Why don't you just go for a couple of days to that model railway conference? Find Neil. It's this weekend, and I happen to know he's there. If you go tomorrow, you can still catch the last day and get some time to talk to him."

"I'll see if Eugene can stay with you," she said with relief. She realized she'd been waiting for permission to leave. It would do them both good to be away from each other for a day or two, and it had now been over a month since she had seen Neil.

A few hours later, she settled things with Eugene. Before she left, she decided to take one last shot to change Sandy's mind before she went to take care of her own mess. Her friend had returned several days earlier to pack up her house and get it ready to go on the market.

She asked Nora to come with her, and they went that afternoon while Jock was resting.

"Hi, Sandy," Doris said, as she and Nora stepped into the condominium. "We're here to help you."

"Oh, you didn't need to do that," said Sandy, smiling hard, though it was clear she hadn't been smiling before they came. Her eyes were bloodshot, and she was thinner than the last time Doris saw her.

"How are you?" Doris asked, hugging her and looking around at the piles of books, clothes, and other belongings. There were a few boxes packed in the corner, but Sandy wasn't making much progress.

"Where would you like us to start?" asked Doris. "Which room are you working on today?"

Sandy's eyes shifted from Doris to Nora and back to Doris. "Oh, Doris. I thought I could do it. I thought I could pack up, leave, go south to be nearer my sister, but…"

"But you'd be leaving your home?" asked Doris.

"Yes," Sandy choked out. "It was hard enough to move from my old house to this place after Blake died." Her sobs got louder. "What was I thinking?"

"Come here. Sit down. Nora, go make us some tea."

Nora nodded and left. Doris turned to Sandy.

"Now tell me what's wrong."

"I miss him. I miss the store. I miss our old lives. Why did he have to take up with Virginia?"

"Sandy, I've been here for weeks, and Virginia hasn't phoned, texted, or visited. I think you have it all wrong about her."

"But…"

"The man is miserable without you," said Doris. "He misses you. And he's grumpy."

"He's always a little grumpy."

"And when I told him you wouldn't want to look after him, that you want a partner not a patient, he started working hard to get himself walking again. He's much better than he was even a few days ago."

"Are you serious? He's walking on his own?"

"He's using a walker if we go very far, and a cane around the house, but he's working hard. Improving."

Nora came back into the room and set a tray of tea things on the coffee table in front of them.

"Nora have you decided to stay and help Jock with the store?" asked Sandy.

"Yes, and we've updated the systems in his absence. He hasn't complained."

"Even the stock system?"

"Uh-huh."

"What about Virginia?" Sandy asked Nora.

Nora looked between them then. "Sandy, I'm going to tell you this, but if you ever tell Jock, I will deny it."

"Tell me what?" Sandy's concern was written on her face, and Doris held her breath, hoping Nora didn't have information that contradicted what she had just told Sandy.

"He's been giving Virginia voice lessons. That note you saw —the envelope on his table—it was a check. Not a love note."

"Why would she need voice lessons?" Sandy scoffed. "I'm sorry, but you're wrong, Nora."

"Sandy, why do you think Jock has been working so hard to get better? He wants to be good enough for *you*. Not Virginia. You."

"What about him going somewhere else, like up to Canada to live with you?"

"He's not coming north," said Doris, "except to visit for Christmas. My brother has no intention of leaving. Not now that Eugene and Nora are taking over the store."

Sandy looked doubtful, but hope sparked in her eyes. "You really think he'll stay?"

"Sandy, that man has been miserable," said Doris. "And he has been trying my patience. I'm close to the end of my rope."

"He does get crabby when he doesn't get what he wants," said Sandy. "And he hates sitting around."

"He's even talking about traveling."

"Traveling?"

"It's his turn, he says. As soon as Eugene gets back from his brief tour."

"So Eugene is still going with the band?"

"Until they can find a replacement, yes."

"And how do you feel about that, Nora?" asked Sandy.

"Nora is fine with it," answered Doris. "Nora is fine no matter what happens with Eugene. And I couldn't be prouder of her."

"You're absolutely sure Jock doesn't have anything going on with Virginia?"

"Positive," said Doris. "And you know, he would love it if you visited him. Give him some hope so he stops grumbling at me?"

"Nora, there are some cookies in the cupboard above the stove. Do you mind grabbing them for me?" asked Sandy.

"Sure." Nora shrugged then got up and left.

"We don't need cookies."

"I had to get you alone for a moment. Have you heard from Neil?" asked Sandy.

"Not for a couple weeks, but I do know that he's at a model railway conference this weekend. I'm going to see if I can find him."

"I like that plan, Doris. You two need to be in the same place if you are going to solve your problems."

"And so do you and Jock," said Doris.

"When you were in Santa Barbara, we hired that PI to look for Neil. I want you to know that he never found any indication that he was playing around on you. He was just visiting clients and friends. No women. Just some old friends from college. I recognized the names. Oh, and he spent a week at a silent retreat. Here." She leaned over to the side table and pulled out a drawer. "He put a file together for you."

"You had him followed?" Doris asked, taking the envelope.

"Technically my sister had him followed, but I wanted to know for sure that you weren't going to get hurt. You're like a sister to me."

"Thanks for this." Doris slipped the envelope into her bag just as she heard Nora coming into the room.

Nora returned and placed the cookies next to the tea.

"Thank you both for coming. I appreciate it," said Sandy. "Tell your brother I'll be over to see him tomorrow morning, so he'd best make sure the place stays tidy after you leave."

"I will," said Doris, rising. "You have the address?"

"Of course," said Sandy. "I did my research."

"What about the cookies?" asked Nora, when Doris motioned to her that it was time to go.

"Changed my mind," said Sandy. "I'll put them away."

"Do you need help with the rest?"

"No, I'll be fine."

When they left, Nora said, "What was that all about?"

"She just needed some reassurance, that's all. I think things are going to be fine now. And tomorrow I am off to see your father."

"It was good to see you, Mom. Tell Dad to drop by soon too."

"We'll come soon. I promise." She just hoped she could keep that promise.

Then she dropped Nora off at the store, packed her bag, told Jock that Sandy would be there in the morning, and wished him well.

"Let me know if you need me to come back, but I think you're going to be okay now," she said.

He stood and hugged her tight. "Take care, Doris. And thanks for everything. I can always count on you."

She left him sitting at the window and pointed her car toward the conference, hoping to see Neil by breakfast.

She arrived at the conference trade show the next day, looking through the sea of people for Neil. It was going to be impossible if she didn't text him and arrange to meet up. Should she?

She pulled out her phone and sent a text. *Where are you today? I miss you.*

There was no answer, so she phoned Robert. Again, no answer.

She decided to phone Kiran, who answered on the first ring. "Hello?"

"Kiran, it's Doris. I'm phoning to see how you are doing."

"Thank you for calling," said Kiran. "My dad is much better. He's coming home soon."

"Your dad?"

There was silence on the other end of the line. Then Kiran said, "I'm in Toronto, Doris. My father had a heart attack."

"Is he okay?"

"He has had surgery and is recovering."

"What about Zack? Did Robert find a new caregiver?"

"I don't know. Robert hasn't contacted me since I left. We didn't leave on good terms."

"What happened?"

"He was upset because I let Zack walk the last few blocks to school with his friends. I shouldn't have done it without talking to Rob first, but Zack said he'd been doing it for months."

"I should have said something to Robert earlier about the arrangement I had made with Zack. I am so sorry. It's been going on so long I didn't think to say anything and now I've dropped you into a mess." This was her fault. Jock was right about her tendency to take things over without consulting people. "I didn't explain enough about how much Rob worries."

"Yes, he does. And it's understandable when you are a lone parent." There was a voice in the background, and Kiran said, "Thanks for calling, Doris. I hope your brother is doing better."

"Yes, thanks," said Doris. "I'm sorry things didn't work out."

"Me too," said Kiran before she hung up the phone.

Where was Robert? She had to trust that he was okay. She had the urge to call someone else next—Esther?—but

decided to take Jock's advice and try not to worry.
Besides, she had come to find Neil. He was her priority.

CHAPTER 26

That afternoon, just before Robert was due to pick up Zack from a visit with his friend Josh, the door to the store opened and the last person he expected to see that day strolled in.

"Dad? What are you doing here? I thought you and Mom were in California." His father had obviously been somewhere warm. His skin was tanned a deep bronze, and he looked rested, relaxed. "Where's Mom?"

"She's in Cataluma helping Jock," said his father, looking around the store. "I thought I would come and help with Zack. It's been a while since we spent time with each other."

"That's great! And you're just in time. I was off to pick him up from his friend's place."

"I'll come with you, and then he can walk home with me. I can help him with his homework and then drop him by around six. Might even pick up a pizza for my first day back. You used to love pizza."

"Still do," said Robert, grabbing his jacket from the back door and throwing it on. "I'll be back in a bit," he said to Max. "Just need to pick up Zack and tell him our afternoon plans."

"I'll be here," said Max from across the room, where he was shelving new books.

"Zack will be excited to see you," said Robert as he and Neil walked to Josh's. "He's really missing Kiran, our childcare worker, and he blames me."

"Did you give her father a heart attack?"

"No, but before she left, I accused her of not looking after Zack well enough."

"Was it true?"

"No, it was something Yvonne told me." He proceeded to tell his father all about Yvonne's interference over the past few years. "I wish she'd said something. Maybe April would have beat it if it had been caught earlier."

"Son, you know how April was. She was stubborn, and she wouldn't have listened anyway. Her mother died of the same thing, and I expect she was in denial."

"I've been thinking a lot about it, and I think you're right."

"You can't blame yourself, or Yvonne. Though it's too bad you didn't trust Kiran. From the conversations I have with Zack, I think he really likes her."

"You talk to Zack?" Was there anything else his son was up to that he didn't know about?

"Of course. Every few days I send him a note on the computer, and he tells me how things are going here. We have a deal."

"He's never said."

His father shrugged. "Probably didn't think to say anything. We just swap train stories, and he tells me about dinosaurs and such. Kid stuff."

"I'm glad he has more than just me to talk to. Sometimes I feel like I'm doing this all alone."

"You aren't alone, Rob. You have me, and your mother, of course. But you should know that Zack had ideas of Kiran becoming his stepmother. She must have made quite the impression. She was only here a couple of weeks."

"It was amazing how quickly she hit it off with Zack. She's a teacher, so she's already great with kids."

"He probably felt safe with her. And maybe he's looking for a mother figure, especially since Doris left."

"I can see how that would be," said Robert.

"What did you think of Kiran?"

Robert walked a few minutes, considering his answer. "I liked her. She brought some life back into the house. That had been missing for a while."

"So Zack was right."

"About what?"

"You liked her as more than a childcare worker."

"Maybe," said Robert. "Though it still doesn't feel right. April's only been gone for a little while."

"Robert, she's been gone for four years. More than a third of Zack's life."

"I suppose that's true." He hadn't thought of how long it had been in Zack years. "But I'm not sure I'm ready to move on. I've dated a bit, but it's all still so hard. And with Zack to consider…" He shrugged his shoulders.

"You're still having trouble moving forward. I can't imagine how hard it is."

"I don't want to forget her."

"How could you, when you see her in Zack every day? It isn't about forgetting her. It is about moving forward with her alongside."

"But Kiran may not think so."

"Who said anything about Kiran?" His father laughed. "Sounds like she moved into your life in more ways than one."

"I can't stop thinking about her," admitted Robert. "But she left, and she hasn't connected again, even to tell us how her father is."

"Well, you either have to figure out what else you can do or let her go. Maybe find someone else who makes you feel alive again. It sounds like you're almost ready to try."

They arrived at Josh's door and knocked. Josh's mother opened the door and barely had time to greet them when Zack came out, saw his grandfather, and rushed toward them. "Grandpa! You came!"

"Told you I'd see you soon," said his father.

"Did you bring the new train set?"

"I did indeed. And I have a new place to put it. Want to come and give me a hand?"

Zack turned to his father.

"Go ahead," said Robert. "I'll see you both for dinner."

"We'll bring the pizza."

"Pizza!" said Zack. "I love pizza even more than chicken curry!"

"You'll have to tell me all about this chicken curry. I didn't know you liked that."

"Kiran makes it," said Zack, and he proceeded to tell his father all about how to make chicken curry as they walked away.

Robert smiled and headed back to the store.

"Nice to see your father back," said Max when he stepped into the store.

"Zack is pretty pumped."

"It'll give you time to find a new caregiver."

"Wish I didn't have to."

"Still haven't heard from her?"

"No, I screwed that up," he said. "Wish I knew how to solve it."

"You could always apologize."

"She ghosted me."

"You mean you tried contacting her and she didn't answer? That doesn't sound like the Kiran I know."

"No. I haven't texted her since the day she left, to let her know I'd updated Louise about her departure. But I've heard nothing from her since."

"Sounds like you ghosted her. Why don't you try sending her a text to ask how her father is doing? Or you could send her a card. Esther was going to get the choir to all sign one so she knows they're thinking about her. Maybe she's been in touch with Kiran."

"Thanks, Max. Oh, and Max..."

"Go ahead. I'll stay a few more minutes while you go next door," he said. "By the way, how's your mom? Is she back too?"

"Mom's still in Cataluma."

"Hopefully she'll be back soon."

CHAPTER 27

*D*oris surveyed the center where the model train convention was being held. It was massive and held hundreds of tables. If he didn't text her back, her chances of finding Neil here were nearly nil. She looked at her phone just to be sure she hadn't missed his response and, disappointed, she put the phone back in her pocket. At least she had time to think and wander. So she spent the next hour perusing the different models and some of the new developments with 3D printers. She purchased a toy for Zack and a custom gift for Neil she arranged to have shipped home when it was ready.

When she had procrastinated long enough, she purchased a cup of coffee from a food stall and sat down at a table again to try to connect with Neil. She hoped he was alone, and they could finally have a heart-to-heart talk. She wasn't sure he even wanted to talk to her. It had been weeks of uncertainty, and she was exhausted from worrying about him and what he wanted.

She scrolled through her emails and message apps on the off chance that Neil might have contacted her that way, and found she had missed two messages while she was driving the day before, one from Zack and one from Eugene.

Eugene, she was relieved to discover, reported that all had gone well. Jock was fine and looking forward to Sandy's visit, so at least something was going well. Then she pulled up Zack's message.

Guess what Grandma! Grandpa is here. We're having pizza tonight.

What was Neil doing in Sunshine Bay when he was supposed to be here in California? She had driven all the way to San Jose for nothing. Now what?

She sent her grandson a message back: *That's great. I thought he was at the train conference.*

Zack replied quickly. *Oh, he was. But he came home to help Dad. He said you were helping Uncle Jock, so he came to help me.*

He had given up his conference to travel back—for Rob. She had traveled for hours, dying to see him, and now he had turned around and gone home. But not to see her. To help Robert to look after Zack.

After telling her she spent too much time helping out their kids, *this* is what he did as soon as Kiran was gone? She smiled grimly. It would be good, of course, for Neil to spend time with Robert and Zack—she just wished he had said something. If he had, she would not be at a conference full of model train buffs. Why had she even bothered?

She looked through her texts again and found one from Sandy. The visit with Jock had gone well, and she asked how things had gone with Neil.

Doris texted back. *Neil has gone home to help Rob with Zack. I missed him.*

Sandy: *He what? Why would he go home without telling you?*

Doris sent an emoji of a shrugging woman and felt her head getting lighter. Dizzy, she leaned forward on the table and held her head in her hands. Her world was upside down, and Neil, the one person who should have been her rock, was acting as though she was an afterthought, if he even thought of her at all.

Her phone dinged.

Sandy: *What are you going to do?*

Doris: *I don't know.*

Sandy: *What do you want to do?*

Doris: *I don't know.*

Sandy: *Do you want me to come there? Stay with you for a bit?*

Doris: *No, you should stay with Jock. He'll work harder if you're there. Maybe I'll just go home.*

Sandy: *Or you could do something else—give him a bit of tit for tat.*

Doris: *I don't like to play games.*

Sandy: *Don't. Just let him know you need a break. You've been working hard, and you can take a week or so getting back. Let him take care of things at home for a while.*

Doris: *I have to think.*

Sandy: *Well, keep in touch so I know where you are. If you need anything, let me know. I'll come.*

Doris: *Thanks. That means a lot.*

She stayed where she was for a few minutes longer until she felt able to stand. It meant a lot that Sandy would come if she needed her. It was more than she could say for her own husband. Maybe she should take a week or more to get home. She hadn't driven the Oregon coast in a long time. And she could go to San Francisco for a day or so. Napa Valley, Carmel.

Yes, there were a few places she would like to see. She was here anyway. So she texted Robert to let him know her plans.

Robert texted back quickly. *What are you doing at a model rail conference? Dad said you were in Cataluma.*

Doris: *Your father and I haven't spoken in a few weeks. We keep missing each other. Just wanted you to know I am en route, but it will be a few days.*

Rob: *So you'll be back in four days or so?*

Doris: *I'll let you know how far I get tomorrow. I'm staying here tonight.*

Rob: *What should I tell Dad?*

Doris: *You can tell him I'm on my way home, but it will be a few days.*

Rob: *Okay, safe travels.*

Doris: *Thanks.*

She considered sending Neil a text too but decided to wait. She didn't trust herself to be civil. Instead, she decided to head back to the hotel and plan her route home. A route that would take her at least eight days.

They would be fine in Sunshine Bay. After all, as Neil always said, Zack was an easy kid, and the store practically ran itself.

CHAPTER 28

Robert slept badly after pizza night with his father and Zack. When Zack finally went off to bed, he and his father had sat down in front of the television to watch a movie, and he learned his father had not actually seen nor spoken to his mother in over a month.

"What? Why haven't you been in touch? Did you leave her?"

"No, I haven't left her," said his father. "I just needed a bit of a break."

"She must have been upset." He thought how distracted his mother had been before she left. "Is that why she went to California?"

"She went to help her brother." His father scowled.

"Right," said Robert. "After sending Nora down to help, and with Eugene there too, she decided she also needed to be there. You don't think it had anything to do with you being in California?"

"She went because her brother needed her," he said.

"And I suppose that's why she went to the model train convention in San Jose?"

His father looked genuinely shocked. "What do you mean?"

"She told me she went there to meet you. She didn't know you had come home."

"She went to the conference?"

"Yes."

"Well, I'll be damned," said his father, looking inordinately pleased.

"You're happy she went miles out of her way to find you?"

"Not happy about that, no," said his father slowly. "But it is kind of nice to have someone come after you, especially after all these years. Do you know when she'll be back?"

"I imagine it'll be a few days. When she drove down, it took her four days."

"That will give me time to spend with Zack," said his father, smiling.

"Aren't you going to at least text her and tell her you are okay?" asked Robert.

"She knows I'm fine."

"Dad, why are you treating Mom like this after all these years? Communicate! You need to communicate with her. If this is the way you treat her, why would she even want to come back?"

"What are you talking about? She'll be back to run the store."

"Dad, she started the paperwork to make me the managing partner. She's not planning to work the store anymore."

"Huh," said his father. "What is she planning to do? Look after Zack?"

"I don't think so. Zack is my responsibility. I'm going to hire another caregiver for him to help out."

"Well, what is she planning to do?"

"I don't know, Dad. From where I'm sitting, she can do anything she wants to do. She's got a great investment portfolio, and the business is strong, and she doesn't need to stay around here. Why don't you ask her?"

"You're one to talk," his father shot back. "Have you even asked that girl how her father is doing?"

"No," said Robert. "But I'll do it tonight."

"Let me know how it goes," said his father, finishing the last of his beer. "I'm going to walk home now. See you in the morning."

"Right," said Robert, scowling at his father's back and mumbling to himself as he locked to door after him.

He put the beer bottles into the recycling bin and cleaned up the room before heading to his bedroom. His cell phone was plugged in near the bedside table. *Communicate. You need to communicate.*

He picked up the phone and texted Kiran. *How is your father? I hope he is well.*

Then he looked at what he had typed and decided to continue. *I'm sorry for how I left things between us. I've spoken to Yvonne, and I know what happened. I hope you can forgive me. We miss you.*

Then he lay down on the bed and stared at the ceiling in the dark.

Did Nora know their parents' marriage was on the rocks? If so, why hadn't she said something? He would phone her in the morning and see what he could learn. Maybe she would see their mother before Doris headed north again.

He turned over and punched the pillow. His father could be so selfish sometimes. His mother had given up so much for him. And she'd stayed home to give her kids a stable home.

But as he drifted to sleep, he knew she would do it all over again—just as he had given up the orchestra for

Zack. He only wished he could share the burden and the joy of family life with someone else.

He wished he could share it with Kiran.

CHAPTER 29

Kiran saw the text when she woke the next day and had to read it three times before she fully comprehended what it said. She had been up the night before with her aunt and uncle, playing games and laughing until one in the morning. It had been a long time since she had laughed so hard.

Today she would be moving back into her father's house, and she was no longer dreading it. She and Rajani had shared another long talk, and she was looking forward to seeing her stepsisters that evening. Maybe being home again would work out well after all.

She had convinced herself of that—until Robert's text came.

He was sorry. They both missed her. And she missed them.

What could she say in reply that sounded neither desperate nor standoffish?

She dressed and packed her bag, then picked up the phone.

Kiran: *My father's surgery was successful. He's going to be fine and is coming home in a couple of days. Thank you for everything.*

She pressed send and then looked at it again. Should she tell him she missed him too? Or wait for a response first?

She didn't have to wait long. *Glad to hear your father's surgery was successful. How long are you planning to stay in Toronto?*

Good question.

Kiran: *I'm not sure. Depends on where I get a job. Meanwhile my dad will need help, so I'm staying here for a few weeks at least.*

Robert: *Where are you applying?*

Kiran: *Ontario mostly. He wants me to be close to him.*

He didn't reply, and sadness seeped into her mood. Their relationship couldn't work if she stayed close to her father. But family was important, and she hadn't been treating it as precious. She had instead run away. Now, though, her cousin was returning, and she was getting to know Rajani better. She was building connections again. And it felt good to belong.

She went to the hospital and spent an hour with her father, then on to the house where she spent another hour unpacking her clothes and putting them in drawers. Rajani and her sisters were away for the day. Rajani had gone to her office to put in half a day's shift, and the girls were in school so she went to the garage and pulled out a couple of her mother's boxes of fabric and found the old sewing machine. While she was waiting for a job and for her father to get well, maybe she could do something creative. Maybe make a quilt. Maybe knit.

She sorted through the colours, arranging and considering them, before she put them back into the box. All she could imagine was a landscape of beaches and waves, like the island she had grown to love in such a short time. She had sat at the beach nearly every morning since arriving in Sunshine Bay, and she missed it.

She pulled out her phone again, and found a new text from Robert. *Is there anything that would make you come west again?*

I don't know, she answered, though she did know. If there was a chance she could get to know him better—that she could date Robert instead of working for him—she would definitely be tempted to return.

Robert: *Were you happy here?*

Kiran: *Yes. I love it there. But I have to honor my father's wishes.*

Okay, he answered, and that was the end of their discussion. He didn't try to engage her again that day, or the next. She was just going to have to get used to not having him or Zack in her life. She had made her choice, and she would have to live with it. Try to find happiness in her career and in her family. A family that loved her as much as she loved them.

A family who would be hungry if she didn't go upstairs and start dinner as she had told Rajani she would.

By the time Rajani and the girls got home, she had a pot of chicken curry simmering on the stove, along with rice and a salad.

"Smells great," said Rajani when she walked in.

"Kiran! You're home!" said Priti, coming to hug her.

Sima looked at her mother first and, after receiving a nod, went to Kiran and gave her a big hug as well.

"Are you ready for dinner?" she said. "Go wash your hands."

They ran off, and Rajani came into the kitchen. "Thanks for doing this," she said. "It smells great. I didn't know you knew how to make curry."

"Mom taught me some things, and when I went to school, I took some cooking lessons from the mother of a friend of mine. She was happy to show me. I think she thought I might become her daughter-in-law, but then I met

Jacques." She shrugged. "And my friend married a girl the family loved, so it all worked out."

"Has there been anyone since Jacques?" asked Rajani, before turning to the girls. "You two set the table."

Kiran relaxed as the girls ran over to get water, placemats, and cutlery and placed them on the table. She didn't have to answer the question. Instead, she dished the rice and curry onto plates, set them on the table with the salad in the middle, and listened as the pair told them about their day. "I'm doing grade four in my piano now," said Priti.

"Wow, that's great! You must be practicing a lot."

"I'm practicing too," said Sima. I'm doing grade two in the violin."

"You two will have to play for me later on," said Kiran. "You can show me how much you've learned."

"But first you need to clear the table and do your home-work," Rajani added.

The girls made quick work of the dishes and left them alone in the kitchen. "Chai?" asked Rajani.

"Yes, please," said Kiran, going to the cupboard to get some biscuits.

"How was Bhapa when you saw him this afternoon?" When Kiran had visited him in the morning, he had looked tired and complained about not getting enough sleep.

"He is looking so much better," said Rajani. "It is such a relief. He'll be home in two days."

"That's great news," said Kiran. She watched as Rajani added tea and spices to a pot on the stove and poured in the evaporated milk.

"We'll set him up in the spare bedroom." Rajani pointed to the room off the kitchen. "Then he can avoid the stairs for the next few weeks."

"That's a good idea," said Kiran. "He'll need to take it easy for a bit."

"Yes, though not too easy." Rajani laughed. "We don't want him to become a potato."

Kiran laughed too. "No, we definitely don't need him to be a couch potato."

They talked about her father's health until the chai had come to a rolling boil and Rajani judged it was strong enough.

"Do you want sugar?" she asked, as she poured the chai through a sieve to catch the loose tea leaves and whole spices.

"One teaspoon, please," said Kiran. "It smells so good. You make the best chai."

"Your father says it is what he is missing most about my cooking while he's in the hospital," she said.

"A tea bag in water doesn't match this," said Kiran, as she took her first sip.

"Now tell me," said Rajani. "You didn't answer my question earlier. Has there been anyone of interest since Jacques?"

Kiran took another sip of the tea and considered her answer. She still wasn't sure how much to trust Rajani, but she couldn't see the harm in telling her about Robert and Zack.

"I've been looking after a young boy for the past few weeks since I arrived on Vancouver Island. His father is a widower. I suppose I entertained the idea there might be more to our relationship if I stayed on longer. But it wasn't meant to be."

"Because you came home?"

"That, and because he didn't seem to trust me with his son." She told Rajani about how Yvonne had reported on her, and how he had made her feel irresponsible. "I can't see myself with another man who makes me feel small," she said.

"Why was this woman following you? That's strange behavior. Is she interested in him?"

"I don't think so. All I know is he didn't trust me and assumed I was in the wrong."

"You liked him otherwise?"

"Yes. He's funny and a great musician. He's got friends, and he helps out his neighbors. He's even running a fundraiser. And he is a good father. His son is a nice kid."

"You learned to care for them," said Rajani. "You will find someone else. If not him, then someone with qualities you can admire. I did."

"I hope you're right, but I'm beginning to worry about my judgment. I trusted him, and he didn't trust me."

"Was he right?"

"Technically," said Kiran. "But his mother didn't even do what he was asking me to do, and Zack wanted some independence. I didn't see the harm in it."

"Did you apologize?"

"Yes. But I could tell he was questioning everything after that."

"Maybe he has a hard time trusting people where his son is concerned. It's hard to be the only parent. You are always convinced you're doing it all wrong."

"Is that how you feel?"

"Not so much now, but before, yes. I blamed myself for everything that went wrong. Even things I couldn't have controlled. I'm better now. Your father helped me."

"I did get a text from Robert this morning," she admitted after a few minutes. "He said he spoke to Yvonne—the woman who told on me—and he was sorry he hadn't got all the information correct. He asked if I would come back."

"And would you like to go back?" Rajani picked up a biscuit and dipped it in her tea before taking a bite.

"Maybe. If I had a proper teaching job. But not as his nanny. It was okay for the summer, but I wouldn't want to do it forever. I want a proper career with a pension plan, benefits. One where I can learn and grow. And I love teaching."

"They need teachers here. I'm sure you will find something soon."

"Yes. But I am not sure if I want to stay in Toronto. I liked living in a smaller place. It was more community-minded."

"You could find a smaller center here. Somewhere not so far away."

"But if I go out of town three or four hours, it's almost as long to drive there as it is to fly to BC."

"Your father really wants you to stay out here."

"I know, but you could visit me. You and the girls would love it. They have beaches nearby."

"But you would need a job there."

"I had an interview the day I left, but I haven't heard whether I got the job or not. They said they would tell me next week."

"Did you like the town? Were the people nice to you?"

"I did. I was helping with the choir, had started making a few friends, and beginning to feel like I belonged. Until he made that accusation. Then I just wanted to run away. And I got the call about Bhapa later that day, so I had a good reason to leave."

"You didn't have a chance to talk about the accusation before you left?"

"No. I just wanted to go. When he made that accusation, it reminded me of Jacques. I thought maybe I was just destined to attract the same kind of man in my life."

Rajani took another sip of tea. "You know, all relationships will have conflict. Your dad and I don't always agree on things. We fight sometimes. But in the end, he always wants to work things out. And I never feel unsafe with him. Did Robert make you feel unsafe?"

Kiran thought about all the time she had spent with Robert. "No, not unsafe," she admitted. "But that immediate lack of trust. It didn't feel good."

"Sounds like you both had a part in the misunderstanding. If this happens in the future, you will have another perspective to consider," said Rajani.

"I suppose," said Kiran. They heard music coming from the living room, and she smiled. *Saved by the violin.* "I promised the girls I would listen to them practice. Thanks for the tea."

Rajani nodded, picked up another biscuit, and stayed where she was, leaving Kiran to join the others and sit through what was, all in all, not a bad performance. Though, she had to admit, they didn't yet have Zack's skill.

CHAPTER 30

*D*oris set off toward Monterey Bay early the next morning, after checking her emails and texts. Neil had sent one at two in the morning that simply said, *Sorry.*

That was the best he could come up with?

She responded. *Sorry for what? Could you be more specific?*

There. He could chew on that. After forty-one years of marriage, he owed her that much at least.

Meanwhile, she would enjoy her trip, stop in small towns, peruse shops and museums, and listen to music as much as she could. She hadn't been on a vacation by herself— that didn't involve visiting family—in decades. This was something new and, as Jock said, she wasn't too old to try something new.

She stopped for a late lunch and looked at his reply.

Sorry for being an idiot. I never should have left you hanging like that. You didn't deserve it.

Well, she couldn't dispute that. She texted him back.

Doris: *Thanks.*

He responded right away.

Neil: *When are you coming back?*

Doris: *Not sure. A week or so. I'll let you know when I get to Monterey Bay.*

Neil: *That's not on the way here.*

Doris: *You're right. But it has great whale-watching tours.*

He didn't answer for a few minutes, but then he sent a text asking where to find the list of suppliers for the store so they could place orders. She stared at it for a moment, the lovely meal she had just finished threatening to make an encore. Did he think she was okay now? He really was an idiot.

Doris: *Ask Rob.*

Neil: *He's gone to a meeting.*

Doris: *Max would know.*

Neil: *He has the day off.*

Doris wondered if she should just go home and forgo her plans to see the whales, the redwoods, and the Oregon Coast.

It sounded like Rob needed help, and Neil, though skilled at his own work, had never been involved in the store. She put her hand on her stomach to settle it and remembered what Jock had told her. She needed to stop trying to save everyone and give them the chance to do it themselves.

Doris sighed. *Look in the top drawer of the desk. There's a binder with all the operational information there.*

Neil: *Right. Thanks. When are you coming back?*

Doris: *Not sure.*

Neil: *Well, hurry home. Zack misses you.*

Zack misses you. Not *I miss you.*

Doris: *Gotta go. Say hi to Zack for me.*

Then she started the car and set off to Monterey Bay, determined to enjoy her holiday and leave the work to Neil. People learned from doing hard things, and, contrary to his belief that stores ran themselves, running Making Sweet Music was hard work.

For the next nine days, Doris booked tours, enjoyed meals by the sea, took pictures she thought Zack might like, and enjoyed her trip. But finally she pushed open the door of Making Sweet Music to find Zack practicing his performance piece.

The bell over the door announced her arrival, and she stood and listened for a few moments until he noticed her.

"Grandma!" Zack jumped up and ran to give her a hug. "Grandpa! Grandma's back."

"So I see," said Neil, coming out of the back room. He was dressed in a pair of jeans that hung loose on his hips and a black T-shirt that contrasted with his nearly white hair. If he tried to hug her right now, she didn't trust her body not to betray her and hug him back, squashing the anger she still felt over his betrayal and letting things go with just a brief apology text. But she couldn't do that to herself.

Or their marriage.

"Hello, Doris," he said. "You look great. I like the hair, and the new outfit."

She glared at him, inwardly pleased he had noticed but still furious at the radio silence he had maintained for weeks. "Where's your father?" she asked Zack, who was still hugging her.

"He's on a trip," said Zack.

"Had to go to Victoria to pick up supplies?"

"I think so. Said he would be back in two days this time, but Grandpa is here, and Max just left."

"I see," said Doris, looking at Neil from over Zack's shoulder. "So he left you two in charge?"

"Yes. Grandpa took a couple weeks off from his job and said he would look after me and the store."

"He did, did he?" She continued to glare at Neil. He had never done that before, not in all the years they had been married. "Did he make dinner too?"

Neil was watching her with a placid smile on his face. It was a smile she knew well. He wanted her to think he was confident, that everything was fine, but she could see the wariness in his eyes and imagined he was very thankful Zack was here to act as a buffer.

Even with Zack there, she felt an eruption brewing. Sure, he had apologized but he hadn't even had the courtesy to pick up the phone and talk to her. He had just moved on with questions about the store. Nothing about how she was doing or what he could do to make it up to her. How dare he look so self-satisfied when he'd left her hanging for weeks?

"Did Curtis go with him?"

"No," said Zack. "He went by himself. Said he'll be back in time for the MMFC, though. So not to worry."

"It isn't for another week. Does he think he'll be gone that long?"

Neil shrugged and shook his head. What did that mean? Did it mean he didn't know, or that he didn't want her to ask any more questions in front of Zack? What was going on?

"Zack, why don't you go upstairs and get ready?" said Neil. "We'll go out for pizza tonight. Grandma might like a night out."

Zack whooped and ran upstairs, leaving them alone in the store.

"I am glad to see you, Doris," he said taking a step toward her. "I wasn't expecting you until tomorrow or Thursday."

"I wanted to see the boys."

"I'm glad. I've missed you."

"You sure have a funny way of showing it."

"I'm sorry I left the way I did. I was feeling… I don't know. Old, I guess."

"Old?"

"There's a bunch of new blood in the organization, and people have been asking me if I'm going to retire soon."

"And are you?"

"I went to a conference. Presented a paper. People were interested in what I had to say. Clients still wanted to hear from me. They even deferred to me instead of the recruit I'm supposed to be mentoring."

"You found out you've still got it?"

"Well, instead of leaving like they were hinting for me to do, I took three weeks off to help out Rob. You know how many calls I've had from my boss to ask questions?"

"Several?"

"Daily. They figured out they do need me after all."

"It must feel good to be needed."

"Yeah, it does."

"So you aren't retiring?"

"I'm in negotiations to work part time. A few days a week or a couple of weeks a month."

"What do you plan to do the rest of the time?"

"I thought I would spend it with you. Maybe we could travel a bit like we've talked about."

"Well," she said, glancing at the clock and walking over to flip the sign on the door to *closed*, "I've had a lot of time to think while you've been gone, and I've decided to make some changes of my own."

"What kind of changes?"

There were footsteps on the stairs, and Zack appeared, hair combed and jacket on. "Are you ready to go?" he asked.

"The deposit needs to be done first," said Doris.

"We'll help," said Zack. "Won't we, Grandpa?"

Neil was looking at her with a worried expression. "Um."

She looked away from him, willing the tears filling her eyes to stay put. Even after his time away from her, he had been thinking of only himself, his career, and his needs.

How had they grown so far apart?

"I'll cash out," said Neil, looking at her. "You can go home and freshen up a bit. We'll pick you up in about forty-five minutes?"

She shook her head. "You two go ahead without me. It's been a long drive, and I have a headache. I'm going to go home and go to sleep early."

"Aww…"

She turned to look Zack in the eye before he could protest further. "I'll see you tomorrow, Zack."

"Will you take me to school?"

"Depends on how I am feeling. But I'll see you tomorrow. Okay? Now lock the door behind me." Then she walked out the door without a backward glance, wishing she hadn't bothered to come home tonight after all.

She had been hoping to see Robert, not Neil. She wasn't ready, even after rehearsing all the things she wanted to say to him for the past ten days. She wanted to rail at him, scream, stomp her feet.

Where the hell was Robert?

CHAPTER 31

Robert's plane landed in Toronto at ten in the morning, and he walked out of the airport with his carry-on bag to find a shuttle to the hotel he had booked the evening before while he awaited his connecting flight in Vancouver.

On the way to Toronto, he played his latest conversation with his father over in his mind. It was all about how his dad had gone to New York to find his mother and tell her how he felt. He'd asked her to come home. It had all sounded great and noble yesterday, as he was rehearsing things in his mind on the way here. But he had landed in a city he hadn't visited in over a decade, without checking first to make sure he could see her, and he felt like a fool. He wanted to turn around, rebook his return ticket, and go right back home.

This was one of his stupider ideas.

He joined the long line waiting at the counter. An airline employee was walking down the line, asking questions and trying to sort customers. Robert explained that he wanted to rebook his flight from Thursday to later that day.

"All the flights leaving for Vancouver are fully booked," the agent said. "There was a maintenance issue on the plane that was supposed to leave an hour ago, so all those passengers will need to be accommodated first. I am sorry."

"Thanks," said Robert, picking up his luggage and berating himself as he walked toward the shuttle. This really was one of his stupider ideas.

When he arrived at the hotel, he showered and changed. Then, unable to avoid the reason for his visit any longer, he texted Kiran.

I'm wondering if you and I could speak?

She didn't answer right away. Why would she? She was busy with her father. He should have thought of that. He added a second text: *I hope your father is well. Is he home now?*

Thirty minutes later, he received an answer: *I'm picking the girls up from school. Dad is coming home today.* She'd added a smiley face emoji.

He flopped onto the bed. He really hadn't thought this through. He wasn't his father. Kiran wasn't singing in a band, and he couldn't sit in the audience until her eyes found his. Kiran was home, surrounded by family, and if he wanted to see her, he would have to go there, knock on the door, break into their family time, and risk looking like a complete fool. What had he been thinking?

He hadn't been thinking. He had been missing her, and he'd gotten carried away after listening to his father wax on about how he had gone after his mother, won her back, and married her. His grand gesture.

Robert didn't want to marry Kiran. At least not yet. They hadn't known each other long enough. He couldn't ask her to marry him, so what was he going to ask her?

And what was he going to say to her when she asked him why he was there? Because of course she would ask him. It was a perfectly good question, and he needed a perfectly good answer. And he had to think of one quick because she had just texted back.

Kiran: *But we could talk tonight. About eight? That's about five your time.*

He stared at the phone. She wanted to talk to him. That was encouraging, right? Yes, definitely encouraging.

Kiran: *Would that work?*

He nodded. Yes, eight would work.

Robert: *Do you have time to meet me at eight?*

Kiran: *Meet you?*

Robert: *I'm here. In Toronto. I thought we could meet over a coffee or a drink.*

Kiran: *You're in Toronto? What are you doing in Toronto?*

What did he say to that? That he came to see her and ask her to come home? Instead he wrote, *I'll explain when I see you. Gotta go. Should I pick you up?*

Kiran: *You know where I live?*

Robert: *I sent you your last check. Remember?*

Kiran: *I haven't received it yet.*

Right. He had found her address in the employee records his mother kept and put the paperwork in the mail only the day before.

Robert: *Your check is in the mail.*

Kiran: *Okay, we can go to a coffee shop near my dad's place. I'll see you at eight.*

Great. He shot up, punched the air, and decided to go for a walk to burn off the burst of energy overtaking him. She was going to meet with him. He was going to see Kiran tonight.

He wanted to dance down the street but instead took a leisurely stroll before taking out the phone and texting his father. *Arrived. Hope all is well there.*

His father texted back: *Zack is in school, the store hasn't burned down, your mother is home, and I am in the doghouse.*

Robert: *Say hi to her for me.*

Ha! thought Robert. He was glad he wasn't in his father's shoes today, and he hoped his mother showed him no mercy.

CHAPTER 32

*D*oris stood in the kitchen, folding a load of laundry she had started the night before, when Neil came into the room.

"Rob says to say hello," he said.

"Where is he?"

"Toronto."

She paused. "Toronto? Why?"

"He's gone to ask Kiran to come back."

"I hope he's not too disappointed if she says no. Or if she's not there."

"I'm sorry. How many times can I apologize for not keeping you up to date on my whereabouts? How was I to know you would come looking for me? I said I would be back."

"No, you didn't. You said you needed time to think. You were taking a sabbatical. And when I asked when you were coming home, you never answered me." She put the folded shirt onto the pile of clothes she was building. "What were you thinking?"

"Doris, I never meant to hurt you. I thought you wouldn't notice if I was gone. You always look after things when I'm figuring out work stuff. "

"This isn't work stuff. This is life stuff."

"I told you. They were trying to push me out, and I needed to figure out what to do next."

"And I always look after things, so you just went off, expecting me to pick up your slack. Do you think you're the only one feeling uncertain about what to do next? Did you ever consider that I might not know what to do either? That I might feel like life passed me by?"

"Life hasn't passed you by. You've got your store, the kids, Zack."

"Neil, you asked me to give up the store. Told me the kids were grown and didn't need me. You wanted me to make all these changes so we could be together, and then you left. Took a sabbatical from our marriage. How do you think I felt?"

"I'm guessing not good?" he said tentatively.

"Not good?" She folded another towel, wishing, not for the first time, that she had chosen instead to bake bread.

She wanted to punch something right now. Or someone. "It made me think, Neil. What would I do if you didn't come back?"

"You didn't think I had left you." He scoffed, and then stopped when she turned her angry gaze on him. "Did you?" he asked quietly, rising from the chair to walk around the table toward her.

"What did you think? That you could walk out and find yourself without it impacting me at all?"

"I guess, yes, that's exactly what I thought."

"Why would you think that?" she asked, banging a folded towel onto the stack she had made. "And why didn't you do your own damned laundry when I was gone?" She picked up another towel. "Did you use every towel in the house?"

"I was going to do laundry tomorrow. I hadn't gotten round to it yet. You always have so much under control I never realized how much work it was. Especially with Zack."

"That's because even when you're here, you don't help. And while you were away, I started to wonder what I would do if you didn't come back. In fact, I've been considering a plan B for my life. A plan that doesn't include you."

"Yeah? Tell me about it." He leaned on the table between the pile of laundry and Doris. "What would you be doing if you didn't have me?"

"Well, for starters, I wouldn't have so much damned laundry to do."

"That's true," he said, looking at her in the eye. She tried to get around him to the pile and he grabbed her by her arms, forcing her to look at him. "Tell me."

"I'd sing again. Not in the shower, or at least not just in the shower. I would sing at open mic nights, maybe join a little band, and do gigs sometimes. I sang when I was in Santa Barbara in a jazz club. I miss it."

"I'm sorry I missed that. I bet you were great." He rubbed his hands up and down her arms, and for a moment she wanted to just let him hold her. "What else?"

"I would travel more. There's a solo travel club I was looking into. It's a group of women who travel all over the place. I would like that."

"You enjoyed your trip, then?"

"I would also visit my brother more often. It was good to see Jock. And Nora. She and Eugene are happy running the store."

"What else?"

"I would teach music more. I stopped doing that when the store got so busy. Administration isn't my favorite part of the job, but I am good at it."

"I could see that," he said. "Anything else you might like to be doing?"

"More laughing. More dancing. More fun. I stopped having fun, Neil. I would also like to spend more time with friends. It went out with Sandy and her sister Rose. We had a great time together shopping and going to a spa. I need more frivolous things to do in my life."

"Things where you aren't responsible for everything."

"Yes," she said.

"I'm sorry. I thought you liked the responsibility. I never realized you wanted help. You never said anything."

"What would you have done? It wasn't like you were going to change your job, move home, and look after things here."

"I suppose," he said, pulling her into an embrace. "Can you forgive me, Doris? For leaving like I did? For behaving so badly?"

"I don't know," she said, stiffening. She stepped away from him. "In the last few days, I was wondering what it would be like to have a life where I could do anything I wanted, where I didn't have to worry about you and your job and your mood and your laundry. A life where I had a partner I could trust."

"You don't trust me?"

"Why should I? You walked out for nearly a month with nothing but a cryptic, 'I have to find myself.' You left me, and you never thought for one minute how it would impact me. And then you had the gall to tell my brother! Do you know how embarrassing that was?"

"I didn't leave you. And that's not what I told Jock. I told him I was thinking about what to do next, that's all."

"Did you know Sandy's sister hired a PI to look for you?"

"Why did she do that?"

"Sandy figured I should know what you were up to. What were you doing at a silent retreat, anyway?"

"You had me followed?"

"I didn't know about it until after they hired the guy. I haven't even looked at the report."

"I went to the retreat because a friend told him it helped him when he was going to retire."

"And did it?"

"I was bored at first, but after a couple of hours I started to get more comfortable. I did think a lot, though. There's nothing else to do, really."

"And what did you come up with?"

"I realized I wanted to spend more time with family. I've traveled so much over the years, and I've missed so much."

"That's why you came home to spend time with Zack and Rob."

"Yes. And in a few weeks, I plan to visit Nora to see how she is."

"And?"

"I also realized I didn't want to retire just because someone decided I'd hit an arbitrary expiry date on the calendar. I like what I do, and I'm good at it."

"And?"

He looked at her. "I would also like to have some more fun."

"So most of your life is exactly how you want it to be."

"I guess so, yes. I realized I don't have to change just because I took another trip around the sun. They're already asking me to work seventy-five percent of the time. They still value me."

"I'm glad for you, Neil." Doris stepped away from him, slipped on her shoes and her jacket, picked up her purse and keys, and opened the door to leave.

"Where are you going?"

"I'm leaving. Everything you just said was all about you. Your kids, your job. I haven't been part of your life for a month, Neil, and maybe it's time to admit that we need to call it quits. I want more in my life than this, especially since I just transferred the business to Robert."

"Doris, come back. Let's talk about it."

"No. It's my turn. Now I need time on my own."

She left the car in the garage and set out on foot. With all the driving, she hadn't had enough exercise in the past two days. Hoisting her purse over her shoulder, she set out for the beach. It usually had a calming effect on her, and it was a good thirty-minute walk away.

When she got to the seaside, she walked to the far end of the park, away from the children's playground and crowds, to the bandstand that was abandoned this time of year. She climbed the stairs and sat on the top step, looking out at the green space and beyond, to the sea. Then she took out her phone to see how Jock was doing. She needed to talk to someone who cared about her.

"Hi, Sandy," she said when her friend picked up the phone.

"Doris? What's up?"

"I just wanted to let you know I'm home," said Doris, "and to see how Jock is doing."

"He walked for fifteen minutes without a walker today," said Sandy. "Here, why don't you talk to him?"

"Doris, are you checking up on me?" Jock teased when he came on the line.

"Yeah," said Doris, swiping away a tear. "I wanted to see if you needed me to come back and read you the riot act again."

"No. I think I've got everything I need right here," said Jock, and she heard a smile in his voice. Sandy giggled in the background. "Thanks for coming, Doris. I really appreciated it, even though I was a jerk most of the time."

"Glad I could help," said Doris. "Maybe I'll come down this summer to visit if you're around."

"Or we could take a trip together," said Jock. "I enjoyed your visit despite the circumstances."

"Let's compare calendars when you're feeling better again. I'd like that."

"Sounds good. Talk to you soon."

She hung up and thought about who else she could talk to. Sandy and Jock were back together and didn't need her bringing down their mood. None of her friends needed that. Maybe she should get a professional to help her figure out her next steps.

She opened her purse and rooted around for a tissue to wipe away the tears that were slipping down to her cheeks. As she did, she became aware of someone approaching. She hoped they would keep walking. That last thing she needed was to be discovered crying in a public place.

"Hey," said a familiar voice.

"Neil, I don't want you here."

He ignored her and stood in front of her, so she had no choice but to look at him.

"Dory, I know you think I take you for granted. Maybe I do. But it's only because I've always known you were there for me."

"You aren't making things better."

"You asked me what else I learned at the silent retreat." He sighed and climbed up to sit beside her, staring out toward the ocean. "I learned that I don't like silence."

She smiled at that.

"It's too much like how I grew up. You remember how my parents were. Studious academics who were always quietly discussing the latest paper or research, as though we lived in a library. And then I met you, and you brought music into my life. Music and laughter and love."

"What changed?"

"What do you mean?"

"We don't laugh anymore. And while music is my business, I don't actually make music much. Love is about respect, caring. I haven't felt a lot of that in the past few months."

"Wow," he said. "I had no idea you were questioning our relationship, Dory. I thought we were just figuring out retirement and aging and our third act. I never dreamed you would think I didn't love you anymore."

"Or that I didn't love you anymore?"

He twisted toward her and grabbed her hands in his. "No. We've always been solid. There for each other."

"Except for the last month."

"If I could do it over, I would. I am so sorry. I just didn't want you to watch me flounder. I hate floundering. It felt, I don't know…"

"Vulnerable?"

"Yes. I guess I wanted you to think I was still in control, that I still knew what I was doing."

"I get it," said Doris. "Change is hard, especially when it's all about your identity."

"Can you forgive me for mucking it all up?"

She wanted to put it all behind her like a bad dream. But could she?

"How do I know you won't run off again?"

"I won't. Not now that I know how much it hurt you. I would never hurt you like that again."

"And will you include me in your plans from now on?"

"I promise. And I don't make promises I don't intend to keep."

"Okay," she said. "I'll try to forgive you."

"Thank you," he said. "Let's go home. It's cold out here today." He stood, grasped her hand, and pulled her to her feet.

"We should probably go and relieve Max for lunch."

"No need. Jorge is back this week. We have four hours until I need to pick up Zack."

"And what do you want to do with those four hours?" she asked.

"Come home with me and find out," said Neil, waggling his eyebrows at her.

She laughed, and they walked home, hand in hand, talking about their plan C—the plan they could do together.

When they arrived at their house forty-five minutes later, Doris had gone a long way toward forgiving him.

"Come." He took her hand. "I have something to show you." He led her upstairs, and she was disappointed when they stopped at the door to the train room. Had the man learned nothing in the last few hours?

"Zack has been helping me put it together." He opened the door and brought her to stand in front of the latest complete installment in the room. "We finished the model of the Zephyr."

"You wanted to show me a train right now?"

His smile faltered, and he searched her face a moment. "This isn't about the model. I wanted to show you this."

He reached up to the top shelf, pulled down an envelope, and handed it to her.

"What's this?"

"It's two tickets for two weeks from now. We can finally go on that train trip we always talked about."

"What if Robert doesn't have childcare by then?"

"Something tells me Rob will be just fine," said Neil. He bent to kiss her, and she stopped him.

"Wait, I almost forgot. I got you a present too."

"Having you back is enough for me, he said, following her to the bedroom. She rooted at the back of the closet to find the parcel she had found waiting for her on the counter the night before. At the time, she had been too angry to open it.

"Here it is." She held up the little box and rushed back to the train room, where she found a knife to slice open the lid then looked inside. "Oh, it turned out better than I expected," she said, lifting it out and placing it on the train platform in front of the Zephyr. "What do you think?"

He looked down at the model she had commissioned at the train show: the pair of them waving to everyone as, arm in arm, they set off on their next chapter together.

"I love it." He pulled her into his embrace, and this time she didn't resist. "Thank you."

He held her for a long moment. "So, by my reckoning, we have at least three hours until we have to pick up Zack."

"That's quite a bit of time. What do you think we should do?"

"Well, I hate to suggest this, knowing that you hate laundry, but…" He kissed her on the throat. "How would you feel about messing up some sheets?"

"As long as I have help, I think that sounds wonderful," said Doris. She laughed when he grabbed her hand and pulled her toward the bedroom.

Wonderful indeed.

CHAPTER 33

Kiran looked at the clock. It was nearly eight. She glanced nervously at her father. He wasn't smiling, just sitting on his favourite chair looking at her with a sad look on his face.

"I don't like it Kiran," her father said.

"It's better this way Bhapa. And it isn't going to be as bad as you think."

"We can talk about it tomorrow," said Rajani. "After we all have a good night's sleep."

Kiran smiled her thanks and wished again that her father had agreed to rest in his room and hadn't overheard the phone call she had received an hour earlier. She would have to talk to him longer. Make sure he really understood things from her point of view. She swallowed nervously, wishing she had texted Rob not to come today.

"How are you feeling, Rahul?" Rajani asked. "Maybe you should go and lie down. You must be tired."

"I'm fine." Bhapa looked from Rajani to Kiran and Priti and Sima. "I am happy to be home and to have all the women in my life getting along. I have missed you."

"We've missed you too. So much," said Kiran, bending down to hug him.

There was a knock at the door, and before Kiran could stand and answer it, Priti yelled, "I'll get it!" She ran before Kiran could stop her.

"Hello?" said Priti. "Can I help you?" She opened the door, and Kiran could see the shadow of the tall man she had been expecting. Her heart pounded. He was here.

"It's okay, Priti. It's for me," said Kiran, putting her hands on the girl's shoulders and guiding her away.

Priti swiveled her head back toward the door. "Who is he?"

"A friend of mine," said Kiran, smiling up at Robert. She found it hard to believe he had actually come all the way to Toronto to see her.

"Who is it?" asked Rajani though Kiran had told her earlier that she was going out with Robert.

"A friend," said Kiran more loudly.

"Bring them in," said Bhapa.

"Bhapa, you should be resting. I'll be back soon." She reached to grab her coat from the hall closet.

"Bring them in," her father said more sternly. Kiran looked at Robert and mouthed an apology. "Come in and meet my family," she said.

Robert nodded, wiped his hands on his slacks, and stepped over the threshold into the huge entranceway.

"Let me take your jacket," Rajani said, as she bustled toward him. "I'm Rajani, Kiran's stepmother, and these are her sisters, Priti and Sima." She pointed to the girls, who were now both standing near the door, looking up at Robert. Robert looked more nervous than she had ever seen him.

"Smile," she whispered, and poked him in the ribs before turning to face the family. "This is Robert," said Kiran. "Robert, this is my dad, Rahul." She motioned for him to come into the living room, where her father was watching him from a reclining chair. She wished she could poke her dad to get him to smile too.

"Hello, sir," Robert said, walking over to her father to shake his hand.

Her father shook his hand in return, examining Robert in the same way Robert had examined her when they first met. It was… uncomfortable. She looked at Rajani with wide eyes, pleading for help.

Rajani nodded. "Please, sit down. Sima, go and fetch pani."

"Yes, ma," said Sima, walking slowly out of the room to fetch water.

"Yes, sit, sit," said Kiran's father, motioning to the seat across from him. "Tell us how you know Kiran."

"Bhapa. This is my boss," said Kiran.

"Kiran," said her father, "I have known many bosses, but none fly across the country to visit their employees."

"Especially when their employees no longer work for them," muttered Rajani, just loud enough for him to hear.

"Um, I came to talk to Kiran."

"About what?" asked her father.

"Bhapa, can you just let us go and have coffee like we planned?" She mouthed sorry again.

He smiled. "I suppose if a man came thousands of miles to see my daughter, I would have questions too."

Her father raised his eyebrows, waiting for an answer, and Kiran cringed in mortification. She had no idea why Robert was here, but she wanted him to tell her first, not her family. Why hadn't she suggested he meet her somewhere?

"Well, actually, sir…" Robert smoothed his pant legs with his hands. "I came to see if Kiran would consider coming back to Sunshine Bay."

"She can get better paid work here," said her father. "She is a teacher, not a childcare worker."

"That is true," said Robert. "She is very talented. And I'm sure she will find a teaching job soon."

"So why are you here?"

He looked at Kiran. "I wanted to ask her if she would consider coming back to Sunshine Bay to live. She was only there for a few short weeks, but she is very much missed."

"A town misses my daughter?" her father asked skeptically.

"No," said Robert, "though I think Esther and the choir miss you, and so does Max." He looked at her father. "Max is one of my employees, and Esther is her neighbor." He turned back to Kiran. "Zack misses you so much he asks about you every day."

"Zack is a child, and children are resilient," her father said. "I still don't understand why you are here."

"I also wanted to apologize for everything I said the day she left. And I hoped she might reconsider coming back to Sunshine Bay, because no matter how much everyone else misses her, it isn't anywhere near how much I miss her."

"Do you want to marry my daughter?"

"I'm not sure we're quite ready for that yet," said Robert, directly to her father. "We don't know each other well and, because she has been my employee, we haven't even had a chance to have a proper date yet. But I do know I care very much about her and want to get to know her better."

"You want her to come back with you and be unemployed? You aren't even offering to give her job back?"

"Well, given how I feel about Kiran, I probably shouldn't be her employer."

Kiran swallowed hard and looked between her father and Robert. "Robert, I was just telling—"

"Wait," said her father, holding up his hand and the turning to Robert. "If Kiran were in Sunshine Bay, and not working for you but for someone else, then you would want to—what? Date her? What are your intentions toward my daughter?"

"Stop it," said Rajani, hitting her husband playfully on the arm and laughing. "He is teasing you," she said, and Kiran breathed a sigh of relief that the awkward moment was over.

Robert looked at her in confusion. "What am I missing?"

"I was just telling Bhapa, who should not have been listening to my private conversation"—she glared at her father, who just smiled back—"that about an hour ago I was offered a job teaching in Zack's school. And I want to accept the position," said Kiran. "I was planning to return at the end of August, because by then Bhapa will be feeling better. Though, by the looks of things"—she glared playfully at her father again—"he seems to at least have his sense of humor back."

"And I was telling her that she should do what makes her happy," said her father, looking between Robert and Kiran. "And it seems, young man, that you are part of that happiness."

Relief registered on Robert's face, and he smiled. "And Kiran has become central to my happiness as well."

"Go now," said Rajani, shooing Kiran and Robert toward the door. "Go on your first date."

Robert walked to the door, and Rajani took his coat from the closet to hand to him while Kiran wished her father a good night's sleep.

"I am so sorry about that," she said to Robert as they walked down the front steps.

"They care about you. No wonder they want to know about me."

"Well, you passed. Bhapa told me he thought you were okay."

"Good to know," he said. When they rounded the corner, he reached for her hand. They fit together so well she was sure a passerby would think they held hands all the time, not that this was the first time they had really touched.

She looked up to find him watching her. "So you came to ask me to come back?" she asked.

"Yes. When you left, I found a hole about your size in my life, and the longer you were gone, the bigger that hole became."

"I see." They walked a little further before she asked, "So what *are* your intentions? You never really answered my dad's question."

He stopped and faced her. "Well, with your permission, of course"—she nodded her head in assent—" I'd like to take you out and get past the awkward first-date phase."

Kiran laughed. Awkward was an understatement. "And how did you plan to accomplish this Herculean task?" He was holding both her hands now, and making little circles on them with his thumbs. She held her breath, waiting for him to continue.

"Well, most first dates, or, in some cases second dates, end with a kiss. I thought that we could perhaps—again, with your permission—just jump ahead and do that. You know, to get past all the awkwardness."

"That's an interesting option," she said.

"What do you think? Is it worth a try?"

"Yes, I think it is definitely worth a try."

"Come here," he said, leading her over towards the plaza where the coffee shop was located and to a set of steps.

"What are you doing?" she asked looking around her to see if anyone was watching them. But then she realized this wasn't Sunshine Bay and she didn't know the few people who were walking past. He lifted her easily to the second step, so she was at his height, and gazed into her eyes. She licked her lips and gazed back, waiting.

"Ready?" he asked, and she nodded slowly, not taking her eyes from his.

His lips met hers and he pulled her close, making her feel safe and loved. And cherished.

After a long while, they finally broke the kiss.

"Well, did it work? Do you think we can take this relationship to the next level?" he asked.

"What is the next level?" Kiran was still a little dizzy.

"Well, since it's so late, I thought maybe decaf coffee. You can tell me about this new job, I'll tell you about my life, and we can get to know each other better. Maybe see where things could lead next."

"I'd like that," said Kiran. "I'd like that very much."

CHAPTER 34

Zack stepped down from the stage after his MMFC performance and ran toward Doris, leaving his father and the rest of the band to pack up their instruments. Doris noticed Robert had been smiling a lot more often and seemed to be enjoying the banter with the rest of the musicians.

"What did you think, Grandma?" said Zack.

"You were fantastic! You must have practiced for hours."

"I did!" Zack said, eyeing the buffet of baked goods in the next room. "Dad said all my hard work paid off."

"It did," said Neil, squeezing him on the shoulder. "You're almost as good as your grandma here."

"Dad said I can get cake now if you come with me, and he'll meet us. Are you coming to get some cake?"

"We are," said Neil. "You lead the way."

Neil walked beside her with his hand on the small of her back. He'd been doing that more often lately. They greeted a few friends as they passed and congratulated choir members on their performance, all the while she felt like she was his priority.

It was good.

They were good.

They joined the line behind Zack, who had made a beeline for the chocolate cake decorated with musical notes. Doris scanned the table. Esther had really outdone herself this year.

"You get the cake," said Neil, "and I'll get some coffee and join you. I see Curtis over there. He's saving a seat."

After gathering cake and other goodies on a plate for them, Doris and Zack joined Neil and Curtis at the table.

"Where did Rob get off to?" asked Neil.

"Oh, he stopped to talk to a fan," said Curtis, nodding toward the opposite wall where Robert was standing with his back to them. He'll be along in a moment."

A couple stopped by and congratulated Zack and Curtis on their performances. Zack blushed, but Doris could tell he was pleased.

"You've raised a real performer," said Neil, squeezing Doris's knee. "I'm proud of you both."

Rob was coming toward them now, and when he got past the crowd, they saw he had someone with him.

"Kiran!" said Zack. "You came back!"

"I couldn't miss your performance, could I?" she said, giving him a big hug. "You did a great job. The audience was enthralled."

"Enthralled?" asked Zack.

"It means they were all paying attention because they enjoyed it so much," said Neil, standing and holding out his hand to Kiran. "It is nice to finally meet you, Kiran."

"Kiran, this is my father, Neil Hudson," said Rob.

"Hello," said Kiran, with that winning smile Doris remembered from their first meeting.

"Come and sit," said Doris.

"We have lots of cake!" said Zack.

"Yes, a lot of cake," said Kiran, as she sat down next to Zack while Robert went to get coffee for them both.

"How long are you here?" asked Doris, glad to see how pleased Zack was to see her.

"Just for the weekend. I have a job teaching at a summer camp in Toronto this year so I can stay close to my father until he's feeling better."

"But then you will move back here," said Zack, "to that little house near the school that Dad showed me, so you can have a sewing room and a place for your piano and…" He looked at Kiran. "What else did you tell me?"

"And a garden," said Kiran. "Where I can grow some of my very own vegetables."

"And cilantro and garlic," said Zack excitedly. "For curry."

Kiran smiled and then shifted her chair for Robert, who had arrived with their coffee.

Rob sat down and took a bite of cake. "You two ready?" he asked Doris and Neil.

"All packed. We leave first thing in the morning."

"Hope you have a fantastic trip," said Robert.

"And bring back another tree for the model," said Zack. "There aren't enough trees yet."

"I'll keep an eye out," said Neil. "I'm looking forward to it," he said to Robert. "Your mom has found open mic nights in two of the places we're stopping. I feel like a groupie."

"Don't forget to take a camera. You'll have to send me and Zack updates while you're away."

"We've got our phones," said Neil. "I'll send you some footage of your grandmother singing."

"How is your brother?" Kiran asked Doris.

"According to my friend Sandy, he's almost his old self again—though, miraculously, not quite as grumpy as he was before his fall." She laughed.

"He and Sandy are going to meet up with us in San Francisco when we get back from our trip on the Zephyr," said Neil.

Curtis and his sons joined in the conversation then, asking Kiran about Toronto and her plans and making suggestions about the places to take her family, who were planning to help her move in at the end of August.

Doris listened to their discussion for a few more minutes, then squeezed Neil's leg under the table. He looked down at his watch. "We're going to head out now," he said. "We've got an early start tomorrow."

"Okay," said Robert, rising and giving them both a hug. "We'll see you in about a month. Have a great time."

"We will," said Doris. She bent to hug Zack. "You be good for your dad, and have fun at the music school next month."

"Josh is coming too," said Zack. "His mom said he can start taking guitar lessons if he wants to."

"Wonderful news," said Neil. "Maybe you two will start your own band one day."

"Don't encourage him," said Robert. "He'll become a vagabond like his grandparents."

Neil laughed and took Doris by the hand. "Ready?"

"Ready," she said.

They walked to the car that was parked a few blocks away. "It's good those two are taking it slow. I think Robert is still working through stuff about April," said Neil. "But Kiran seems pretty special."

"I know Jock would approve. He doesn't believe in love at first sight. Thinks it's hogwash," laughed Doris.

"Well, he's wrong," said Neil. "I knew you were the one the moment I heard you singing on that stage at college."

"And I remember singing out to the crowd. And there you were."

"I fell in love with you that night, and my life has never been the same since."

"Is that a good thing or a bad thing?"

"All good, Doris," he said, pulling her in for a kiss just before opening the car door. "And I can't wait to see what we do next. Whatever it is, I am sure it will have trains and music." He opened the car door for her.

"And love," she said, as she slid into the seat.

"Oh, yes," said Neil, closing the door for her. "Lots of love."

ABOUT THE AUTHOR

Jeanine Lauren is a USA Today bestselling author of heartfelt women's fiction and sweet romance novels with themes of friendship, love, community, and second chances.

While Jeanine has been passionate about writing for most of her life, she frequently directed her literary endeavours towards day jobs, academic papers, volunteer work, and meticulously crafted 'to-do' lists she rarely glanced at.

In 2019, Jeanine embarked on her publishing journey with the release of "Love's Fresh Start," the first instalment in her uplifting Sunshine Bay series. Since then, she has written several more tales and is currently penning new stories with fervour, determined to make up for lost time.

Stay updated on Jeanine's upcoming releases and other news by subscribing to her mailing list at www.jeaninelauren.com.

Jeanine lives and works in the picturesque lower mainland of British Columbia, Canada.